This is an overall lighthearted and happy story, happily-ever-after guaranteed. However, there are some negative events both on the page and in character backgrounds that may be upsetting:

- Both April and Dennis have romantic history involving kink relationships that went wrong, one way or another.

- April is targeted for misgendering and transmisogyny by some unpleasant people a few times, and targets herself sometimes also with negative self-talk.

Additionally, Dennis and April have a Dominant/submissive relationship that permeates the book. For more detail on kink activities and other potential triggers, see pennyaimes.com/afcw.

FOR THE LOVE OF APRIL FRENCH

PENNY AIMES

carina
press

carina
press®

Recycling programs
for this product may
not exist in your area.

ISBN-13: 978-1-335-63099-5

For the Love of April French

This edition published by arrangement with Harlequin Books S.A.

For questions and comments about the quality of this book, please contact us at CustomerService@Harlequin.com.

Carina Press
22 Adelaide St. West, 40th Floor
Toronto, Ontario M5H 4E3, Canada
www.CarinaPress.com

Printed in U.S.A.

This book is dedicated to:

My best friend—who, like Jason in this book,
showed up with a moving truck when I needed him most.

My wife—who did not let a broken neck
get in the way of our HEA.

FOR THE LOVE OF APRIL FRENCH

Part I: Dennis, April

Dennis

Dennis Martin looked around the club and decided to at least take off his tie. He had dressed tonight based on his somewhat limited experience in Seattle kink and BDSM clubs, and here in Austin he was feeling distinctly out of place. As a dominant he wanted to project power and confidence, whether in a suit or fetish wear, and by any measure power suits were more his style. He'd unpacked a sober but lightweight black moleskin Armani blazer from his garment bags—but this place was forcing him to consider he might need to relearn how to be a dom in jeans and cowboy boots. Jason had *not* given him sufficient details. Although maybe a name as simple as Frankie's should've been a tip-off.

On a midweek evening in the middle of May, there were less than a dozen people around. Most of them were white, although there was probably a little more color than in any of his Seattle haunts. Down the scuffed bar-top sat a woman with a cloud of sandy blond hair in a pink leather jacket. A denim-wrapped couple were cozy in one of the horseshoe-shaped booths defining the corners of a makeshift dance floor where a few more people swayed. There was a DJ's enclosure blocking what would have been a window to the street in a normal bar, but no one was occupying it, and something slow and alt-country was piped in, talking about one big love.

There wasn't much staff around, either; a pugnacious bouncer on the door who seemed to be puzzling over a ledger between entries, and a pierced, pale and androgynous goth behind the bar. Even the goth gear was on the casual and breezy side. The club he'd attended in Seattle had tighter security and a much stronger dress code, for employees and members both.

He quickly loosened and removed his green silk tie, folding it up and slipping it in his jacket pocket. He hoped it looked casual and intentional, as if he'd come here from somewhere more formal. Then he felt the flicker of imposter syndrome that suggested a *real* dominant didn't worry about what other people were thinking. And besides, he added to himself, it's unlikely anyone had even noticed.

"Your first time here?" said a husky voice, and he turned towards his only companion at the bar.

Looking at her more closely for the first time, he saw a white transgender woman in clothes as casual as the rest of the room; pink faux leather jacket, a grey T-shirt and tight jeans that wrapped around curvy hips and a tight pinch of waist. Her face, though, was fully and skillfully made-up. Almost airbrushed. She could've been anywhere from twenty-five to thirty-five.

She had grey-green eyes that smiled along with her full lips, which were stained to match her jacket and the bobs of her earrings. She had long nails, painted like a cloudy blue sky except for a large yellow crystal inset in the right ring finger. Her T-shirt displayed a molecular structure and the words: "I survived testosterone poisoning." Cute. Funnier than a Pride pin. He smiled at the slogan, then at her.

"I just moved to Austin," he confirmed. "I know, I'm over-dressed." As a lesbian couple in full latex arrived and were waved past by the bouncer—they were known here, apparently, from the bouncer's reaction and from the woman's quick wave—he quirked his lips and added, "Or under." Fashions might be different here, but some things are always accept-able in a kink club.

She laughed. "No, I just don't recognize you. I'm kind of a regular." She sipped her drink, which looked citrusy. "It's a Wednesday," she said, "So things *are* kinda casual. People just popping in after work." She gestured vaguely at herself. "I look a lot better on the weekend."

"You look good now," he said. It was a tactful first move, and it was true. Good skin. Great hair. The kind of figure he liked, and a face that looked both kind and sensual.

She tossed her mane of honey-colored hair out of her face. "Then imagine how good I look on the weekend," she said. Her lips curled teasingly.

"Maybe I will," he said.

She took another sip. "And what are you imagining?"

He paused infinitesimally, thankful he was already lifting his Jack and Coke to take a drink. She was returning his flir-tation, inviting his imagination, but she was also calling his bluff. He'd been bantering along automatically, but now he was challenged to actually consider it. And suddenly he found himself very determined to get this right. There was some-thing in those warm green eyes—a welcome, like he was a friend she hadn't seen in a long time. This felt different from the times he'd been approached since his breakup with Sonia.

"Hm." He studied her a bit more, and she returned his regard, smiling. Her figure was lush on the bottom, but lighter on top, or at least a bit small for her frame. He could see she was a bit curled up on herself within the depths of her cropped jacket; she had broad shoulders that she was perhaps trying to minimize. Combined with her hips and waist, it gave her a classic hourglass shape, despite her slighter bust.

He licked his lips and tasted the sweetness of the cola. Tried to conjure something that wasn't just generically fetish, but specific to the woman in front of him, the woman whose interest he suddenly wanted very much to capture. "Leather, or maybe PVC. Up to your throat. Sleeveless. Short skirt."

"Like a skater dress," she mused. He nodded.

"Stockings, of course." That was purely for him. He wished he'd noticed her shoes; would she be sensitive about heels? She was sitting, but he suspected she was almost as tall as himself. "Court shoes. No collar. Unless I missed something?" A critical question. Maybe she had a regular dom and just liked to flirt.

"No collar," she confirmed, her smile widening to show white, even teeth.

"But maybe cuffs," he said, trying a slightly more insinuating voice. He let his eyes linger on her boldly, and she colored and looked away, smile still in place. "How did I do?" he asked.

"Depends," she said, and now her voice, too, was changed. Lower; quieter. "Was that supposed to be a guess or a wish?"

"I don't know what's in your closet," he admitted. "Just what I'd like to see you in. Did you like the picture?"

"Yes," she almost whispered. There was an unspoken *Sir* after it that fired his nerves and took him from partially aroused by the visualization to almost painfully hard. It would be a huge red flag if she actually said that now, just like it would've been inappropriate for him to suggest he'd collar her, but the silent subtext was there and charged the air. Most of his self-consciousness evaporated as the dynamic clicked into place. Thank God she wasn't a dressed-down domme!

She let her eyes drop to her drink as she stirred it, sending dark fluctuations through the sunshine. "What color, though?"

"You seem to like pink," he tossed off.

"That," she said wryly, "would be a lot of pink." She gestured to indicate, apparently, the amount of pink it would take to wrap her frame. Her hands were graceful, expressive.

"Black is always acceptable," he allowed, "but I like you in pink."

She colored even more—more pink—and signaled the bartender for another drink. He relaxed a little; he'd passed the test. And that suddenly, unexpectedly, mattered very much to him. For the first time in a good while, he was feeling true desire, uncomplicated by shadows of the past. He wanted her.

April

April French was having what she considered to be a good night. She was lonely and she was horny, but the lovely thing about Frankie's, even on a Wednesday, was that she was probably not the only one. And the welcome wagon gambit was working. New doms always responded well to a little attention. She wondered how many of the hookups in her limited sexual history it accounted for—post-transition, of course. Her sexual history pre-transition was not only limited but singular.

On second thought, that was a depressing thing to contemplate. She decided to steer her mind back to the present, because her present was damn good-looking. He was Black, looked to be about her age, dark-skinned and tall, with narrow hips and shoulders that were probably narrower than hers, too.

There were clear hints of lean muscle under his suit, and

the suit looked expensive. She didn't really care about the name brand, but she had to admit the cost was reflected in how well it draped his body. He had short-cropped, wiry hair and that sexy kind of two-day stubble thing happening. A reassuring bass voice and an unreadable calm that made his face a handsome mask. The tightly wound dominants were almost always the most fun to see come unraveled with desire.

"So. You can flirt," she said, trying to keep her voice even despite the smile tugging the corners of her mouth. It wouldn't do to tip her hand just yet about how attractive he was. "And you wear nice suits. What else should I know about you?"

"Well, I just moved here," he said. "Which you also knew. My name is Dennis. I came here from Seattle."

She nodded, as Aerith set down a new Painkiller in front of her. "I'm April. Grow up out there?"

"No," he said, shaking his head. "Illinois, actually. Little tiny town."

"Oh hey," she said, her smile shifting to be a little less flirtatious and a lot more genuine. It was always a treat to meet someone from the same basic context; someone she could count on to get it. Not that she expected to spend much time talking about growing up in the Midwest, but it was still a nice bonus. "Ohio. I went to school out East, though, and worked there for a while."

He laughed. "So a lot like me, but in the opposite direction. UC Santa Barbara."

She bobbed her head. "Wesleyan."

They exchanged graduation years; she guessed he was probably thirty-five or thirty-four to her thirty-two. "What took you out there?" he asked.

"It was as far away as I could get without driving into the

ocean," she said with a laugh. "And they had good financial aid. You?"

"About the same, about the same. Lots of loans, in the end." She nodded as he went on. "While I was getting my masters, a couple of my friends got a start-up going and brought me in, and we headed up the coast to Seattle."

"Ooh," she said. "A techie. I should've known."

"Oh? Why's that?"

"Well, most of the folks who come here from the West Coast are," she said. Especially the ones who could afford that suit.

"You're right, anyway. I was the support team, not the talent, though. My degree's in technology management." He sipped. "Start-up life isn't for the long haul, so I came here to take a job as CTO for a small firm. What about you?" he asked.

She fidgeted with the little straw in her drink, then drew it out. Chomped a cherry deliberately. "Poli-sci major. I don't use it, though."

"Hm." His eyes watched her mouth. Good. "So weird, isn't Austin where they have that political particle accelerator?"

He was smirking at his pun, and she snorted. "Queeons and Kingons?" At his blank expression, she added, "You don't read Terry Pratchett, do you?"

He shook his head. "No, I was just teasing."

Her smile snatched at the corners of her mouth again. "Teasing's okay." She was fighting herself not to relax fully into the moment, to keep up her boundaries until they crossed the preliminary hurdles. This might not be anything, yet. But he was cute, and he was funny, and he was—so far—gentle. She thought she could really like this guy. She knew she liked the way his eyes settled on her, the weight his gaze seemed to have.

"So what do you do?"

"Oh, I work with data," she said offhandedly. Her job was a definite conversational dead end, simply because it was both hard to explain and deeply boring, even to her.

"Doesn't everybody, these days?" he asked, and she shrugged. "So how long have you been in Austin?"

"About three years. I got a job after college in New Haven, and then… I transferred from that office after I transitioned." Time to make sure he knew. She knew he probably knew—people could usually tell just by looking at her—but she liked him so far, and she liked where this seemed to be going, and she didn't want to be in a situation where he hadn't figured it out.

(It wasn't just that, either; it was also making sure that he knew she was cool about it, that it wasn't a secret taboo topic, that she could just mention it. Making sure her voice was pitched just right, brisk and level and bright, when she mentioned it. It was about projecting *comfortable, casual* and *totally untraumatized*, and God, it was exhausting.)

She watched his face, and from his brief nod she unpacked a great deal of information in return. He knew. He was cool. They were cool. She took another drink, letting the relief settle in before she continued.

"Everyone at my company was actually great about it, but there's just a relief in having co-workers who don't vividly remember who you used to be. And I'm less client-facing in this role."

He frowned at the last. "Did people ever—"

"No," she said quickly, setting down the drink. *Not really.* "I was just…more comfortable."

He nodded again. A moment ago, she'd been thinking she liked his poker face, but right now she wished she could read him better. "I want to make sure I've got it right. Trans woman, she/her?"

"Yep. Just...treat me like any other girl." On the one hand, it felt humiliating to have to specify that. On the other hand, every trans person was different, and the question did indicate he knew something about the topic. She just wished she could download the FAQ into his brain.

Now, please God, if he was just not a chaser. Sometimes it seemed like the band between people who weren't attracted to trans women and the people who only wanted her *because* she was a trans woman seemed impossibly narrow. She felt good about this guy, but people she'd felt good about had disappointed her before.

She tried out a smile, but it felt uncomfortable, almost pleading; she crushed it and pivoted quickly to another topic. "So where are you living in Austin?"

"Well, right now I'm staying with my friend," he admitted. "I bought a house in the same neighborhood, and I'm having it renovated. I was supposed to at least be able to move in, but..."

"Not so much?"

He laughed; it was a good, rich laugh and after the awkward moment it lightened her heart as much as the rum. "Not so much. It turns out that there's a lot they have to *undo* from the previous owner before they even start on what I wanted."

"Oh boy," she said. "That sounds expensive. What neighborhood?"

"Just south of Oltorf, near Congress."

"Oh, by St. Edward's?" she asked, referring to the small private college south of town. "You know what's really good down there?" she continued, when he nodded.

"No, what?"

She rattled off a few favorites, a fried chicken place and

a little Indian restaurant tucked away in a converted house, and spared a moment to mourn a departed Tex-Mex favorite. "*And*, if you zip over to Lamar on Oltorf, you're pretty close to the best barbecue in Austin."

"Hang on," he said, smiling. "I think I heard of that. The truck, right? I thought it was on the Eastside."

She paused and raised her hands to gesticulate, forgetting for a moment she was supposed to be a docile submissive. "Okay. So. *Technically*, technically, that *is* the best barbecue in Austin, you're right, but this place on Lamar is so close... I mean, this is the best barbecue in Austin that you don't have to wait four hours for." She cocked her head as she corrected herself. "Well, there's some places south of town that are pretty good, but they're barely in Austin."

He laughed again, and it made her feel warm and loose; she rolled her shoulders a bit. She always hunched up like this and then suddenly realized she'd given herself a headache. She could see he was relaxing, too, some of the wary tension that had made him stand out to her as a newbie seeping away.

He smiled, and said, "So am I going to be in trouble if I say I don't really like barbecue?"

Dennis

She looked scandalized, then suspicious. "Hang on. You're from *Illinois*. Describe barbecue to me."

He chuckled a little. He knew he was in for it now, but there was nowhere to go but forward. "You take some beef, and you cook it, and you chop it up and mix it up with sauce. My grandma used to make it for Christmas."

"No. Wrong. Disgraceful," she said. "That's just chopped beef. In fact—what cut of meat?"

He shrugged. "I don't know, chuck roast I think."

"No, no, no, no. No. No, Dennis." She put a hand on his shoulder. "Oh, Dennis. I have such wonders to show you."

He could feel the warmth of her hand through his clothing and he liked it. He wrapped his hand around her wrist, feeling her pulse leaping there, and leaned towards her. Her hand pressed into his shoulder as he tightened the distance between them. "I would love that."

She tilted closer until her pink—very pink—lips were inches away from his, and said in a low, sensual voice, "Barbecue...is not when you cook in the backyard with your friends. And it's not, I'm sorry, whatever your grandma made."

"Makes," he said, stifling a smile. "She's still alive."

"Well, thank God," she said, not missing a beat, and he laughed again. He couldn't help it. "Barbecue is a special miracle that happens to a cow or a pig—most places it's a pig, but in Texas they like cows—over the course of several hours. Brisket. Sausage. Pulled pork. Short ribs. The sauce is optional. The smoke does the work. There's also—" The voice, somehow, was still making the hairs on the back of his neck stand up. "—potato salad."

"I see," he said, matching her bedroom voice. Her teeth caught her full lower lip and worried it. The pink stain didn't move, and he couldn't tear his eyes away from her lips or stop thinking about kissing them. All he said was: "Haven't you only lived here three years?"

She raised a finger, then deflated, blowing her hair out of her face, and drifted away, leaning back the other way on her stool. "Yes, but it's been an *instructive* three years."

"Apparently so." He inspected her closely. She seemed a little giddy and loose, but not drunk. He saw her twist slightly on her stool, reacting to his gaze. Positively, he thought, if he knew anything about reading women. (And a shadow flickered over his mood at that thought—had he ever really known Sonia?—but he pushed it aside easily.)

"So." She fidgeted with her drink, then set it to one side. "How did you find out about Frankie's?"

"A friend recommended it," he said. She seemed to be waiting to see if he would say any more about his friend, and when he didn't, she moved on. Privacy was important in these settings, which was exactly why he didn't mention Jason. He should be here soon anyway, and could introduce himself.

"Well, welcome," she said, another warm smile spilling out over her face. She gestured at the space as if it belonged to her. It wasn't much compared to others he'd seen—an L-shaped room, bar and dance floor and a few tables and booths—but she seemed proud of it. "This is the main room. Sometimes there's a DJ. Sometimes there's...people." She laughed—she seemed to laugh easily, and he found he liked the sound. Like her voice, it was unaffected, with no artificial attempt to retune the deeper qualities. Instead, she had a musical lilt, bouncing naturally between extremes. "I'll admit, this is slow even for a Wednesday. But we got a few folks. It gets busier on Saturday...or when there's theme nights."

"What kind of themes?" he asked. His experience with these clubs didn't involve theme nights, either.

"Oh, like, ladies' night for us sapphics, or leather parties or what-have-you," she said easily. The part of him that was still wary of misreading the situation clocked *sapphics*, a careful word choice to include bi and pan women. She wanted him to know she was into women; she wanted him to know it wasn't exclusively women. Good news. "Sometimes there are demonstrations or shows."

"In here?" he said, looking around the room again.

"No, silly." She laughed and gestured towards folding doors along the back wall. "There's more space, but they only open them up on the weekend."

Now, *that* was interesting. He looked more closely now. "How big is this place?"

"Two or three times this big, altogether," she said. "With the roof, too."

"And it gets full?"

She shrugged. "Sometimes. Hey." She put her hand out

on his shoulder again, and he felt warmth bloom in his chest from her touch. "Can I show you something?"

Was she proposing a demonstration of her own? He wasn't sure how to take someone saying *can I show you something?* in a kink club. But he wanted to see where this went; see more of her. Whatever this was, he felt sure it wouldn't be boring.

He finished off his drink and set it down. "Of course."

April

He still seemed calm, unperturbed, and it was hard to imagine what *could* perturb him. A hungry part of her wondered what he'd look like when he came undone, and she swallowed it.

She liked this guy. She definitely liked him. That wasn't strictly required, but it did wonders for her self-respect afterwards. "Come with me." She beckoned him to one of the doors, one that wasn't locked, and up the stairs to the roof of Frankie's.

"Pretty soon it'll be wayyy too hot up here, but right now it's just...perfect." She did shrug out of her jacket, though, and so did he, and they draped them over their arms while he bought her another drink. There was a second, smaller bar up here, where Manny looked deeply bored. He roused himself enough to tip her a wink and give Dennis a once-over, which Dennis acknowledged with a brief smile but did not return. He replaced his Jack and Coke; she just got a Sprite.

"Estrogen wrecks your tolerance," she said confidingly. "Unadvertised benefit."

They settled on a chaise under an unlit heater and looked at Austin's endlessly multiplying skyline. Some of Austin's oldest skyscrapers complained about losing their views to the new high-rises, but Frankie's had always been low to the ground and the lights of the city *were* the view here. The more hotels and condos they put up, the prettier it got. The other buildings on the block, built up to the sky, towered beside them and sheltered the rooftop from the wind.

She looked out at the glimmering skyline. "In the winter it's almost too cold to breathe up here sometimes, but this is still my favorite."

"It's beautiful," he said. His arm slid around her perfectly and she twisted the soles of her sneakers against the rooftop to ground the thrill that ran through her.

She wanted, desperately, to ask what he was looking for, what he was into, if *this was going to happen* and if they were at all compatible. But, she told herself, she'd done enough. She'd started the conversation. She'd initiated coming up here. If he wanted her, let alone wanted her in the way that brought them both to this club, he'd take it from here. All she had to do was surrender to the moment and be honest. Wasn't that what had attracted her to the submissive role, even when she hadn't known she was April yet?

Say something, she willed. *Say anything.*

He didn't at first, just let her nest in the crook of his arm, and then his hand, large and warm and well-manicured, moved from her waist to the back of her neck and squeezed; not forcefully, but tenderly. "You're tense," he said, in a low voice that kicked her in the libido with steel-toed boots. "Do you need some space?"

She smiled; her face tight at first, but it loosened with the rest of her as he continued to rub her neck. "I know how to say no."

"Of course you do. But there's a difference between yes and the absence of no."

So he knew that one already. Thank God. She let her eyes flutter closed as her heart rate picked up and arousal sluiced through her. "Yes. I mean—no, I don't need space. Yes, I want to be here with you. It's just—"

"This is the tricky part," he filled in.

"Yes," she said again, and felt another electric zing from his hand to the center of her. Was he going to actually make this easy?

Dennis

Dennis took a deep breath. He decided he was glad she'd closed her eyes; she couldn't see his face. But how would he ever regain his confidence in this if he didn't do it?

"When I came here tonight," he said, "I just wanted to see the place my friend recommended. Have a drink and get the lay of the land. But, you know, it crossed my mind—I might meet someone and go home with them tonight. I mean, I think we all think there's a chance of that whenever we come to a place like this, right?"

"Yes," she said, tipping her head forward and sending an avalanche of hair over her face. Something about it sent a pang through him.

"Yes, there's always a chance, or yes, you hoped you might meet someone, too?" he pressed. The distinction did matter.

"Yes… I did hope," she admitted. Her shoulders rolled, and finally she uncurled. He couldn't help noticing the motion pushed her breasts up and out, and since her eyes were still closed, he let himself stare. "I was...looking."

"But it's trickier finding a one-night stand in a place like this. More compatibility questions than a normal pick-up. Or maybe we just worry about them more."

She laughed. *"Yes."*

"I love hearing you say that," he growled. What did they say? Consent is sexy? Vanilla people had no idea. He knew he was probably more assiduous than he needed to be, but he didn't want to make any wrong moves, and every *yes* told him she was with him, she was onboard, she wanted more. There was a purr and a promise in the way she said it that was driving him wild, as if he was reading her mind.

Her lips moved, inaudibly.

"Hm?" he said, tilting his head towards her.

"I said, *fuck* you're good at this," she laughed, and inwardly he preened a little. Negotiating the hump between chat and leaving together was a skill he'd been good at once, but that had never been in a kink space. It was nice to know he still had the knack.

"So we talk about it," he said, more easily than he felt. "If we aren't compatible, I'll be disappointed, because...well, because you're hot." Even as he said it, he realized he'd be more than *disappointed*. He'd been trying, yes, but this was the quickest he'd felt a real connection to someone in a long time. And without that sense of connection, there was just... not much for him, in casual sex. But now he felt engaged, present and drawn to her, and along with that came arousal and hunger he hadn't felt in a while.

His voice was still light, still under control. "But that's just how it goes, right?"

He felt her tighten up again and wondered what it was. "Right," she said, taking a deep breath and lifting her head;

opening her eyes to look into his face. "We talk. Have you been with a trans woman before?"

"No." He'd known some trans people in the course of his life, especially in college and in Seattle, but he'd never hooked up with one. "Is that a problem?" he asked, suddenly wary of a new way to fuck up.

"That's a 'you' question," she said, with a brave little smile that just about broke his damn heart. She seemed like she was waiting for something, but he didn't know what. Finally, she sighed and said, "I mean..."

"Is this about your genitals?" he said, as lightly as he could manage. Did she seriously expect him to start firing questions about her medical history at her? Did people *do* that? "Because you're not going to chase me off that way. I can work with anything."

"Yeah, but you've got to be hoping for something, right?" He could feel the mood slipping. It seemed like she'd had a script in mind; maybe he should've let her go ahead. But it didn't feel right. Instead—

"Hey." He fixed her eyes with his. "What if you let me worry about that?"

Her sudden mounting brittleness seemed to melt just as quickly. "I'd like that," she said quietly.

"I know I'm asking for you to trust me," he said, thinking it out even as he spoke. Working without a safety net. "In fact—that's exactly what I'm doing. Do you trust me? *Will* you trust me, for tonight?" *Because if not...this can't happen.*

Her smile came back. "Yes," she said once more, and that admission of trust, the gentle web of connection building between them, set him on fire.

Maybe it affected her the same way. She closed her eyes again, briefly; when she reopened them again, she was more focused. She tapped his shirt front. "*We* still have to talk about limits and interests. And I can't be all subbed up for that. It's

bad enough I'm as horny as I am." She gave a little demon-
strative wiggle, and he laughed, but there was an edge to it.

"Maybe we ought to carry around laminated kink sheets
so we can't edit them on the fly."

She smiled back. "Maybe so." She was waiting for him to
lead, so he launched into it, let his hand slip away from her
neck. In the past comparing notes like this had sometimes
felt like an interrogation (hot in theory, felt shitty in practice) or begging for permission (not his thing *at all*). But it
was necessary.

"First, do you have preferred safewords?"

"Can't go wrong with traffic lights," she said cheerfully.
"A classic for a reason."

"Do you like dirty talk?"

"Oh *hell* yes," she giggled. "Get creative. I'll let you know
if you misstep."

"I like lingerie and dress-up," he admitted.

"What girl doesn't? But it's a Wednesday night and some
of us have work in the morning." He nodded in concession.
He hadn't really expected they'd get to that tonight; just information. He didn't care what she wore, because he was increasingly focused on tearing it off of her.

"I'm a big fan of discipline—" he said, and she laid a hand
on his arm.

"Don't take this the wrong way, but I could tell that about
you."

He felt that warmth and energy spreading up his arm again
from her touch but continued. "—and while I don't enjoy punishment as much, it has its place." He put some weight on that
and enjoyed seeing her eyes darken. She got a little less chatty.

"Let's talk about *punishment*," she said, in the same voice
she used to talk about barbecue. "I actually love impact play."

"I'll be honest," he said carefully. She seemed like she
may have been doing this longer than him. "My experience

is limited to spanking, mostly. Some experimentation with nipple clamps."

She smirked mischievously. "On you or others?" She wasn't quite a brat, she was just...having fun. At first, he had felt a little wrong-footed, as she seemed to have totally dropped out of role. Yet he found he enjoyed laughing with her like this almost as much as he had enjoyed watching her melt.

"On others," he said firmly. "I'm more experienced with bondage."

Her eyes lit up. "Yum," she said, then regretfully, "But not on a first date."

"That's very reasonable." Regrettable, but reasonable. She was so *mobile*, so alive, a flame dancing on a candle, and he ached to pin her down and make her scream with pleasure.

"Do we need a flag for when the scene starts?" he asked. Most of the time, kinky experiences had a defined beginning and end, with one set of rules during the scene and one the rest of the time. It was always important to have clarity on which set of rules applied.

She bit her lip again, and again his eyes zeroed in on her mouth. "For tonight? Let's say it starts the first time you kiss me." So she did know what she was doing with that little trick. He nodded his agreement, and she leaned in closer.

"So...do you want to hear the good news?" she said, almost humming with controlled excitement.

"What's that?" he asked. His jitters were trying to come back, but when he remembered each trembling, whispered *yes*, his pulse picked up. This was what he was meant to do. This *was* sex, for him.

She grinned. "I live just down the street from here."

He grabbed his jacket. They could finish the conversation on the way.

April

"I like orgasm control, too!" she admitted, as they walked down the street. "But I don't think we have time for that."

"You'll come tonight," he said confidently, and she laughed even as sparks sizzled through her.

"The estradiol giveth and the estradiol taketh away. But we can sure as hell try." She felt nervy and charged; felt like she was talking too much. There'd been a moment—one clean, perfect moment—where she'd hit exactly the right subby vibe, but then the inevitable crushing reality of her body had shattered it. He'd recovered well. *God, he's good at this*, she thought once again. He was new in town and he might be inexperienced, but he was a goddamn natural, and for tonight he was all hers.

Word's going to get out and he's not going to need the welcome wagon anymore, said an unkind part of herself. *But I got there first*, she snapped back.

It was only a few blocks to her apartment, but downtown was always crowded, even on a Wednesday. A small pack of drunks was wandering up the sidewalk from the moustache-themed hipster bar around the block. Dreadful little scenarios painted themselves on the walls of her mind like the murals around the Mexic-Arte Museum; she'd never been harassed on the street, not really, but there was a first time for everything and—

He squeezed her hand and rumbled, "Hey," and she felt it in the center of her body. As if he could read her hurtling mind, he pressed her to the side of her building and kissed her deeply, capturing her mouth with his and plundering it.

In an instant, she felt so attracted and grateful and protected that her brain began to overheat. Through the steam, that same unkind, unwanted voice reminded her: *this is a game, an experience. You're going through second puberty and you're feeling a lot of things and sure, that's the point, but remember this isn't real. Remember he's not yours.*

Then he nuzzled his face into her cloud of hair and nipped her ear and she shoved that voice out of her head and locked the door. She'd be sensible in the morning.

For what felt like an hour (but was genuinely just enough time for the drunk UT bros to meander past, hoot encouragements at his back, and disappear into the night), they made out there. His hand slipped between her ass and the building, molding around the curve of her hip like it grew there. Her arms went around the back of his neck and she let the edges of her gel tips zip over his scalp. It made him growl into her mouth. Her breasts pressed against him in a way that made her knees weak; something about those sharp aching points being thrust out into the world and being so very excited to find her lover got to her every time, whether the answering chest was broad and flat and firm like his or soft curves that fit together with hers.

Then his free hand closed over one of them; searched for a moment against her bralette and found and tweaked, and it was good, and he *twisted*, and something like lightning shot up from the pit of her stomach and made her weak all over. She was somewhere else entirely, on another planet. "Please," she said incoherently, and he finally guided her the last twenty yards to the door.

They got through the door and kissed in the entryway for a while. Got in the elevator and kissed there long enough for the doors to close and open again twice on the second floor. Got to her apartment and kissed, counterproductively, while she tried to find the key.

And then they were in her studio and they were kissing and there was no second part of the sentence. They let their jackets drop to the ground and tumbled into the bed together. His hands slid over the softness of her stomach and he growled, "I want to take your shirt off. Do you want that?"

"Yesss," she hissed. And yes, and yes, and yes, until he was fully dressed, and she was in only her best (pink) club-going panties, and his hands felt like they were everywhere. But mostly on her tits. Either he was monomaniacal about consent or it was some special technique of his, but she felt drunk on *yes*. She said *yes* to calling him Sir. Then she said *yes Sir* to being needy and slutty and gorgeous and helpless.

His dark brown eyes were black with need and she saw herself reflected in them, tiny there in a way she never felt in real life. Yet when his hand touched the waistband of her panties she tensed, a feeling she would've sworn she'd forgotten how to feel.

"I want to take these off," he said, finger curling around

the elastic, and then, with ingenious sensitivity, "Does that scare you?"

"Yes, Sir." She gulped, grateful that he hadn't knocked her off the tightrope of *yes*; grateful and scared. She hadn't told him the details. She always told people, because not telling people got you killed.

"What if you let me worry about it?" he asked; the same words he'd used before, and then he smiled—it was devilish on that hungry face, with those hungry eyes—and he said, "Seriously. Genuinely, my dear. What would happen if you let me worry about what I find?"

She took a deep shuddering breath. "You might not like it," she said, plaintively. "You might not know what to do."

"I want you," he said, like an anchor dropped into a stormy sea. Like a fact. "I want whatever you have to give me. And I will learn. I'm a quick learner." He pressed a kiss to her mouth and tugged the waistband down, angled across her hip. "Are you ready?"

Dennis

"Yes, Sir." But she closed her eyes as he slid them down her legs, inhaling slowly through her soft, blurred pink mouth. She was afraid, he knew.

Dennis was not. Maybe he should be—he wanted to not fuck this up, the need to not fuck this up and the need to have this woman twisted around each other and towered over him and filled his world. But he felt the way he did sometimes playing sports, or in a boardroom, or with a willing woman who called him Sir so prettily. He felt immense and powerful and capable of anything—not at will, certainly, but like everything was possible if he played his cards right, and his sleeves felt full of aces.

He was certainly not afraid of anything in April's underwear. He didn't know a great deal about surgeries available for transgender women, or the effects of hormones, and he supposed that he had either imagined he would find something much like he'd seen with other women or much like the genitalia he saw every day. This was something…else, but it was the opposite of frightening. What he saw was small, and pink, and, "Cute," he said, with delight in his voice. "My God you're cute." And he leaned forward and kissed it.

"I had an orchiectomy, so I don't have testicles or produce androgens anymore," she recited; she seemed determined to give this speech eventually. "But I haven't had genital reconstruction surgery. I'm not, um, prepared for anal tonight. I didn't expect—"

He took back control of the interaction easily, calmly. "And what do you call this precious thing?" he said, running a finger over it. It was sunken back into itself, half-hooded like a clitoris would be. He might have been concerned she wasn't aroused if it weren't for the wetness he found.

"M-my clit. Please," she said.

"That's not something you have to say please for," he said easily, and let his fingers explore the wetness that had spilled out of her into the folds of skin below her clit. No depth there—well—maybe. There was a sort of something there after all, behind the skin. He pressed and was rewarded with a moan and a roll of her eyes.

His shirt had come unbuttoned along the line somewhere and he let it hit the floor, as well. "Show me how you touch yourself," he said, his voice firm. Commanding. She inchwormed her way back to the pillows, while he stayed sprawled across the foot of the bed and watched as she sat up, exhaled shakily, and pulled a Magic Wand from an end table.

"I sort of—" She sort of let her legs fall open and pressed the head against the top of her mound and the powerful vibrations pulsed through her indirectly. There was a tattoo on the front of her upper thigh, an explosion of watercolor wildflowers in reds, purples and yellows. It wrapped around her leg, stretching up to her hip and trailing vines and foliage along her inner thigh. It rippled as the muscles of her legs jumped with tension.

She closed her eyes, and he told her to open them. Her panting mouth trembled. "You keep *looking* at me," she said plaintively, and added *Sir* when he raised an eyebrow.

"I like looking at you," he said, and it was really that simple. He liked watching her manipulate the wand over her body; liked the way the vibration made her high, conical tits wobble. Liked watching her breath come faster and her eyes, pinned to his, darken with arousal. As she approached something resembling an erection, she shifted the wand around; pressed it against the folds of skin at the base of her clit for a long lip-biting moment, then ran it teasingly along the underside until she dripped.

He slid forward and, putting his hand over hers, steered the pulsing head of the wand back to her mound. He took her into his mouth easily. He'd made a conscious decision to see if men were his taste, back in college, and he'd ultimately concluded it wasn't really for him; this was not a man's body, a man's cock. It smelled different, felt different, fit differently in his mouth. It was a long way from the iron bar currently trapped in his slacks.

She yelped. She'd closed her eyes again, the bad girl, and she hadn't expected it. He would chastise her in a moment, but right now she was coming, as he'd promised her, pulsing in his mouth. Her spend was thinner, too, tasting only of salt, and he swallowed it easily.

She wasn't expecting it when he moved up the bed to kiss her while she was still shuddering, or when he slung her around and over his lap, ass up. "Whoa!"

"Now, somebody came without permission..."

"You *surprised* me!"

"Yes, because you closed your eyes, doll. And this is talking back. How many for that, do you think?" He was always going to spank her, of course. Had been dying to since he watched her ass go up the stairs ahead of him at Frankie's. But it was good of her to walk right into it.

"Three," she said tentatively. "Sir."

"No, that's silly," he laughed. She made a put-upon noise. "Try again."

"Ten?"

"Ten it is," he said cheerfully. "And two more for trying to undercut."

She scoffed and gave him a look of such sheer indignation that he wavered. "We green?" he asked. Suddenly it caught up to him that he'd been pushing her limits a bit, and now he was manhandling her.

She blinked. "Yeah," she said softly, looking back over her shoulder. "All green over here, Sir."

"Good," he said firmly, schooling his face into implacability again. "Count them off."

April

April wasn't exactly afraid of twelve bare-handed spanks at this point in her journey as a submissive. Her headspace was a little thrown, though, by the unexpected safety check, and without that lovely pink cushion, the first one stung like hell.

"One, Sir," she said, wincing, and tried to sink back. It was always harder just after she came, too; her refractory period had changed dramatically on hormones, but it wasn't entirely gone, either. And—

"Two, Sir." God damn it! She'd even thought of mentioning the paddle she'd bought a year ago and never properly broken in—dismissed it as topping from the bottom—and now she was grateful she hadn't. Her—

"Three. Sir." Her fucking *brain* was too fucking *busy*, and every time his hand landed, it jolted her back to here and her body, and for a moment she was annoyed with the whole thing—

"Four! Sir." *Fuck*. "I'm better than this," she snapped. Angry with herself maybe; angry at him, maybe, for breaking the rhythm when things were *so good*. Angry at the tears stinging her eyes.

"I know you are," he said, his hand moving gently over her burning ass. "I figured you could do a dozen standing on your head." It was a gentle observation, but it felt like an accusation.

"I lost my vibe," she said grumpily.

"Should we stop?" he asked, real concern beginning to cloud his face, and she put her foot down. Mentally. Putting her foot down right now physically would not accomplish much.

"No!" She grinned back over her shoulder with wicked, artificial glee. "Spank me back into compliance, Sir." In her head it was an overdone, porn-quality airhead voice, but God knew how it sounded through her poor testosterone-poisoned vocal cords. She felt something throb against her stomach, though, and that eased her self-consciousness.

"Compliant," he mused. "What a good word."

The fifth smack caught her on the exhale, so her voice choked a little on *Five*, but it didn't hurt as much. Heat spread through her instead, trickling back up her spine and into her busy brain.

"What's another good word?" he asked, as he slid the Hitachi between them and pressed it up into her core.

"Obedient," she said with relish, and barely flinched. "Six, Sir."

"Mm-hm?" he said, his hand hovering, waiting, and she picked up the game. Picked a really *good* word.

"Controlled. Seven, Sir." And gasped as the wand switched on.

Eight was *broken*. Nine was *dripping*. Ten was *needy*. Eleven was *slutty*, which came out with a crack in it from her second orgasm. She spasmed and moaned into the bed, barely aware of her body, let alone its specifics. The orgasm felt like it came from outside, ripping through her like lightning.

Twelve was *desperate*, and by then she was. She was desperate to please him, to know his body like he'd learned hers, but she stayed bonelessly slumped over his lap and waited for direction, blissfully.

I'm under control, she thought with the kind of delightfully hazy thinking only available on a major endorphin rush. How good to let herself go, be totally out of control, and then be brought back under control by someone so kind and handsome and thoughtful. For once, she didn't have to control herself, because this gentle stranger was doing it for her. She should thank him.

"Thank you, Sir," she murmured into the sheets. If she ever made her bed, they'd be on top of the comforter, but she hadn't made her bed in…years. Decades. "Centuries," she said.

"Hm? Are you all right, doll? You seem a bit out of it." He pulled her upright in his lap.

"I'm *good*, Sir," she affirmed. "Green as hell."

He kissed her nose, and she was so moved that she burst into tears.

"Okay, that's sub drop," he said pragmatically, and she shook her head vigorously, whipping both of them with her mane of hair.

"I'm just *happy*," she said, and cuddled against him.

"Okay." He smiled. "So it's just subspace. C'mon, let's tuck you in."

"Ohh. Maybe." Yeah, that checked out. Brain cloudy and feeling like it had had a hot bath. Body slightly sore, slightly buzzing, feeling strangely like it belonged to her and not some hulking ugly stranger. The pretty illusion that she was absolutely in love with this person whose name probably started with a *D*. "You're good at this," she muttered into her pillow.

"I'm really glad you think so," he said sweetly. Fuck, he was sweet.

"Wait, I didn't do—didn't do anything for you," she realized.

"I did notice that," he said; his voice was amused, smugly superior in a way that would make her want to squirm if she wasn't too tired to squirm. He drew the comforter up around her, murmuring sweet words, and she drifted into sleep still waiting for his next command.

Dennis

Dennis woke up to a mouth on his cock and for the first confused moments after waking he thought he was back in Seattle. Back in time. *Sonia?*

No. April. Austin. Right. Wow. *Wow.*

It was dark—not pitch black, not with windows facing the streetlights of the city, but certainly pre-dawn. For a while, he just let it happen, let her simply pump up and down his length and felt the pressure build. It was amazing, velvet and warm. Then he fisted his hand in that beautiful sandy cloud of hair and pulled her up.

She looked startled in the half-light, then grinned at him, mischief in her eyes again.

"I didn't ask for this, doll." His voice was rusty. He waited to see her reaction to the cues and was rewarded by a widening of her eyes and a softening in her expression.

"I took some initiative, Sir," she admitted, clicking back into the role easily, sparking an answering smile from him.

"Carry on, then."

She nuzzled down, played with him for a moment. "Do you want me to tell you how big and beautiful your dick is, Sir? Or how hard you made me come last night?" He knew all about that. There was a stain on the leg of his slacks and a taste in his mouth to remember by.

"I think—" A shudder as she nipped him. "I think I just want to use your mouth, doll." She hummed her agreement and sank back down, and he leaned his head back to let it happen.

Sometimes he found it hard to take his pleasure. Well—there was certainly pleasure in dominance, in putting a pretty and willing woman through her paces like he had last night. But sometimes when he was being pleasured, or even when he was having sex and clearly in control, he found it difficult to hold on to the thread. He'd rather make his partner orgasm than have his own, sometimes. The problem was many submissives felt the same way.

Did she know? She seemed experienced, but did she know that what he'd done last night was as much for him as for her, even if his pants had never come off? "Good girl," he moaned. "You're such a good girl. You were fucking amazing last night."

Not just in the scene, he thought. Just. Fucking amazing. Her ability to move fluidly between the roles of a new friend, even a guide to Frankie's and this new city, and a submissive squirming for his commands. Her bravery and her beauty, her fragility and her trust. Her *fucking mouth*. Some women were uncertain with an uncircumcised cock, but she seemed to know exactly how to tease the sensitive glans without overwhelming him.

"I'm going to come," he warned her, and then he did, with a stifled gasp and an all over clench of his body. He felt the explosion of pleasure rise from the tips of his toes and tear his mind apart.

He lay there and panted. He still felt half asleep and completely wrung out now. She looked up, after a while, and smiled at him with a dreamy look in her eyes. "I'm going to brush my teeth," she whispered. He chuckled, because after all he still could taste her from last night, so who cared? But she was already moving, the bathroom door closing behind her and leaving a thin thread of light beneath it.

She was in there a while—he realized she'd never gotten to take her makeup off last night—and by the time the door reopened he'd shaken off his doze, found the lights and begun to dress. In the light he could see her apartment more clearly; a tidy little studio, with a kitchen partitioned by a long counter and lots of bookshelves and one very crammed closet. Big windows, and good light, now that the sun was beginning to climb. But small—the trade-off for living downtown, he supposed.

"I'd offer you breakfast," she said as she emerged, "but I really have to get in the shower and get to work." She was wiping water off her face with a towel.

"Of course," he said easily. His grip of one-night stand etiquette was pretty solid. "Can I get your number before I go? Or will I see you again at Frankie's? I want to see if Saturday night is all you made it out to be." She'd been quick to get out of bed, and he hoped she wasn't regretting him. He didn't regret her.

"You'll definitely see me there," she said, beaming, which was a relief. It wasn't quite a date, but he had something in mind to lock that down. "But sure, got your phone?"

He caught an Uber back to Jason's house as the sun was

rising and tried to sort his head out during the ride. He didn't start his new position until Monday, but in the meantime, he needed to meet with the contractor at his house, and the CEO of his new firm was inviting him to dinner...this suit absolutely needed to be dry cleaned, as well.

But first—he popped open his newest contact.

Dennis: How do you feel about presents?

April: what kind of presents?

Dennis: Mysterious ones.

April: mystified i guess ☺
seriously tho you definitely dont need to do that

The *April is typing* dots began to dance, but stopped dead when he sent:

What if I wanted to?

And then began again:

April: that would be really sweet and would make me feel very special ☺
and embarrassed!

Dennis: Isn't that a good thing?

She *ought* to feel special; she was a bona fide miracle. And embarrassed could be…very fun. There was another long pause before she sent:

April: yes Sir ♥

Dennis grinned in the back of his Uber and began to look for a boutique in Austin with delivery. Time to let her see what he was capable of with a little time to prepare.

April

April tried to keep the goofy smile off her face at work. At work, she was one bland, industrious cube in a whole floor of bland, industrious cubes. At work, the game was put away and all the dizzying heights and crushing lows of her kinky microcosm were forgotten, and she was thirty-two, not sixteen for the second time. That was the rule.

It was a hard rule to keep up when someone kept texting her:

Dennis: I was supposed to move into this house a week ago.

It was accompanied by a photo of a kitchen with no backsplash, no cabinets and no top to the island.

April: wow thats half of a very nice kitchen ☺

A brown face in a headscarf appeared over the wall of her cube—although not very far above it—just as she did. Fatima looked as tired as April felt, but probably not for the same reason. Probably. At eight months pregnant that window had presumably closed. Fatima was normally a tiny Pakistani woman; she currently looked like a tiny Pakistani woman who had swallowed a basketball whole. "Ready for lunch?"

April's eyes panned over her triple-pane monitor setup and the spreadsheets that were no closer to being reconciled than they were when she opened them this morning. "Absolutely," she said. Maybe lunch would reboot her brain.

"Who are you texting?" Fatima asked in the elevator.

"Nobody." She shoved the phone away in her purse.

"Big plans for the weekend?" her friend teased. When April's eyes widened, Fatima chuckled and said, "Going to slay some dragons?"

Right. She'd made the mistake once of mentioning at work that she occasionally played a role-playing game with friends from a support group and now that was her "thing" in the office. She'd gotten a birthday card with Legolas on it.

Absolutely no one in the office, not even Fatima, seemed to suspect April had a sex life whatsoever, let alone one that involved its own kind of role-playing. Sometimes that felt safe. Sometimes it stung. People seemed to assume she was straight—they teased her about Orlando Bloom, not Liv Tyler—but mostly they assumed she was kind of a eunuch.

"I'm not sure what I'm doing yet," she said, as they walked to the cafe down the block with the good pastries. The May sunshine felt good; at least there were no more jokes about her name.

"Do you want to go to that nail salon again? That was fun."

April glanced down at her nails. "Yeah, maybe. These are lifting a bit." The rainbow-swathed queer-friendly salon was her biggest (visible) indulgence in life. Some women bought shoes. April paid a lot for Japanese gel nail extensions. People wondered how she could type.

(Occasionally women at Frankie's wondered how a pansexual woman could function with nails like that, but that's why God made tongues and dildoes, right?)

She shook off *that* train of thought and tried to focus on what Fatima was saying about the new CTO. Fatima maintained databases for their company, working on the fourth floor on the opposite side of the net from the analysis and modeling April did on the tenth, and she had been a part of his interview. Apparently, he'd been extremely handsome. "And intense! Girl, if I weren't already pregnant, I would've been by the time that interview was over."

April snorted and looked down at her soup; apparently it was her fate to be awash in hormones today, either hers or Fatima's. "Now don't you tell anyone I said that," Fatima said with mock seriousness. "HR's gonna have a field day with that kind of talk."

"You know you can trust me," April said. She meant it. She and Fatima shared more than lunch two or three times a week. They shared facial hair woes—Fatima had told her about an electrology clinic in Dallas that had eradicated Fatima's wispy moustache and chin whiskers in two eight-hour visits. They had celebrated together when April's name change was final, and when her divorce was, too; when Fatima's oldest got into A&M and when her pregnancy test came back unexpectedly, impossibly positive. They didn't share everything—there was *no one* who shared everything in April's carefully compartmentalized life—but they shared a lot.

Her phone buzzed again. She had a package at her apartment, a mysterious present. She looked up from the notification and bit her lip.

"I'm—seeing somebody," she said abruptly, and instantly regretted it; regretted saying anything, and regretted saying *that*, especially. "I mean. We went on one date." *Yes. A "date."* "But. Um."

She looked back at her soup, and peeked up to see Fatima's face, which looked thunderstruck. But in a good way. "*Girl.* Why did you wait until we had ten minutes left to get back? You have to tell me everything about—him? Is it a him?" Of course; Fatima, unlike everyone else at work, knew about her ex-wife.

"It's a him." She felt a smile pulling on the sides of her face. "Very much a him." Her face flamed and she decided that was probably enough honesty for one day.

"You have to tell me. *Everything.*"

Well, *that* wasn't going to happen. Fatima was broad-minded, the only person at work she would discuss a date with at all, but there were limits to how much she was willing to discuss with anyone. She'd rather be a eunuch than the office pervert. She'd just have to choose her words carefully.

Dennis

"So did you go to that place I told you about?" Jason asked.

Dennis looked up from his laptop. "What, Frankie's?"

"No, man, the barbershop." His oldest friend and temporary housemate rolled his eyes.

"Shit, like I'd let you find me a barbershop. I'm *sure* you
know the best place to get a fade 'round here." Not only was
Jason white, but he had shaved his head since his forehead
started growing at twenty-two.

"Yes, Frankie's. You check it out? I got there around ten
like I said I would, and I didn't see you."

"I got your text," he acknowledged. He got it eventually,
in the Uber in the morning.

"While you were out trolling the sex shop parking lots?"

Absent: "You are nasty and a bad friend." Dennis clicked
through his emails and confirmed April's package had been
delivered. Excellent.

"You are—" Jason sighed and dropped into an armchair that had clearly been relegated to this guest room for being offensively ugly "—being squirrelly."

"I went," Dennis said. "I met someone."

"Before I got there?"

"Yes."

"Fuck, I knew I'd regret telling you about my spot. So I guess you liked it?"

"I was overdressed," he said, closing the laptop.

"Yeah, it's not like the place you took me in Seattle. A little more working-class, I guess. No fancy NDAs or membership fees."

Hmm. He'd chalked it up to the Austin heat versus the Seattle freeze. Was it about money? He wondered if he'd spent too much on April now, if she'd be uncomfortable. Well. It was done.

"But obviously that didn't stand in the way. I guess an Armani suit rarely does." Jason smirked.

Jason had just as much money as Dennis. More, probably; they weren't in the habit of comparing checkbooks, but Jason had leaned in on start-up life instead of running away. They'd grown up together in the more tattered kind of suburb; dangling from the bottom rung of the middle class, where people hang on as tight as they can to keep from dropping into WIC checks and government cheese. But for whatever reason, Jason had grown up to have the bigger chip on his shoulder about money. The mismatched, leftover furniture of the guest room told the story; his wardrobe colored it in.

He was the tech start-up stereotype who wore hoodies to investor meetings and preferred Cap'n Crunch to sushi. Which was silly, because *everyone* could afford sushi these days.

"Are you insinuating I hooked up with a gold digger?" Dennis said, raising an eyebrow.

"I have no idea who you hooked up with, you cagey fuck. Do you want to tell me anything or just leave me twisting here?" He softened. "I mean, good for you. I'm just surprised. You've been a little gun-shy about kink since your breakup."

"Now I don't think I'm going to tell you shit." But Jason knew him better than that; he waited.

"She said she was a regular there. April."

"Ohhh, April. Okay. Huh."

"What?"

"I just didn't know that's what you were looking for."

Dennis gave him what Paddington's Aunt Lucy would call a Hard Stare. "What does that mean?"

"Nothing! Nothing. She just…she's very friendly with new doms who come around. You're easing yourself back into things, that's great. Good for you, man."

The words landed in Dennis's stomach like a kick. "I liked her. I like her a lot."

Jason rolled his eyes. "Everybody likes her. She's very sweet. She helps schedule events and makes sure the demonstrators have a bottle of water. I'm just saying, you didn't get to meet many people yet. This is not the time or place to be Mr. Serial Monogamy. Play the field a little. There're some girls I can introduce you to. They've been asking me if I had a straight brother for a long time."

"You can introduce me to them on Saturday." A beat. "I'll be the one at the bar with April." He appreciated Jason looking out for him, but he knew he wanted to see where things with April were going. First person he met or not, there was too much potential there to not see it through. See where it led.

Jason sighed deeply. "All right. Fine. I'm going to go work," by which he meant code in the basement. Jason only used about 15% of his three-story house, even with Dennis occupying a guest room, and he spent about 25% of his time as CEO doing his employees' work and the rest avoiding meetings. He paused a beat, then asked, in an offhand manner that did not at all fool his oldest friend: "Did you call any of those therapists on the list I gave you?"

"I don't need therapy," Dennis said flatly. He didn't want to have this conversation again.

"Dennis…" Jason just looked at him. "You've been through some shit the last couple years, man. I saw your apartment in Seattle when I came to get you, remember? You were in a bad place."

"I was feeling sorry for myself," Dennis said brusquely. "I don't need someone to tell me to feel better about what happened with Sonia, I need to not fuck up like that again. Feeling bad when you make mistakes is a good and normal mechanism."

"Yeah, all right," muttered Jason. He paused at the door. "I'm gonna order Instacart, anything you want?"

"Yes." He waited until Jason met his eyes. "Literally anything but Code Red and Hot Pockets, you monster. Your refrigerator is a nightmare."

April

April's apartment building had a posh office on the ground floor that was manned by the rental company, from nine in the morning to five. Since her work hours ran from 8:30 to 5:30, she was pretty much never able to interact with the front desk staff, although she did enjoy the fancy free coffee machine.

Most of the time it wasn't a problem; most packages fit in one of the self-service lockers. But she hadn't gotten a message about that this time, so she slipped out of work slightly early to make sure she got it. She brought home her laptop and promised her conscience she would get in some work before bed.

A front desk staffer hunted in the mailroom a moment and returned with a package. "Here you go. April French, right?" He sounded either stoned or mildly concussed.

"Yes," she said, feeling a little concussed herself. It was *way* too big for a locker.

"Yeah, like, a courier dropped it off earlier." No wonder he'd been able to get it to her so quickly.

"Thank you," she murmured, and headed for the elevator.

"Have a nice night, sir."

She whirled back in shock and disbelief, looking for a sneer on his face, but he seemed spacey as ever and unaware anything had happened. She got on the elevator without saying anything and studied herself in the reflective door. She searched for a reason it was her fault, although she knew that was pointless and cruel.

Makeup perfect: eyes, lips, and foundation. Wearing a dress, sober enough for the office but still bright and cheerful. Everything just right. She didn't pass, she knew, but surely it was clear to anyone what she was going for. And it didn't make a difference. Her reflection squinted its eyes at her, holding back humiliating, infuriating tears.

Maybe he said…something else. Or he was just…on autopilot, she tried to argue with herself.

That's…not really any better.

She looked down at her present and decided to focus on that, pushing the injury to one side. She hurried back to her apartment, dumped the rest of the mail onto a little table by the door and set the box on her bed. It was square, and wide. She opened it up and found several other boxes. The largest appeared to be a dress box.

"No fucking way," she breathed. It was a PVC dress, about two notches more fetish-y than anything she'd ever worn even to Frankie's, black with pink piping around the skirt and along the zipper on the side. Ornamental buckles crossed over the zipper and at the throat. She held it up against herself— her size, more or less, although incredibly short, maybe even more so than it was intended to be because of her height. It was a sleeveless skater-style dress, draped from the shoulders then flared in the skirt. There was an opening in the front that would probably be obscene if her bust was any bigger. Overall, it would minimize her shoulders and emphasize her waist. She hadn't lost any weight on hormones, but she did like how it had moved around, and the dress would play into all her strong suits.

She laid it down and dived back into the box. Stay-up stockings, black with thin pink seams up the back. No bra, but a pair of pink hip hugger panties in silk. Pink and black round-toed pumps with a buckle on the top and a kitten heel. And finally, black leather cuffs with buckles and stainless-steel D-rings.

She exhaled and reached for her phone.

April: oh my GOD this is TOO MUCH

Dennis: You got the package. Do you like it? Does everything fit?
The panties are optional.

April: of course i like it thats not the point
i didnt try it on yet how did you know my sizes??

Dennis: Either I guessed or I looked in your closet before I left.

April: i cant tell if thats sweet or creepy but i want to say sweet because i want to keep these

Dennis: If you need a different size for anything we have two days.
That's why I had it delivered.

April: I cant believe this
why would you do this?

Dennis: What if I just wanted to see you in it since the moment I made that outfit up?

Well, what if he did?
He was typing again:

Dennis: I don't want to make you uncomfortable. But I would love to walk in the door to Frankie's Saturday and see you in that. Will you do that for me?

its too much money, she typed, and then hesitated. He knew exactly how much money it was, didn't he? Was it her business? She cleared the message and wavered. Her eyes flickered back to the previous message.

Dennis: What if I just wanted to see you in it since the moment I made that outfit up?

Then...that would mean she was more than just the welcome wagon, more than just a convenient body. It would mean he wanted her. Her specifically. Her in all her...herness.

yes, she typed. And then before she could chicken out, she added Sir.

There was a long beat with no response, and then:

Dennis: Good girl.

The words felt like a hug, like strong arms shielding her from the world.

Dennis

The restaurant was downtown, with high-end steakhouse vibes and a game-heavy menu that went along with the taxidermy-heavy décor. It was too tasteful to call kitsch, yet there were enough antler light fixtures to give a vegan a panic attack. Dennis got a steak, while O'Reilly ordered an Idaho rainbow trout.

Ed O'Reilly was a florid white man in his sixties, missing some hair but not bold enough to wipe the slate clean like Jason. He looked like he might be between his second and fourth heart attacks. "I know you were making a lot more in Seattle," he said. "But we're going to be glad as hell to have you."

"I was," Dennis admitted. "But I didn't like the work. I'm interested in what you're doing here."

And he still had stock options from his old job, but that didn't seem politic to bring up.

Growing up, both his folks had worked jobs that they hated over the years to keep them in shoes and hot meals, and come home from those jobs to plant tomatoes and zucchinis in a backyard garden, to make the food stamps go a little further. It wasn't until he was in high school that things had smoothed out a little for his family, and the result was twofold; he didn't know how to stop working, and he was determined not to work in a job he didn't like.

He continued: "The work you do with Medicaid and other public agencies...it's important. I'm doing well now, but I know from experience those programs make a difference in people's lives. And I think by sharpening your technological approaches, you're going to be able to make your clients' money go a lot further."

O'Reilly agreed eagerly. "Absolutely. Things are scattered all over the place, redundant programs and departments, and frankly, our internal developers treat us more like nuisances than clients. And the Help Desk!" The CEO shook his head. "Not a day goes by I don't get a complaint about the Help Desk."

"We're going to solve those problems and we're going to do great things together, Ed," said Dennis seriously, and cut into his own steak. He tried not to let money go to his head, but he had to admit that a high-quality steak, aged, minimally seasoned, still cool in the center was worth the spend. A crust of sea salt flushed out hidden reserves of flavor and reminded him why people used to be paid in the stuff.

O'Reilly continued: "Now, officially we're headquartered out East, and we've got more offices scattered around the country. You'll be doing some travelling, especially the first six months. But most of the tech folks are here in Austin rather than back at corporate."

Dennis nodded. He did his research before he took a job;

most of this he knew. "Do you spend a lot of time down here?" he asked.

"Not as much as I used to." O'Reilly smiled. "Our COO is located here. Since we promoted him, I don't have to spend quite as much time flying back and forth. Except when we have a new addition, haha."

Dennis chuckled politely. "I appreciate you taking the time. Did I meet him during the interview process? There were quite a few interviews." He smiled to show it was a joke, but internally he knew if the chief operations officer hadn't been mentioned until now, there was a reason. "I know I saw the name somewhere—Graham, isn't it?"

"Leo Graham, that's right," said O'Reilly. "Hell of a guy. Came up through the consulting side but decided he was more interested in the how than the why. Did a lot to modernize our operations. Hell, half the reason we wanted someone like you to fix our tech issues was because Leo showed us the way with Ops."

"I'm sure I'll enjoy working with him." *And I'm damn sure there's another shoe waiting for me somewhere...*

Damn it. Dennis had never expected to find himself sitting on millions of dollars in stock options, let alone in the first ten years of his career. Alicia and Sanjay's little company had blown up beyond anyone's imagination. But he knew, however much money he was making, start-up work was going to kill him.

On top of that, Seattle had no longer felt like home after Sonia left; without her to come home to, the overbearing whiteness and Seattle freeze had gotten to him. Taken altogether, the standing offer of Jason's guest room had been a lifeline. Yet he wasn't ready to retire midway through his thirties. This job had seemed like a nice, safe option.

The last thing he wanted to do was come down here and

butt heads with someone…well, someone like himself. *Or yourself before you got the wind knocked out of you,* he thought ruefully.

"I was actually hoping to introduce you two over dinner, but he had other obligations," O'Reilly offered, which also didn't bode well.

"Well, there will be plenty of time for that," Dennis agreed.

He decided to text April from the restroom; the package had already blown any "play it cool" protocol.

Dennis: And what are you doing with your evening, doll?

April: nothing exciting…ate some leftovers and now im trying different jewelry and makeup with my new clothes ☺

Dennis: Is that arousing for you?

April: yes Sir ☺

Hm…she had said she was into orgasm control, hadn't she? He picked his phrasing carefully.

Dennis: I'd really like it if you didn't touch yourself until I see you again.

There was a significant pause before the next yes Sir. Excellent. He'd *certainly* be on her mind until the weekend. He sighed and kicked his brain back to business mode, thinking as he returned to the dining room of the steakhouse that he'd rather be eating barbecue from a crappy truck with her.

After dinner, riding back to Jason's, he was still on his

phone, restless. He wanted to text April again, but surely that would be coming on too strong… He found himself browsing Instagram. He didn't follow Sonia anymore. Had she protected her account?

Apparently not.

No evidence of a new boyfriend. She was living in the Bay Area now, and there were lots of pictures of food, of monuments, of buildings. Not many of friends. Not many of her. He found one, only a few weeks old, and stared at it. She was growing her hair out, in a natural puff that suited her, and wore a yellow dress he wouldn't have picked for her. It looked good, though, her dark skin popping. That long, graceful neck had worn his collar. Here was the woman he'd almost asked to marry him.

She didn't look happy. But then, she didn't look scared, either, the way she had the last time they spoke. He squeezed his eyes closed for a moment, then closed the app.

April

For April, Friday passed in a blur of rapidly intensifying horn-
iness. She didn't even masturbate *that* much, in a normal
week; even once a week was more than she managed sometimes, since her orchiectomy. But now she *wasn't allowed to*,
and that changed everything. Her mind went in a predict-
able circle…she thought about cheating, she thought about
Dennis's dark, commanding eyes, and *even though* that only
made her more turned on, she refrained, until her mind inevitably cycled back.

Thank God she was allowed to wear jeans on Friday and
thank God for compression garments. Her crotch still felt
pinched and achy. She shifted uncomfortably in her chair and
shot Fatima a message:

AFrench: I need to get out of here for a minute. I'm going
to run to the drugstore, do you want anything?

FNayeem: Not really, but do you want company? We can hit the smoothie place.

That wasn't going to work. The shaving cream was fine, but she didn't particularly want to talk about buying an enema.

AFrench: Really just have to run there and run back. Lots to do.

Already, walking outside at noon was like walking face first into a wall of heat. Instantly she felt so gross that sex seemed impossible. She made her purchases at the drugstore down the street and returned to the office, sternly telling herself to pull it together. She worked late to make up for Thursday and managed to keep her mind mostly off Dennis.

She reserved Saturday to prepare. She had an emergency haircut, where her stylist left the length alone but pared off a lot of volume and layered the remainder, then piled it up in a glamorous bun she tried her best not to touch for the rest of the day. She had her nail appointment with Fatima, and a last-minute wax of places she couldn't reach and a touch-up of her brows. Then she took a long bath and got the rest with a razor. The enema happened, never a particularly pleasant experience.

She was ready by seven, which gave her an absurd amount of time to sit around her house dressed like a fetish doll and try not to feel ridiculous but also not aroused, which was hopeless. She was wearing panties but not spanks, and she checked herself in every mirror to see if her clit was visible. (The stiff PVC was on her side there.)

She wiped her face clean and re-did her makeup three

times, finally reaching for the Dermablend, the absolute gold standard for a smooth, shadowless base of foundation. It was a pain to clean off, but if you wanted absolute perfection…

By nine she was posted up in Frankie's, staring at her new nails and trying to breathe. Compared to Wednesday, Frankie's was a whole other world. The main room was packed, and the rear doors had been folded back to reveal the additional spaces that weren't used during the week, including the room with the stage, although there was no formal demonstration tonight. As she'd promised Dennis, the dial had also been turned up when it came to fashion; although there were still plenty of jeans-and-cowboy-boots holdouts, more nightclub styles and more leather, PVC and latex moved among them. The usual DJ was in his cockpit, cranking out EDM and dance remixes. It wasn't anything she'd listen to on her own time, but it was fun for dancing.

She felt skittish and giddy. She hadn't dated much in high school and she hadn't known she was a girl yet then, but this was how she imagined it felt to be a schoolgirl waiting for her prom date. She stopped to talk to Vic; he worked the door like a bouncer, but he was actually the bar manager, and she wanted to touch base with him about an upcoming Shibari training event Frankie's was hosting.

She made her way to the bar, where Aerith—gothic finery cranked up for the weekend—had been joined by one of the weekend bartenders. Aerith had a Painkiller ready for her before she got there. As she sipped it, other friends passed by, several complimenting her look. She was too nervous for much conversation, and most of them took the hint and wandered on. Caroline, however, grabbed a stool near her, hitched up her bustier and started a long recitation about babysitting her sister's kids.

"And then the *other* one was throwing up and—whoa, who's *that*?"

It was just after ten when Dennis arrived. She felt a needy pang shoot through her. He wore another tailored suit, this one dark as a hole cut in space, with a sliver of charcoal shirt and a pink tie visible under his jacket. The only leather he wore were his shoes, the color of blood and a lot of money, not brand new but gently worn in and obviously cared for.

He arrived with Jason Beaumont. That must be his friend. April knew Jason, not well, but enough to recognize his smooth pale skull and wiry frame. True to form, he hadn't dressed up at all, although he was rocking some *very* expensive sneakers and his hoodie was clean. Despite his low-key look she knew he had a reputation among the gay doms as a sub who was anything but casual.

She was on her feet immediately but waited at the bar for Dennis. God, she was buzzing. He was looking around, taking in the transformed space impassively, but once his dark eyes settled on her they didn't move. He moved towards her like a homing missile, drawing Jason along in his wake. He didn't stop until his arm had snaked around her waist. "Hello again," he rumbled.

"Hi," she whispered. His body was hot against her and she could feel an erection pressing through his slacks against her thigh.

"This is my friend I mentioned. Jason. I'm staying with him while my house is finished."

"We've met," Jason said, smiling in a thin way that made her nervous. "We're both practically charter members." Like her, he was regular, involved in a lot of bar activities which had thrown them together. Unlike her, he was rich, and she'd heard rumors he'd invested money in the club. "Hi, Caroline," he added.

Oh, right. Caroline was there. Suddenly very there, soft and curvy in her corset-style bustier, which she filled out the way April never could, all creamy flesh pressed up and spilling out of the top and smooth shoulders that were not in any way similar to a linebacker's. "Hi, Jason," she said in a sultry voice. "Who's your friend?"

"This—" Jason and April spoke at the same time, and she bit her lip and dropped her eyes to let him proceed. Looking down gave her an excellent view of the low-heeled court shoes that had made her so happy when she opened the box, now positioned next to Caroline's strappy six-inch stilettos that brought her up to approximately April's shoulder. There was a tiny patch of hairs near her knee she'd missed.

"This," said Jason again, "is my best friend, Dennis. We've known each other since we were kids. He's new in town and we're trying to show him a good time." In a dozen words, he had reframed the evening—it wasn't a date, how could it ever be a *date?*—and April felt her already precarious mood shatter and fall around her fancy buckled shoes. She just prayed it didn't show on her face.

Dennis

He drank her in from the moment he found her at the bar. She looked *fantastic*. Of course, he'd provided the clothes, and he was pleased to see that they fit her and *how* they fit her, but she'd brought a thousand alluring grace notes to his basic idea.

Her blond hair was piled on her head, emphasizing her long throat rising from the buckle of the dress's neck and making space for delicate pink crystal drop earrings. Her face was made up expertly in the colors of her outfit, with dark smoky eyes and the pink bitable lips. The skirt was shockingly short, giving a glimpse of the tattoo wrapped around her upper thigh, and his hand itched to check if she'd worn the panties. Her arms were bare from the shoulders down to the cuffs, but on her long fingers there was a scattering of rings, and as he raised one hand to kiss them, he saw the black-to-pink ombre that ran the length of her long nails.

Her flush burning through her foundation, her dropped

eyes, her immaculate style, and most of all the sight of her in something he had picked out for her all added up to a submissive gift he'd like to bend over the bar right now.

"Seems like he's having one," said a girl with dark hair, in a tone that told him he was staring, and he dragged his mind from inappropriate fantasies to the here and now.

"I'm sorry," he chuckled. "I met April earlier this week and I was captivated by her look tonight."

The girl looked sideways at April, eyes widening. "Oh, she's a total cutie. I was wondering where all this came from. It's not your usual style," she said, addressing the cutie in question.

"I think my style is a work in progress," April answered, her voice tuned up to a squeak. She did seem a little anxious, Dennis realized, pushing back his libido. Was she uncomfortable? With the clothes? Or with the possessive moves he'd made since he'd come into the bar?

"No, totally," said the girl, who was possibly named Caroline. "I mean, isn't everyone's? I'm just glad you found something that makes you feel hot, yeah?" He couldn't tell if it was just a thoughtless remark or a calculated jab, but he saw it hit home.

"Hm," he said. "Do you feel hot, April?"

She turned within the curve of his arm to meet his eyes. She was tall—by far the tallest woman he'd been involved with, nearly matching his height, and he found he loved being eye to eye with her. "Yes," she said quietly, repressed passion in her voice.

His hand tightened momentarily on her hip before he remembered that they weren't alone. He ached to hear her say *Sir*. But even if he had been 100% clear how she felt about exhibitionism, he knew he was being rude. "And I agree," he said, clearing his throat and pivoting out of the two-person universe they seemed to be generating between them. "How long have you two known each other?"

April and Caroline exchange glances. "A few years, I think," April said. "I know I was already a regular here when she started coming."

Caroline nodded. "I was still in college. April was great, she always looks out for the new subs. Lets you know who to avoid, or at least not to get stuck next to in a crowd."

Jason frowned at that. "Anybody like that ought to be reported to the club."

"Well, yeah," said Caroline. "But wherever you draw the line someone's going to get right up next to it, right? I'm just saying, we can always count on Mama April to look out for us."

April looked away and whispered something.

"What was that?" Dennis asked.

She looked back and smiled, or at least her lips turned up. "Wendy Syndrome."

"I don't think I've heard of that."

"It's sort of like the opposite of Peter Pan Syndrome. Even among the Lost Boys there's always somebody who has to remember to be sensible."

"And you're Wendy." She nodded.

"It's not a bad thing," Caroline protested. "I mean, everybody loves her, right, Jason?"

"Of course," Jason said quickly.

Dennis tightened his jaw; he was no student of mean girl logic, but with three sisters he knew words like *everybody loves her* could land like a punch in the right context. He studied her face, looking for traces of the impact, and didn't like what he saw. Abruptly he said: "Would you like to dance? I feel like dancing."

Her expression cleared instantly. "Yes, I'd like to dance. That sounds great."

He smiled and saluted the group. "We'll be back. Order me a drink, Jase?" he said, and with a hand on the small of her back escorted her into the crush of the crowd. The two of them were tall enough and took up enough space to carve out their own bubble.

He pressed his mouth to her ear. "Are you okay?"

"All green, Sir," she murmured back. That wasn't exactly what he meant, but it surely wasn't the time or place to push her about it. In the noise and heat of the dance floor he just put his arms around her and pulled her in close, trying to fill that bubble with affirmation; with the sense that she was enough.

April

Dancing was a good chance to reset. She was getting lost in her own head, forgetting to be sensible. She knew perfectly well Caroline wasn't trying to intrude or push her out or show off. Caroline wasn't *competing* with her.

Caroline didn't have to. She was seven years younger, curvier, prettier, and cis. Caroline just had to show up.

She was getting clingy with someone who she had no claim on. He was handsome, and sexy, and deeply kind—and their kinks aligned. That was fantastic. He would be a good friend, and if he wanted more sometimes that would be a lovely bonus, but she had known from the start that the club was full of Carolines and he would meet them eventually. She just happened to be there first. Being jealous was a waste of time; she just had to enjoy this while it lasted.

The sooner she got her head around that, the sooner this could go back to being fun. His arms around her and the lean heat of his body soothed the agitation in her heart even as it stoked the tensions further down.

When they came back to the bar, Jason and Caroline were still there, and one of Jason's irregular doms had turned up to flirt, Tony Something. Dennis took a Jack and Coke from Jason and they slid back into the conversation, which was about the upcoming Shibari demonstration. April was able to give some helpful commentary. "We aren't getting the whole show, actually," she said, "because the bar doesn't have the right hard points for suspension."

"I have to pee," Caroline announced. "Are you coming, April?"

"Yeah, sure." She grabbed her purse and followed. She did not in fact have to pee—she'd barely touched her drink—but she appreciated being included and used the time to check her makeup.

"So quick work with the new hottie," said Caroline approvingly, from inside a stall. "You met him earlier, huh?"

"Wednesday," she agreed, inspecting her face for shadows or roughness under her foundation.

Caroline audibly rolled her eyes at her reticence. "Uh-*huh*. And what happened?"

"Some stuff, you know. We hooked up."

"*What*. Girl. How's the dick?"

"I'm not going to…"

"*I* would tell *you*," said Caroline pragmatically. "So, this is a second date?"

"What? No. We just… I told him I'd be here tonight. We'd both be here either way. I don't think he's…" It seemed too complicated to mention the dress. He had money. Some people got off on spending it that way.

"You sure, hun? Because he seems a little smitten."

"Don't make fun," April muttered under her breath.

Louder: "No. It was just a hookup. He's a free agent. Nothing exclusive." It was never exclusive for her. It was safer that way, because no matter what was *said* sooner or later it *would* stop being exclusive. No expectations meant no one got hurt.

"Huh. Good to know." A beat. "You sure, though? I mean, I know you don't have—"

Oh Lord, the last thing she needed was pity. "We're all grown-ups, Caroline." *Some of us for longer than others.* "Do what you want." She pushed her way out of the bathroom and back into a solid wall of noise.

When she returned to the main room, the cluster at the bar had become a crowd in one of the club's large circular booths. Jason's group of friends, along with a healthy number of curious regulars and strangers, were squeezed into seats or lounging nearby.

She thought seriously about just leaving. He obviously didn't need her anymore. But—she looked down again at the dress. He'd made a simple and clear-cut investment. She would stay, and she would hang around, and maybe if he didn't leave with someone else—

"April!" He was calling her over, flagging her down, and she came over to the booth. "Let me—" He looked around, but the young man behind him chatting with Jason didn't seem to hear him and the girl sitting next to him showed no inclination to move. "Hm, come here."

"It's fine, I'm...fine," she heard herself saying, but he leaned across the table and grabbed her hand and pulled her into the booth. Onto his lap.

"Dennis, I'm too big for this," she whispered.

"No you aren't." He turned her sideways, wrapping an arm around her waist to hold her up. Helplessly she put an arm around his neck to stabilize the arrangement and leaned her head forward against his. She realized he'd brought her drink and took a big gulp. He dropped one large hand high up on her thigh as he resumed his conversation.

She exhaled and let herself fold into him; closed her eyes for a while and let the buzzing of her thoughts subside. Part of her was waiting for him to realize that she was indeed too big, or that he wanted privacy. But it never came. He wanted her here, and she was where he wanted her. It was…perfect.

Dennis

April was quiet at first; at one point he thought she might have fallen asleep. He was fine with it. She certainly wasn't petite, but she was no burden. Holding her on his lap felt good. Felt dominant and tender all at once. He had placed his hand on her thigh exactly over the tattoo just at the hem of her skirt and could feel her pulse rushing under his fingertips.

She came to life suddenly, waving as a lesbian couple walked past, both dressed in latex. One was a plump older Latina woman, and she had a college-aged white girl on a leash. "Mistress Sandra! Grace! Hi!"

"April! How are you, my dear?" The older woman reached out a hand to stroke April's crowning bun delicately and stole a speculative glance at Dennis. He met her gaze but tightened his arm around April's waist infinitesimally.

"I'm wonderful," April said, clicking into her deferential

submissive tone immediately. "This is Dennis. He's new in town—he's a friend of Jason's."

"And yours, it seems." Sandra smiled and handed the leash to her companion, who smiled back and immediately circled around the back of the booth to get closer to April. The domme had a firm handshake. "Sandra Barreras. How are you?"

"I'm good. Getting used to Austin. I like your club," he said.

"It's a nice place," she agreed. She definitely had *presence* as a domme, from her statuesque curves to her waterfall of black hair. An undefinable air of sternness. "And are you enjoying our April?"

"I'd say we're enjoying each other," he said cautiously. Was this an ex-girlfriend? Or a meet the parents–type scenario?

"Well put," she said, with a rich laugh. "What do you do when you aren't a throne for pretty girls?"

He could live with being April's throne, he thought. "I'm in technology. What about you?"

"My wife and I run a restaurant, Deedee's Place. Keeps me pretty busy, but I try to swing by here now and then."

"Ahh, and is this—" He gestured to the collared white girl. She had seemed excited to talk to April, but now both submissives were on their phones, albeit occasionally looking up to make eye contact. April's hands were moving in a more subdued version of her usual animation, probably to avoid clubbing him with her phone.

Sandra shook her head and laughed again. "No, this is Grace. My wife is a vanilla woman, but she allows me…"

"A little grace?" said Dennis, quirking an eyebrow.

"Dear God. April," Sandra said, in a firm voice, and he felt April jerk as her head swiveled around. "If he makes another pun like that you must leave him." April looked back and forth between the two dominants and ducked her head.

"I'll take it under advisement," she muttered into his lapel.

Sandra snorted, and relaxed back into a smile. "Disobedient creature. But yes, she gives me a little latitude to indulge myself, when I can spare the time. Grace is my current indulgence."

"Yes—" Dennis twisted his head to try to include the fourth person in the conversation. "Pleased to meet you, Grace." But Grace was looking at her phone and didn't respond. He slanted a look at Sandra, surprised. He wasn't offended, exactly, but the domme seemed like the kind to demand more discipline than that.

"She's Deaf," Sandra explained, just as Grace raised her head and gave Dennis an embarrassed wave and inclined her head. She signed something to Sandra, who nodded and translated. "April told her what you said. She's pleased to meet you."

Ahh. That certainly made sense of some things. "Have you been together long?"

"Less than a year," said Sandra. "Part of my arrangement with my wife is that the commitments don't last long. Although we may play together again sometime." Her eyes flicked to April again, and Dennis nodded.

He'd known couples with arrangements like that before. And that made sense of the relationship with April. He filed her subtle prickliness as a protective feeling for a former sub, which made sense. He felt sure he'd feel that way about April if he saw her with someone else, even after their short time together.

He also found he didn't like thinking about seeing her with someone else. Hmm.

"Well, if your time is limited, I shouldn't take up too much of it," he said. "Very pleased to meet you, though."

When Sandra and Grace made their way on to their own

table, April settled back against him and put her phone back in her clutch. She made a pleased sound but didn't say anything.

"They seemed nice," he said. "Have you known them long?"

"I met Mistress Sandra when I first came to Austin and found Frankie's," she said. "She's lovely, the nicest sadist you'll ever meet. We had a lot of fun but like she said, she has an expiration date. Grace, I don't know very well; they haven't come in that often. Sandra doesn't have a lot of time away from the restaurant, so they usually make it, uh, impactful, while it lasts." She giggled.

Dennis narrowed his eyes at her. "*Impactful.* Does that make us even on the pun front?"

April blinked demurely. "I don't know what you mean, Sir."

"Disobedient creature," he growled in her ear, and was rewarded with a little shiver.

As the night wore on, a tidal drift of clubgoers flowed around the booth. From her perch on Dennis's lap, April greeted and introduced old friends, recent arrivals, various subs and doms and switches of her acquaintance. Other times she settled back, curled against his chest, and allowed him to make conversation without her; Jason had a lot of people he wanted to introduce as well, and she seemed happy to be ornamental when she didn't have anything particular to say. Spaces in the booth came and went, but she didn't make a move to reposition herself and neither did Dennis.

Close to midnight, a baby-faced white man in casual clothes entered the bar, looked around and headed straight for their table. He slumped into a recently vacated chair, only the top of his tousled dark hair visible, and April sprang forward once again. "Oh no, Max, what happened?" she asked. She glanced back at Dennis. "This is Max. Max, this is Dennis."

"Gavin broke it off," the young man muttered to the table.

"Oh no," April said. It sounded heartfelt. "I thought things were going so well."

Dennis kept his arms around her waist, not sure he had a part in this conversation.

"He's been chatting with some other dom on FetLife," Max said, and Dennis winced. The boy was a stranger, but that was a blow any dominant could empathize with. April's response was more dramatic; she braced one hand on Dennis's shoulder as she half-stood in the booth and waved at the bartender.

"Aerith, I think we need some shots over here!" She turned back to the young dom and began to commiserate. Dennis smiled inwardly; he could absolutely see what Caroline and Jason meant when they described her as the den mother of the club, but if that was supposed to mean she wasn't desirable, then there must be something wrong with him. She was an effervescent mix of warmth and kindness and sweet submissive heat.

When the shots had been shot and his sorrows poured out, Max wandered off glumly. April turned back to Dennis with an apologetic smile. "Poor kid."

"Another old friend?" he asked.

"Well, I've known him for a bit," she said. "We haven't played together if that's what you mean. He's only interested in boys. Sorry if I got distracted."

"Absolutely no problem," he assured her. He liked seeing her like this. He wondered if she was like this at work, too; if she was the person who always had five minutes to get coffee when you needed to talk, or an aspirin in her desk, or an idea of where to find a shark costume for a fifth-grade pageant on short notice. Or was this place her element in some unique way? "So, have you always been a Wendy?"

"Oh," she said, and looked thoughtful. "Not always. It's

a lot easier to like people when they know your big secret
and are cool about it. Before I transitioned, I was kind of a
misanthrope."

"I can't believe that," he said. He hadn't really thought
about a pre-transition April, but he'd assumed she was pretty
much the same.

"No, it's true. I'd worked at my job since I got out of college, but nobody knew who I was. I think I had about six
people on my transition email other than the people in my
physical office. And I think a bunch of them probably said,
'who?'" She smiled crookedly.

"We don't have to talk about it if you don't want," he said.
She nodded quickly, and he second-guessed himself. "We can
if you want, too. But I know your past might be..."

She nodded again, looking brighter, and kissed his cheek.
"It just seems like another life now."

Could he understand that? He wasn't sure. There were
certainly events in his life that drew a line; he would always
have a Before Sonia and an After Sonia; a Before One Million Dollars and an After. But he was still the same person,
still the only Black kid in Pulaski High School, even if now
he was the only Black man in boardrooms and C suites. Still
working like hell and working twice as hard not to let anyone see him sweat.

"Do you think of it as being a different person?" he asked.

"I don't think *he* was ever anyone," she said. "Just someone
who had a lot of problems and wasn't very happy and wasn't
even a real person for the trouble. But he kept us alive until
I could... I could take over. I have to respect that." She took
a gulp of her drink.

He considered. "Where were *you* while all this was happening? Or is that the wrong question? I know it's not really
a split personality."

"I was there," she said, looking thoughtful. Looking vulnerable in a way that made him want to protect her from the world. "I was somewhere, I guess. Nobody ever asked me that before." She studied his lapel. "I was hiding, I guess."

He kissed the side of her head and gave her a squeeze. "Are you ready to get out of here? Should I settle up?"

She leaned in even closer, smelling of rum and citrus and faint feminine sweat. "Yes, Sir," she whispered in his ear. He deposited her gently in an open space and slid out of the booth.

He ran into her friend Caroline at the bar. "So," she said, as the bartender-who-wasn't-Aerith processed his card. "What's the deal with you and April?"

She'd definitely had a drink or three since he last saw her. "She's a delightful woman. I want to get to know her better."

"Mm-hm," she said. "Just her?"

Was this woman asking after his intentions or making a play for him herself? He frowned. "I mostly try to take life one thing at a time," he temporized. *Just her*, he realized. *I think just her.*

"Two at a time can be nice," she mused. "But okay. I hope you mean it. I really do. Maybe Mama April deserves a guy like you for being such a good girl all the time."

"You don't even know who I am," he said with a frown. "You don't know what kind of guy I am."

"Good point!" she said. "Then I guess you better try to be the kind she deserves."

April

For the first time all night, April's butt was on a cushion instead of Dennis's thighs. She felt slightly unsteady. That might be the rum, but she was pretty sure it was the hormones. Pheromones. Whatever. The club was beginning to clear out; the booth certainly was. What a lovely evening this had turned out to be. Dennis was talking to Caroline at the bar and she forgot to even feel jealous.

Then Jason Beaumont sidled around the curve of the booth and leaned in to talk to her. They'd had a few brief conversations over the night, but she still didn't feel like she could add anything to the description she'd walked in with: *rich gay power bottom, more committed to the club itself than to any of his lovers, dresses like he's fourteen.*

"Hey," he said, his breath full of vodka Red Bull. "I wanted to talk to you quick about D."

Oh Lord. She couldn't see how this could be good. "I know he's your best friend," she said.

Jason's mouth moved briefly, as if he was trying to choose his words carefully through alcoholic mists. "Just…be careful."

She stiffened. "I'm always careful, Jason."

"I just meant…he went through a real bastard of a breakup last year. It was his only serious kinky relationship. He's trying to get his head straight now. And I just…"

"I get it," she said, probably too low to hear over the music.

"I'm not sure you…" Jason mopped his hand over his face. "Just be careful, yeah?"

"I'm always careful," she repeated, sliding away, out of the booth. *What if I'm sick of being careful?*

She made her way to Dennis and leaned close to whisper in his ear again; Caroline fell silent as she approached, but she refused to think about that right now. "I want you to tie me up tonight."

He blinked. "Are you sure? We haven't known each other long."

"You've got about a hundred new friends who are about to see me leave with you. I think I'll be fine." She held up her wrists in the leather cuffs. "Were these just for show? *Sir?*"

Something flared in his eyes before being slammed behind shutters of control, and it woke an answering flame in her core. The bartender chose that moment to return his card. "Let's go," he said.

This time they set a record getting from the club back to her apartment.

It was a short way from the door to the bed, and this time he was undressing every step of it and she was not. "What restraints do you have?" he asked, a deeply serious expression on his face.

"Zip ties, nylon rope, jute rope, silly toy handcuffs, realistic handcuffs..." she reeled off.

"Someone is a closet bondage slut," he observed.

"Closet?" She dragged a large suitcase out from under the bed and dropped it on the counter. "I'm insulted."

He swatted her ass while she was bent over unzipping it. "Such a smart mouth you've got suddenly." He looked in the case; picked up the realistic handcuffs and snapped them through the stainless-steel rings on the cuffs, fixing her hands together behind her.

All her senses were singing. Covertly she flexed her arms against the cuffs and shuddered to feel herself restrained. Shoulders back, tits thrust forward. He shoved a hand into the keyhole of the dress to grope her. "Fuck!"

He grabbed a few other things from the case before he pushed her down onto the bed, not too forcefully but indomitably. He leaned in to kiss her; passionately, roughly. She bit his lip in return. "What has gotten into you!"

"Maybe I'm tired of being a good girl," she murmured against his mouth. Even she was a little surprised at herself. She didn't usually brat much, if at all. If she wanted to be roughed up, she'd beg for it. But tonight she felt wound up, ready to snap at anything that got near her jaws. She wanted more of that flare she'd seen in his eyes.

He gripped her locked elbows and rolled her over, kicking her feet apart. He bent her legs up off the ground, using the nylon rope and the cuffs to hogtie her; she could still wriggle and shut her legs, but not very effectively. Since the rope was over her stockings it wasn't that secure, but it's not like she was trying to escape, and she certainly didn't want to wait to take them off.

"Oh fuck," she moaned, as his hand roamed over her ass and groin, hot through the panties. He tugged at them, then she groaned loudly as she felt the cold of the emergency shears from the case cutting them off.

"Sorry about that, doll." He didn't sound very sorry.

"You paid for them," she panted, and that did *something* to him; he literally growled, grabbed her swollen clit and squeezed. She cried out as the cool lube hit her ass and trickled down her legs.

"Shit, shit, yellow!" she panted. "One second, one second. Yellow."

Dennis

Dennis froze and tamped down the fires raging inside of him. "What's wrong, lovely? Are you hurt? Is it—"

"No, no, just—can you put a towel down? This comforter takes forever to dry."

He laughed; they laughed together, and she laughed even harder when he slapped her ass. "You little...yes, one moment." It was BDSM protocol to always thank your partner for using their safeword—for keeping safety paramount even if it was frustrating in the moment—but just this once, Dennis decided to let that go. He shook his head and headed into her bathroom, which was exactly as tiny as he expected but spotless.

He investigated a tiny linen closet and returned with a towel he hoped wasn't one of her good ones; tucked it in place under her body. Her face was pressed into the bed and she had lifted herself up halfway on her bound legs. With her ass in the air like that, the bed was just the right height... "Are you ready, doll?"

"Green as *fuck*, Sir."

He ran a hand over her lubed-up ass and groin again; pressed a finger. "You've been very rude the last little while, bondage slut. Is this your way of telling me you want something?"

Her breath was coming in quick little pants that he could feel all the way to the root of his cock. "Not want."

"*Need* something?" She moaned in response—or maybe that was because of his finger slipping inside. "Do you need to be tied down and brought under control?" He ransacked his memory for her list of good words.

"Yyyyygh," she groaned into the bed. "I need it."

"Do you need to be fucked into *compliance*?" This time her response was a rising, mewling cry.

"Yes!"

A slap on her ass with his free hand. "Yes, *Sir!*"

Holy shit, he was going to lose his mind. Part of him knew he was being deliberately goaded, that this was a game like any other; the part of him that listened carefully for *red* or *yellow* even in her garbled voice. That part of him felt very far away right now. In his head everything was flames and lust and the need for control.

"But if I *fuck* you," he said, timing his words to thrusts of his fingers. "You learn that running your smart—little—mouth—works on me." And he pressed, hard, and she shrieked and shuddered and...didn't come. But he could tell she was right on the edge.

"Did you come since I saw you last?"

"No, Sir."

"Did you touch yourself since I saw you last?"

"*No, Sir.*"

"Did you want to?" he asked. As he fumbled with a condom, he kept up the rhythm of his other hand, preparing her, driving her closer to the edge.

"Yes, Sir."

"Wanted to come for me?"

"Oh, yes, Sir!"

"Wanted to touch for me? Even if you couldn't come?"

"…yes, Sir," she said, as if the words were being dragged from her by his questing fingers.

"Maybe I should just edge you and put you to bed," he mused. Like hell.

"Nonononono," she pleaded, wriggling and pushing back against him fruitlessly. "Please."

"You think I won't do it?" he demanded. "You think I'm ruled by my need to orgasm the way you are?" Her response was garbled but took the general form of a denial and a paean to his self-control and mastery.

He put both hands on her hips, tight, and let the tip of his cock touch her. She almost sobbed with need and pushed hungrily back against him. For a wild, reckless moment he almost considered not letting her come, even if it meant not fucking her. She was just so perfectly needy…

The sequestered part of himself reminded him that she did have limits, and so, for that fucking matter, did he. Even if it didn't feel that way right now.

"Keep begging," he instructed her, as he lined up his cock. Every word that poured out of her now was *yes* and *please* and *Sir*, in no particular order. And then he slid inside of her and he didn't know what she was saying anymore; he didn't know what *he* was saying anymore. Everything was hot and tight and perfect and obedient, and it was both too quick and far too long until he was exploding inside of her. His knees shook; he planted one hand on the bed to keep from falling over.

The fires in his head went out and he turned to aftercare like a drowning man to land.

April

She didn't *really* black out. Probably. Not exactly. Her continuity of experience—if not coherent thought, God knew what nonsense she'd been saying—was good all the way along, from cuffs to cold blades to his fingers leaving prints on her hip bones to being so intensely and perfectly impaled. Then he'd hit her prostate, just so, and two days of frustration and fantasy had gone off like a grenade.

Did they put a towel down? Shit, she hoped they'd put a towel down.

Bed. She was in bed. Felt like she had no bones. The ropes and other restraints were gone, even the cuffs. She was dimly aware of a salve, another staple from the suitcase, on her wrists and thighs and ankles. "Well. Those stockings are fucked," she observed to the dim room.

"Yes, like the panties," he agreed.

"Did we put a towel down?" she asked, and heard a chuckle in return.

"Yes, don't you remember?"

"Heh. Yeah."

"Of course, you ground makeup all over the comforter, anyway," he observed.

"Welp. You win some, you lose some." She felt numb, in a good way. Just generally…floating, some distance from her body. She didn't want to go back there. Some *really excellent* things had happened there just recently, but that wasn't her usual experience with it, was it?

"I'm cold," she said more coherently.

"Sorry, dolly. Just let me get the dress off and I'll tuck you right up."

Her tightly wound bun had finally disintegrated—had he pulled it at one point? Or did she just wish for that? She helped by fishing out her earrings and about a million bobby pins, dropping them on the bedside table. When she looked back, she was naked and so was he, and he was pulling her to his chest and dragging the comforter over them both.

She eased back into her body and let herself experience a broad flat chest with tight curls of hair. Dark little nipples which she experimentally kissed. He purred and stroked her head.

Maybe having a physical form wasn't so bad. "More of that please, Sir." He laughed and kept petting her as she melted into him. The unwrapped rope of hair slowly unraveled as he did.

She drowsed again, soaking up warmth and affection, then determinedly pushed herself up. "Kay. I gotta use the bathroom—and take all this makeup off."

"You sure you're ready?" He seemed reluctant to let her go.

"I'm sure I can't wait a lot longer," she sighed. Pragmatic

Wendy struck again. She rolled out of bed. "I'll toss the condom."

She had stuff to do besides take off her makeup; she expected (maybe hoped?) he'd be asleep when she returned. He was on his phone, though, and immediately looked up. "Hey. Everything okay?"

It would have been so much simpler if he'd been asleep. Or even if he'd ducked out, but that would probably be a little too tacky for a second encounter. Tacky wasn't in Dennis's vocabulary. Dennis wasn't like her usual ships passing in the night, and he kept proving it, even when it was inconvenient.

"Yeah," she said, moving to turn off the light. Keeping her head ducked. "That stuff just only comes off with a special face wash and even then, it's a bitch." She got back into bed, and his hands received her, gliding over sweet bruises and treasured rope burns and cradling her face. And then:

"Are—are you bleeding?" he said, in the most adorably puzzled voice, and her guts turned to ice.

"Fuck, I thought it stopped," she said in a low voice, wiping her chin with the back of her hand. This was what she hadn't wanted him to see.

"The makeup remover can't be *that* strong," he said, blankly.

"I…" She cleared her throat. *Sound normal, sound normal, sound normal.* "I had some… I needed to shave my face, because it's been twelve hours." No! That wasn't normal, that was defensive! Damn it! "It's just…something I have to do. I cut my lip."

He looked like he was absorbing that. "You could've done it in the morning."

"I could've," she sighed. "But I wanted to kiss you."

He looked stunned. "Honey, you can always kiss me." It

was an incredibly sweet thing to say, brought tears to her eyes, and then suddenly it hit her a different way and she *was* crying.

"That's not true," she said, in a horrible sobby voice, rolling away from him. Fuck. Oh fuck.

He wrapped his arms around her. Kissed the back of her neck and the side of her jaw, her hateful fucking jaw she just had to stare at in the mirror. "What if it was?"

"If I could always kiss you," she said shakily, as part of her rose up furiously at the rest of her. *Don't. Don't say it you endorphin-drunk bitch.* "Then you'd be mine. There wouldn't be anyone else."

"Is that something you want?" Which was not "That's what I want."

Be careful. Just, be careful. He was waiting for an answer—even with him behind her, she could feel those rich dark eyes watching and waiting—and she had to get this right. *If you never ask for more than they want to give, you're safe, you can't get hurt that way, so just be careful.* He was very kind, and very gentle, and she was sure he would be kind and gentle as he explained that he wasn't looking to move that fast. That he had just got to town. That he could do better. Well, no. He wouldn't *say* that. Not out loud.

He would be very kind when he let her down, but he would never touch her again. He wouldn't want to lead her on, after all.

This isn't your first rodeo, girl, so just. Be. Careful.

Dennis

As Dennis waited for her answer, he knew what he was hoping for. But when it came, it wasn't a *yes*, with or without her favorite honorific.

"I don't usually…do exclusive relationships," she said. She sounded like she was a long way off, although she was right here; like the words were painted on the bathroom door in a foreign language and she was slowly reading them off. "It just doesn't work."

"Oh," he said.

"You're gonna meet a lot of great people and I don't want to stand in the way of that," she said. "And—I mean, I have various friends with benefits and irregular partners at the club, too. We had…a nice time, a couple times. Some *really* nice times. But that doesn't mean…" She shrugged.

"No. Hey, I get it." He loosened his grip around her and berated himself for misreading the signals. For springing it on her when she was emotionally vulnerable. Right after a scene, and when she was insecure about her appearance. "We just met."

It hurt him to say it, because he felt such a strong connection already, but it was true. *Mr. Serial Monogamy strikes again.* "And I'm not trying to come in and...blow up what you've already got." That was the right thing to say, right? It didn't *feel* right, but he had to use his brain for once. If she felt any pressure, any demands from him—he had to be careful.

She ducked her head. "You make me sound greedy."

"No. Not at all."

"It's really...look, I don't want to get in *your* way," she said, her voice coming quicker now. "If that's really something you want—"

No! She couldn't, could not, change her answer just to make him happy. That was unacceptable. That was the start of another Sonia situation, another Seattle. "No, I'm sorry. I didn't mean to try to push you into anything. I...misread the situation."

She twisted back towards him, still in the loose net of his arms. God, her sides were soft. "I really like you," she whispered.

"I really like you, too." He pulled her close.

Fuck! Get it together, Martin. She's messy and vulnerable and that's because of you, she trusts you to take her here, and that means you fucking well listen when she tells you what she wants.

"We're going to be...such great friends." Every word felt like a knife in his stomach, but he smiled, anyway.

"With the most amazing benefits," she added, in a fragile tone of voice.

"Absolutely." She closed her eyes, and he let his face fall. Later, she would be asleep, and he would lie in the dark and reach for his phone, and he would text Jason: You were right.

April

The rest of the weekend was…bad. The fragile consensus by which April held her sanity in check collapsed into an orgy of self-recrimination, which she medicated with peanut butter chocolate ice cream.

By Monday she was sincerely glad to be back at work. Disentangling hospital general ledgers sounded like a fucking treat after the Sunday she had given herself.

She'd been at her desk no more than fifteen minutes, not even long enough for her first cup of coffee, when the email about the new CTO dropped into her inbox. It took her a moment to remember. Right. A new executive position. Supposed to make big improvements in efficiency and redundancies, which sounded like layoffs to her. She knew the COO passing well and he was far from excited about it. But according to Fatima the new guy was a real panty-melter.

She opened the email and read:

Please join me in welcoming our new Chief Technical Officer,
Dennis Martin.

Ah. Yes. Of course.

Part II: April

Six months later, a lot of things had happened to April. She was promoted. She acquired a completely new wardrobe. She met Fatima's baby. She confessed her kinkiness to her D&D group. She planned and executed three successful events at Frankie's. She told her grandmother she was a woman.

Two things did not happen:

*She did not tell Dennis they worked at the same company.

*She did not orgasm, not even once.

May

Dennis had told her the night they met that he was into orgasm control, and she had agreed she liked it, too. It was one of the first things they talked about after agreeing to non-exclusivity; in the Sunday morning after, before Dennis went home and April threw herself into a tub of ice cream.

They'd made breakfast together, her mostly pulling out pots and pans and food and knives and letting him get on with the cooking. Eventually, there was nothing left to do but watch him cook eggs, and April had hitched herself up on the counter and done so. He was wearing boxers and a half-buttoned charcoal shirt as he coaxed his so-called "perfect scrambled eggs" into existence in a pot.

All other things aside, she considered, he was a damn aesthetic treat. She loved the way his back moved, smooth complexes of muscles gliding over the bones to get out of each other's way when he reached up to turn on the hood fan. He was fairly fit, in the way of someone young with athletic hobbies rather than the relentless cut of the gym addict; he was firm but not hard to the touch, with a layer of cushion that made his stomach a delightful place to lay her head.

"You're staring," he said. He sounded amused.

"You're sexy," she replied, sticking out her tongue.

"I wasn't complaining. Would you like to touch yourself?"

She shifted restlessly on the counter. "Is that an order?"

"Does it need to be?" he asked, still not looking.

She bit her lip. She had tied back her hair and put on a nightgown that wasn't particularly sexy; it had squids on it. Almost thoughtfully, she reached up and palmed her breast. "Like this?"

"I have to watch these eggs," he said mildly.

"Hmph." She brushed her thumbs over her nipples and considered more of what she liked about him. Nice ass. *Good* ass, the kind that made her mind race on to imagine him in tight jeans, or from behind as he pumped into her... Oh...

She slid a hand between her legs, ignoring her clit as she often did when she didn't have a vibrator, and instead pressed her fingers into the folds of skin over her inguinal canal. *Ohhhh.*

She'd felt awkward at first, her bone-deep certainty of her body's wrongness making it difficult to imagine this as sexy, but he wasn't watching her, and if she forgot about her body and thought about his...

His dark skin was so smooth...but she knew from experience the tips of his fingers were slightly rough. Strong legs; powerful thighs. She fixated on the column of his neck rising from the foundation of his shoulders and the angles his shoulder blades made in the shirt.

"Can't you turn around?" she asked, half-joking, half-pleading. She wanted to see his face.

"Eggs," he repeated.

She tried to make a sound of disappointment but let it trail into a little moan. She saw a subtle twitch then and smiled to herself.

"I'm getting all wet," she said breathily. "And starting to… throb."

"Hmm," he said, and reached for the pepper.

"You're very mean!"

"They're ready. Plates?"

She huffed out a breath and pointed to a cabinet. As she washed her hands, he looked around for a table but there wasn't one, just the counter partitioning the kitchen from the room. She grabbed a couple stools. She squirmed her way through breakfast and he pretended not to notice. They were good eggs.

Eventually: "I was thinking about orgasm control," he said, in an offhand way which didn't fool her whatsoever.

"What were you thinking?"

"What if you couldn't come without permission?"

She felt a hot shiver run through her. "That could be fun." She poked the eggs around and asked the necessary question. "Your permission or just anyone's?"

"What would you be more comfortable with?" His voice was carefully neutral, as it had been all along, but was it wishful thinking to hear reluctance there?

"It's your game… You should make the rules." *Only you*, she thought, provoking a sharp response from the voice of reason.

"I'd like it to be me… I'm just not sure that's fair. Hmm…" He took another bite. "Not just anyone. You can't be calling up your friends and begging for them to help." The image of that, of being reduced to that, almost made her dizzy, but he went on. "If you're playing with someone else, I suppose it's fair for them to have that option."

Shut up about fair, she begged silently. "I don't mind," she said. And recklessly: "I've always wanted to try something longer-term. Like a…" She gestured vaguely. "A project." In that moment, it felt like a genius idea; a commitment that wasn't one. A permanent way to keep him in her life, without asking him for anything so dangerous as his heart.

He laughed, and there was a gleam in his eye she considered dangerous. "Fair enough. What if I thought about it and made some rules, and we can negotiate?"

"Okay," she said quickly.

"Do you want to come today? Might be the last time for a bit."

"Yes please. Sir." She pushed her plate away.

"I'll give you one minute," he said.

"Um, that's not really—" That gleam came back, and she inhaled.

She *knew* she couldn't orgasm in a minute, especially not sitting on a stool, but she was pretty sure he knew that, too. It was still her last chance for the day. She was maybe half-hard from her display earlier, and she tried all her old tricks to coax that into something more before time ran out, but all she accomplished was getting her hand sticky.

"Time's up." He looked at her ingenuously. "Didn't feel like it?"

She pursed her lips in a very fake smile. "No, Sir."

"Well, there's always tomorrow." That shiver ran through her again, a lick of fire up her spine.

"Yes, Sir."

"So well behaved suddenly," he laughed.

They finished breakfast and did the dishes together. "I can do it," she protested. "You're the dom. And a guest." But he shook his head and grabbed a dish towel.

"That's not the kind of obedience I want from you. And I'll be damned if I'll be a guest after last night."

"What kind of obedience do you want from me?" she said, eyes flickering to the front of his boxers. "Does it turn you on thinking about me not being allowed to come?"

"Oh, very much," he agreed. Still playing it cool. God, she wanted to see those fires in his eyes again.

"Do you want me to do anything about it?"

He shook his head. "I'll be fine. After all, *I* can masturbate."

She squawked in frustration, to his laughter. For as long as his voice and laughter filled her studio, she could hold it together. It was only when the door closed behind him that she plummeted into despair, at the mercy of the screaming match in her head.

The counsel for the prosecution: *You miserable bitch, do you get off on suffering?* This voice wanted to know what the hell she was thinking, did she ever think, why would she do that, and so on. It hauled in evidence both recent—the way he touched her, that one particular expression, dancing, sitting on his lap—and historical—the GSA meeting she'd almost attended in college then blown off, the fact that she was still in the closet to her grandmother—to make the case that she made bad decisions, that this was a bad decision, and that she should feel bad. That she should take it back.

The counsel for the defense: *Why would something good happen to you?* This voice reminded her that it was only a matter of time before someone else caught his eye; that if they weren't open now, he'd just want to open it up in six months; that soon she would be one among multiple, probably five or six other girls the way he looked and topped and fucked, and while she might just barely earn a place among those five, she would never be number one. Hell, she would never make the top three. That she had sat on his lap all night like a fucking billboard: *this is one of the good ones!*

This side had evidence, too, evidence that she absolutely did not want to look at or even think about or remember existed. The closing argument was a long, detailed self-examination nude in front of the mirror, pointing out all the lingering traces of a man that would always lie between them.

It's not his fault. It's not even your fault. But you're not pretty, French. Maybe he thinks you're pretty when you scream or when you choke on his dick, but guess what? There're a million other girls who want to do that who don't have to shave twice a day. You're aiming too high.

Ultimately, the jury found that she couldn't take it back even if she wanted to because he would laugh in her face, sooner or later he probably would've wanted her to fuck him anyway, and also, she was getting fat.

When she got the email on Monday, informing her that Dennis worked for her company, she knew she had to tell him. It was the only ethical thing to do. Not telling him was planting a ticking time bomb at the heart of their…thing, their thing that was not a relationship.

She had to tell him, and she had to tell him soon, because the longer she waited the more likely it was that telling him meant things were over. It would be awkward as hell, and he might end it right then, but it was the right thing to do and if she didn't, it would just be hanging over her head all the time.

And then she didn't tell him. It was not a decision to *never* tell him. She was just…delaying it. It would be an uncomfortable conversation and it would likely torpedo the best thing she had going, or had had going in months. She still had time to do the right thing. Just. Not yet.

Later that week she got an email with his plans for her, which filled her with equal parts desire and dread. The sexy kind of dread, mostly. He'd left her with very simple instructions not to touch herself until he got back to her, and by Wednesday—between the tension in her core and the anxiety of knowing he was in the same building—the guy in the next cube had asked her twice to stop bouncing her leg.

Her phone pinged with a new email on her personal account, and she looked both ways before pulling it up on her monitor. She had a window cube, one of the perks of her long tenure, and the management offices were around the corner in a different area. All things considered, it was hard for anyone to sneak up on her, but a little paranoia never hurt anyone.

1) You may only orgasm with my permission.

   a) You may ask me to transfer that permission to another dominant.

   b) You may ask for permission as much as you want, without penalty.

2) You may beg.

   a) You will bring yourself to the brink of orgasm and stop at least once per day. ("Edging")

   b) You will stop immediately if you go over, ruining the orgasm. ("Ruins")

   c) You will accept all penalties assessed for ruins or unauthorized orgasms.

3) I will check in a minimum of once a week, virtually or in-person.

   a) I am very unlikely to give permission outside of a check-in.

   I will check in with you this Saturday morning. That will be your first deadline and opportunity for an orgasm. Unfortunately, it will have to be virtual—I have to travel for work.

Okay. She could work with this. She shivered at *you may beg*, but yes, she could work with this. The edging would make things much more difficult; there were times in her past she'd gone months without masturbating at all, when she was still sorting out her dosage of hormones and antidepressants, but constantly teasing herself was something else. She replied immediately.

so fancy! i know the terminology ☺ but i appreciate how thorough you are

i can mostly agree with this, but im not sure i can edge every day...illness, RL stress, etc...whats the rule on that?

She had an eight-hour full-face electrology appointment coming up and she knew from experience sex would be the furthest thing from her mind for a day or three.

The response came very quickly, and that made her feel... weird, thinking about him on a different floor in the same building. Knowing he didn't know.

I can be reasonable. 7 edges a week, not necessarily once a day. If an issue goes on longer than a week we can discuss it in our check-ins. And safewords are always an option, of course.

Do you always type like that? Or is it just for me?

She snorted.

No, I don't always type like that. I actually have to fight the autocorrect to do it. But my earliest kink experiences were on IRC and other chatrooms, and that environment teaches you how to send subtle cues through your formatting and typing style. If you use capital letters people think you're a Dom.

It doesn't cause me problems unless I'm being a pervert and playing at work. Code switching is hard. >_<

I can live with 7 edges a week.

The next email took a little longer.

Ah, I see. That *would* be awkward. (Someone mistaking you for a dom. You typing like a needy sub at work is funny to me, I'm afraid...not that I want you to get in trouble.)
I wanted to make an addendum to our agreement:

b) I will allow you to renegotiate the terms of the agreement during check-ins.
c) Since these renegotiations will be sexualized and in a power exchange environment, you can of course always use your safeword to request a non-coercive renegotiation at any time.

How does that sound?

Fucking hot, is how it sounded. *sounds great Sir, thank You,* she typed, throwing in a little extra capitalization courtesy of IRC etiquette. She bet he'd get a kick out of it.

Good. If you can, I'd like you to edge right now to seal our agreement. I know you're at work…

She froze, then typed furiously.

Like in a public restroom? Like me, a trans woman, masturbating in the women's public restroom in the building where I work?

Almost instantly:

Shit. Never mind.

She exhaled and closed her browser. The whiplash of feelings was making her feel queasy and—now her phone was ringing. She grabbed it and headed for the door, not answering until she had stepped out into the hall. "Hey."

She heard a door close over the line. "I'm so sorry, I didn't think."

"It's okay," she said, trying to keep her voice neutral.

"It isn't, is it?"

"No, it really is." *Calm. Calm. Calm. This is a perfectly normal boundary. This doesn't have to be a trans thing.*

She heard his sigh. "I'm sorry. I've got a lot to learn. That was a really foolish thing to say."

She suddenly felt like she weighed a hundred tons. She wished she could sink through the floor. "You shouldn't have to do research to—" She bit off *date* and replaced it with, "talk to me."

"And you shouldn't have to educate me," he said. "I'll do better."

"I could get arrested," someone said, and she realized it was her. "Like if a cis girl did that and she got caught it'd be embarrassing but I'd go to jail. I'd be on Reddit. I'd be the example TERFs bring up for the next hundred years." Her voice was coming out quick and angry and she barely recognized it as herself.

"I'm sorry," he said again. "I'm sorry I said it. I'm sorry the world is like this. I'm sorry I don't know what a turf is in this context. I'm sorry."

This is another reason it's good you're not serious about him, said her most hateful inner voice. "I... I have to go back to work."

"I know. I—" A pause. "I'll talk to you later."

"Yeah." She hung up and stared at the wall for a long moment before heading straight to the elevator. She punched the button for the fourth floor.

Asshole! You're such an asshole, he's been so careful mostly, he's always checking in on you, why are you such a bitch, you should've just done it, you should've lied, you should've just gone to the unisex bathroom upstairs, you pathetic self-destructive hateful bitch.

She needed to make this right...and now, first, she had to tell him they worked in the same company. Why had she waited? Fuck!

She knew her appeal lay in being easy, undemanding, accommodating. Uncomplicated—or at least, in discreetly keeping her complications to herself. Now she was going to blow all that up, and if she'd told him sooner, at least she could have staggered it out. Maybe then she would've had at least a hope of keeping him.

On the fourth floor, her badge worked to get into the

tech staff area, but she realized she had no idea where the CTO's office was. This space was smaller than the tenth floor, which was completely rented out by her company, but she still couldn't exactly go door-to-door through the offices. She froze in the doorway like a deer in headlights.

"April! Hey! What are you doing here?"

She flinched, then realized, Fatima. It was Fatima. "Did you want to go to lunch today? You usually message first."

"Yyyyes," she said slowly. "Let's go to lunch." *That* was the moment when she truly decided she wasn't going to tell him. She realized now she had obviously already been considering it; it had been three days and she was still sitting on it. Now she committed. It was like lighting a very long fuse, and like all truly self-destructive acts, she found a purity and an inevitability to it that felt peaceful.

Someday he'd find out, and this would all be over. She didn't see how their fragile arrangement could survive it all. She couldn't change that.

But it didn't have to end today.

"You don't have your purse," Fatima pointed out.

"Oh. Shit."

"I'll ride up with you. So, what's going on?"

She blew out a breath as the elevator climbed back up. Of course Fatima could see through her to the storm raging in her skull. She wished she could talk to Fatima about this, but that was a nonstarter. Not only would it mean revealing what kind of freaky stuff she was into, but Fatima probably worked fifteen feet away from Dennis's office. She pivoted to something else that was worrying her, that would pass for the reason she was off-balance.

"John says he wants to promote me this year. He already discussed it with Mr. Graham."

"Well, that makes sense. You've been in your role a couple years now. It's good." Fatima studied her face. "Isn't it?"

She looked around the tenth floor, eyes peeled for coworkers. "Let's talk about it at lunch."

She'd been on this team since she moved across the country; the switch from consulting to operations required it, and she'd been happy to get out of New Haven. She liked what she did, mostly. As a consultant, she'd worked with Medicaid health care providers to help them take advantage of federal opportunities for funding. Now she did the operational work involved in submitting those cost reports.

In practice, she spent a lot of time poring over financial data from health care providers, usually provided in the most inconvenient format possible. It turned out that what had made life easy as a consultant—"Hey, whatever format you've got is fine!"—created a nightmare for Operations staff. Yet on the best days, deciphering and manipulating the data into a usable shape was a bit like solving a puzzle, and she'd learned to make Excel sit up and beg.

Actually entering the data into the massive manual cost reports was tedious, but it helped the Medicaid safety net and that felt good. And because the company was headquartered in New England, her insurance covered virtually all of her transition costs.

A promotion would still be mostly the same kind of work. She would be salaried instead of hourly. More meetings. More money. More visibility. There was no reason to *not* want it. It made it hard to explain why she didn't.

She dressed her salad in the restaurant down the street and tried to explain to Fatima. "I like having my own time. I don't even have work email on my phone, you know? When you're salaried, you're really working 24/7."

"Listen, you don't have to tell me. I'm the one whose phone

is blowing up in Lamaze," grunted Fatima. She took a bite of her lunch. "They *do* expect to be able to get you anytime. But anytime isn't *all* the time. And they're more flexible about your time *in* the office. It's really not that different."

"It feels like it to me. I like leaving work at work."

"So say no." Fatima shrugged. "But I'll warn you...they'll ask you where you see yourself in five years and start coaching you out the door, if you don't want to move to salaried. I've seen it happen."

April scowled. "I like this job. I like this company. I just want to stay where I am."

"Where *do* you see yourself in five years, April?" Fatima's expression of gentle concern looked maternal, although that was pretty much inevitable at this point. She only had a few days until her maternity leave began; she radiated maternal like a leaking nuclear reactor.

In five years, she'd be able to see forty on a clear day. "I don't know. What's wrong with where I am? I like my apartment. I can do this job and I don't hate it. I've got...my hobbies. My friends."

"Whatever happened with that guy?"

"I don't want to talk about him," she said in a rush. That was the last thing she wanted to think about.

"Okay. No boyfriend. Same job. Same apartment. Dungeons & Dragons once a month. That's what you see for yourself five years from now?"

"I guess so." She dropped her eyes to her plate and thought, *hey, don't forget a sex club where I'm known for being* sweet *and* reliable.

Not that there was anything wrong with those adjectives— not that she didn't enjoy her volunteer activities—but event planning sure the hell wasn't why she'd started going to kink clubs. Guys like Dennis and women like Sandra were why she'd started. She loved Frankie's, loved helping make it a community, but it could be hard to hold on to that when she started to feel more like a caretaker of the community than a part of it.

"Is that where you *want* to be five years from now?"

She sat in silence a long time. "I guess I've never...been happy with my life for this long. I don't know why it has to change."

Fatima patted her hand. "Everything changes. And thank God for that. I never expected to be pregnant while Jamil was in college, but I'm happy. I'm going to have my little girl finally. I never expected to end up doing this work when I went to school—I thought I was going to be a nurse! Can you imagine me as a nurse?

"You're not the person you were five years ago, and I know *that's* good. Why are you afraid?"

"The person I was five years ago..." She thought about Dennis asking about her past. "He's dead. I like being alive. That's enough to scare anybody off change."

"It's none of my business," said Fatima, throwing up her hands. This was invariably the sign that came before a big-time meddle. "If you want to throw away a promotion and a perfectly good man, it's up to you."

"I didn't throw him away," she snapped, and realized too late she'd taken the bait.

"So *he's* the one who bailed on *you*? Show me this fool so I can smack him upside his head," Fatima said in a gruff voice, and April found herself laughing.

"He didn't... We just—we're better as friends." *Who masturbate together...*

"Mm-hm. And who suggested that?"

She replayed the conversation. "I mean... I guess I did."

"So you did throw him away."

"I didn't—for God's sake, Fatima. You have to butt out."
Strictly speaking, she *had* been the one to suggest it. But she
knew how this worked. Fatima hadn't been through this cycle
before; Fatima hadn't seen the strings of connections that had
gotten her hopes up and then ghosted or bounced as soon as
things got messy or inconvenient or simply because a better
opportunity came along.

Dennis was lovely. Dennis was under her skin more than
anyone had been in a long time. But she couldn't afford to in-
vest herself into a relationship that was doomed. She couldn't
do it again.

"I don't have to do anything," Fatima said placidly. "I'm
a pregnant woman, the world is my bitch. In a week I'll be
gone for maternity leave, and now it's my chance to set everyone straight before I go while they can't say boo to me."

April sighed in exasperation.

"You were happy last week. I haven't seen you that happy
before. Now, suddenly, it's over. If there's a good reason, fine.
If there's not—then maybe you're getting in your own way,
like with this promotion."

"Wait, is this about my love life or my career?"

"It's about whatever I want it to be. Look…if you don't
want the promotion, don't take it. But find something else.
Think about a job where you *do* see a future and go there.
Same thing with this man. Holding still isn't a plan, April."

She looked down again wearily. "I guess." In the messy
chaos of her divorce and relocation, of her medical and legal
and administrative transition—after a life that had seemed
impossibly long because she hadn't wanted to be living it—
holding still had seemed like impossible grace to April. Why
be in such a rush to give it up?

Was it really time to start moving again? It terrified and
attracted her in equal measure.

The pregnant woman nodded to herself, watching April's pensive down-turned face. "All right, all right. I'll drop it. Hey—you want to hear some gossip? That new CTO, you know what I heard about him?"

April froze. "What?" she asked, tearing a bread roll slowly to pieces.

"Dude's a millionaire."

She choked. Genuinely choked, to the point that her friend half-started from her chair to help. She gulped some water and waved her off. *"What?"*

"His last job was at a start-up and I heard he cashed out with *millions*. Plural. Less than ten, more than five."

"That...can't be right..." She knew he had money, but... *millions?* "Why would he be here?"

Fatima shrugged. "Just a rumor. Who knows, yeah?"

Maybe...maybe that made it seem more fair. *I don't tell him we both work here. He doesn't tell me he's a millionaire. We obviously barely know each other.* Didn't this, if anything, confirm her perception of their relationship? April could just maybe envision a future for herself with a cute, gentle, normal guy with a penchant for ropes. Could she see herself as the girlfriend of a millionaire? Absolutely not. She wasn't sure she could even make sense of herself as the side piece of a millionaire.

And ridiculously, embarrassingly, in spite of all her attempts at distance and the egregious hypocrisy, she felt hurt he hadn't told her. It was kind of a big thing not to mention.

Later that night she sat in her reading nook with a bottle of wine and thought about it all. What did her future hold? She was getting older, and suddenly that scared her in a way it hadn't when she thought she'd be an old man. In truth, she'd always sort of thought she wouldn't live that long. Hadn't wanted to.

Someday I'll be an old woman, she thought, for perhaps the first time. *And I'll probably still have to shave. God. What if my hand shakes too much to do it someday and I look like Santa Claus?*

She picked up her phone and, without stopping to think about it, called Dennis. When he picked up, she knew from the thump of bass he was at Frankie's or some other club. She could hear a crowd of people; she could hear a woman saying his name. "April? Is something wrong?" Why did he think that? Because she was sitting here silently, listening to a future that wasn't hers?

She hung up. The phone began to ring at once and she answered with a text. Sorry. Butt dial.

She decided she was going to take the promotion. Because holding still wasn't a plan and the future looked empty. Because Dennis was just one person, wasn't the answer to all her problems, but he was the first person in a long time to care in that way, the first person to really see her and really want her in a long time, and she'd slammed the door so fast she almost lost a finger. Because Fatima had two kids and a great marriage and a job she loved, and Dennis was apparently a fucking millionaire and she…existed. And once it had seemed like enough, like such a precious thing, just for April to exist, for April to be allowed to exist. But now she wanted more, a huge ugly angry wanting, and she didn't know how to fill it.

Dennis texted her the next day and things seemed…normal. She didn't tell him about the promotion. That weekend they met virtually for their first check-in. It was low-key; she edged for him on camera, studiously avoiding the view of herself and focusing on his praise. He masturbated and made her watch him have what she couldn't. There were no real mind games or coercion involved, despite his emails. She did not talk about her job.

"I have to admit," he said, smiling. "I was hoping you'd be a little antsier by now."

"I, uh…" She paused, then continued. "My ex-wife and I used to play chastity games. Like…with a lock on it and everything."

His eyebrows went up. "I see. You didn't mention that before."

"My ex-wife? Or chastity devices?"

He laughed. "Either, I suppose."

"Well, most chastity devices for people with penises need testicles, and mine are in a jar somewhere," she said calmly. "And I don't talk much about that part of my life." As she knew he would, he took that as a cue, and didn't ask anything further. Good. That was good.

"In that case, let's make your next opportunity a month out," he said, and she whimpered. Bit her lip.

And then with a spark in her eyes, she said, "Let's make it two."

She wasn't sure why she said it. Punishing herself for keeping the secret? Trying to show him that she was experienced at this, that it was going to take more than some hot emails and a webcam view of his dick to get to her? Probably, she thought, this was going to fade into the background. She'd had doms like that before, people who came and went and checked she was still in compliance without being a real part of her life. It was fun, if a bit…self-service. Guided masturbation.

If she was going to shrink into a footnote in his schedule, might as well speed it up. She was going to focus on work, right?

And there was plenty of work. At first, she found herself enjoying the promotion more than she expected. The hours did get worse, but not a lot. She had to do a little development work, which was new to her. She still didn't have to deal directly with clients, but she had more interaction with internal stakeholders rather than just direction from her supervisor, and enjoyed working with the consultants and business analysts, collaborating and working to support them and figure out how to solve their problems. She'd done their jobs in her previous life and knew how to talk to them.

She'd always liked dealing with clients, and doing something similar divorced from the pressure to sell, and in an environment ruled by HR policies, was a huge relief. It felt like maybe, for the first time since she switched from consulting to operations, she had a career path and a future here instead of an eternal present.

At first.

June

As the summer wore on, Dennis continued to be attentive. They continued to check in weekly, either virtually or in person, depending on his travel. With the date set, it was less about discussion and more a welcome opportunity for him to tease her. He asked her how many pairs of panties she'd ruined by dripping in them; watched her edge, drew out the filthiest language she'd ever used making her beg.

On the other hand, in the run-up and recovery from her session of full-face electrolysis she dropped out entirely for a full week—no pictures, no clothing instructions, no edges— and he was gentle with her. During their virtual check-in they played *Mario Kart* and didn't mention it. He was...kind.

What are you? she thought. *What is this? What am I to you?* But those were all questions she'd made impossible to ask.

About six weeks into her denial regimen, she got another email.

I want you to get some new clothes. I'll give you a prepaid card. I want you to spend up to $500 a week. However, I'll have veto power. You'll have to return anything I don't approve.

She fired back:

are you joking?

This is not a joke. It is, however, a game. Do you want to play?

Of course she did. Of course she couldn't. She sat frozen, staring at her screen.

We should discuss it in person, of course. We can talk about it this weekend. I'm back in town. I just wanted to gauge your interest first.

Interested didn't mean she had to do it, right? But maybe he could…talk her into it. He was a millionaire. Was this what millionaires did? Surely not. If they were dating, maybe… not with someone they'd very explicitly decided they weren't seeing exclusively.

im definitely interested, she typed carefully.

He was still living with Jason and the club was too loud for a serious discussion, so they agreed to meet at her apartment once he was back in town. She obsessed for a while about what to wear, but that turned out to be very simple, because around noon on Saturday he texted her.

Dennis: Wear something simple. White. A skirt or dress.

No shoes. No jewelry. No underwear. Makeup if you choose but nothing dramatic.
Wear the cuffs I gave you.

Followed by an emoji of a stoplight.

yes Sir, she sent, adding a green heart.

She looked through her closet and found a white sundress she never wore, and put her hair back in a high ponytail. She really did intend to keep her makeup light, but once she went over her beard shadow with orange concealer, she needed more foundation than she expected to cover it; and then her eyebrows were wiped out, so she needed to use an eyebrow pencil; and then her eyes looked unbalanced without mascara; and then her complexion was flat so she needed blush; and *then* her mouth was washed out, so she went over it with a neutral lip crayon...

It took forty-five minutes, but when she was done, she liked what she saw. It didn't look heavy or dramatic, or even have the bright pops of color she favored for work to really sell the "I'm a girl!" message. It looked like...her, in a kinder world. She liked what estrogen had done with the shape of her face, and now she'd touched up all the things she couldn't ignore.

She painted her toenails; she couldn't hope to match the black-pink ombre still on her fingers, but she could at least get in the same general area.

Even with other general preparations, she was ready by five o'clock. She sat down on her bed and wondered what on earth she was going to worry about if she couldn't worry about her appearance. She decided to clean her apartment. It didn't take long; it was a tiny apartment.

She wondered, as she wiped down the counters and moved

books from their random stacks to their homes in the Ikea shelves, if that's why he felt like he needed to buy her clothes. Was she too obviously broke to spend time with a millionaire? What did that say about the clothes she already had?

I'm not going to think about this. I'm not going to get myself all wound up when he'll be here in a little while to explain. I'm not going to do it.

She did it, anyway.

She sat on the bed, and then she decided that if she did that, they might never end up talking about anything, so she moved to the small reading nook she'd created in one corner by putting a couple of armchairs there. She *liked* her tiny apartment; she liked being downtown and was willing to live in a studio to do it. So there, imaginary Dennis.

She read *The Calyx Charm* for a while and then had to get up when he knocked on her door, anyway.

"Hi." He smiled at her, and she told herself not to turn to mush. Today was not going well in terms of listening to her own mental commands. Today he was proving he could wear casual clothing—jeans, which fit in exactly the way she had hoped for, and a light linen button-down and Allen Edmonds loafers. She was mush. She was ultra-mush. She wanted to go to him and kneel at his feet and lay her cheek against his thigh and just exist there for a thousand years. She wanted to orbit him like a cold planet eternally falling towards the sun; desperate for the warmth, but afraid to burn.

She was staring. She cleared her throat. "Hi."

She brought him over to the reading nook, smoothed the dress over her knees, and looked across at him. "I... I should say, I dressed the way you wanted, but I really think we need to talk about this out of role." Because nothing made her feel like her everyday, out-of-role self like having her dress grazing directly over her excited nipples and clit every time she breathed.

His eyes widened. "You're absolutely right. I apologize, this is a particular fantasy of mine and when you were interested, I admit I leapt at it. I shouldn't have…have I fucked this up already?"

His face looked so dismayed that she wanted to climb into his lap immediately and kiss it better. *Damn it, French.* "You didn't fuck anything up," she said gently. "Have you done this before? I think that might help me feel like it's less…weird…" Because officially, she didn't know he was a millionaire.

"Not less special?" he asked.

"I mean maybe a little?" she said. It honestly hadn't occurred to her, but now she examined it. "I mean, I guess I know you didn't invent spanking just for me, either. There's only so many ways to be kinky no matter how hard we work at it." She grinned, and he brightened in response.

"I did it with my ex. I guess it was different then because we were already living together before we got kinky. In a funny way it was just a kinky gloss on some household budgets. But doing it taught me a lot about what I liked." Talking about this part of his life seemed to take his expression back into darkness.

"So what *do* you like?" she asked.

"I like spoiling the people I—I care about," he said. "We haven't talked about this, but honestly, it's not a lot of money to me."

"But it is to me," she said neutrally. Some less disciplined parts of her brain were howling about the phrase "people I care about" but she was determined to do this right. This wouldn't work for either of them if they didn't do it right.

(*I'm people he cares about!!!!*)

"That's—not what I meant," he said quickly. "Look. I like

to dress women up, okay? It's a huge turn-on. If you did this, ultimately I'd like to have input into what you wear every day, or at least when I have time to plan something. Part of this is so I have a better idea what's in your wardrobe, and so you have some..."

"Nicer things?" she prompted.

"Things in tune with my aesthetic for you. I'd love to just buy you the clothes, but I know I'll get things wrong, at least at first. Maybe after a while I'll know what you like and what I like and we can try that, too."

"My own personal Stitch Fix," she mused, trying different ways to think about it. Seeing if there was one that made it fit in her head. God knew she wanted to find a way forward.

He laughed. "I like that. Maybe I'll use it next time I have to explain it to someone."

She willed her smile not to dim. "Caroline would love this game. For sure."

His own smile faded. "So what do you think? Are you in?"

She thought. "I need you to admit something first. It's at least a little about the money, isn't it? I mean...you have more money than me." She'd had time to think about this. "That's a fact. That's power you have that I don't. And this is all about power exchange, taking those imbalances and making them sexy, but...we can't do that if you don't admit it. We absolutely have to be ruthless about admitting it."

He seemed to absorb that. "Okay. You're right. It's a little bit about the money." He sighed, his eyes roaming around the room. "I didn't grow up with...the kind of money I have today. When I got my first big bonus, I paid off my parents' house. And I could do that, not because it was *so much* money, but because my parents' mortgage in Illinois was that small. But they would've been working on paying it off the rest of their lives.

"I like that power. I like not having to think about whether or not I can afford it when I want to do something or solve a problem." It came out in a flood; not an outburst, but something unlocked from deep within, coming out of his mouth fast and unplanned. "Having options.

"So I like having money, and yeah, I like to show it off a little. Not excessively, and not for its own sake, but because it protects you. It makes things easier. I've heard that Black men have trouble getting into some of the fancier bars on the West Side around here—"

She had not heard that, and was shocked, and then mad at herself for being shocked.

"—but I haven't. Not when I'm dressed up. It's not…a perfect defense," he added quickly. Intently.

"But that's…that's the fantasy," he concluded. She could see uncertainty in his eyes, wondering if she really understood, and she hurried to reassure him.

"No, I get it," she said quickly, searching for her own words now. "I think I do. It's like… I work…really hard. I work really hard on how I look. Because I feel like if I've done everything I can to send the message that I'm a, that I identify as a woman, then even though I don't pass, I… I did my best."

She didn't consider herself totally ignorant on matters of race, but there was a long way between putting a Black Lives Matter sticker in your window and knowing how to be a good partner to someone who faced challenges you couldn't understand. But there *was* something here she could understand.

She knew, she *knew*, she was just as much a woman in sweats and a day's stubble, but it could be damn hard to find her voice to say so. When she was dressed up it was simultaneously more of an insult and that much easier to say, "it's ma'am, actually." Most of the protection was illusory, because nine out of ten times no one said anything anyway, and at the end of the day she knew she didn't pass to anyone looking closely. But if she did her best, she didn't feel quite so much like she was waiting for it to happen.

She went on: "It's probably a little fucked up, but it makes me feel better, and I can face the world as my best self." It wasn't what she would expect of any other trans woman. But it was what *she* needed to go out the door in the morning.

He was nodding "*Yes*. And the money just makes it easier." His eyes found hers again and all uncertainty was gone now; she felt like he was pouring some kind of energy into her that spread to the roots of her hair and the tips of her fingers.

"I want to share that with you. Yes, I want to retain some control of how it's spent. And yes, I want to see you in the kind of things you can't usually afford. It *is* about power— and I want you to feel my power head to toe when you walk out the door in the morning. But I never want you to feel trapped by it. I want you to wear it like armor."

She sat very still, because she felt like if she moved at all she would explode. She felt pinned to the chair by the intensity of his gaze and his desire. Her own desire. She'd never had much of a sugar baby kink, but yes, she could understand this. She swallowed audibly. "O-okay. I'm still interested. I do feel like…it's so much money. It feels a little wrong. But— it's practical clothes, too? I mean, this isn't just a lingerie account, it's work clothes, jeans, stuff like that?"

"I'm absolutely going to veto any pants," he said, quite seriously, "but yes, like that."

"Well… I don't have *space* for an entire second wardrobe. I'll have to get rid of things I already have. I do know some clothing exchanges for trans women that could use them…" She was talking herself into it. "It's *so much*, though."

He laughed. "It's really not," he said. "But we can start

with a lower number if you want. Work up to something more ambitious as you feel more comfortable."

"As *I* feel more comfortable? What about you? It's your money. What if I took it and ran?"

"I think we're worth more than five hundred dollars," he said, and it was like his first confession of desire; simple and stark and a line drawn in the sand, daring her to give a little. "Don't you?"

She stared into her lap until she made up her mind, and then raised her head. "Yes, Sir." It was the *we* that got her. More than anything, she wanted them to be a *we*. A thousand objections and fears fell at the feet of that *we* and surrendered.

"Terrific." He really was beaming. "Can I see your closet?" he asked. "I'm not going to pass judgment, and I won't tell you to get rid of anything. But I'd like to know what I'm working with."

The inventory of her closet went smoothly until they came to her small collection of lingerie, and then the evening took a delightful turn where money didn't come up at all. Of course, neither did an orgasm, because *someone* had had the bright idea to say, "Let's make it two."

July

She threw all of her building sexual frustration into organization; she created an online spreadsheet with a catalog of all her clothing, old and new, organized by type. It took a bit of work, but she rationalized it to herself as fair value for the money she was receiving. She laughed aloud in her apartment alone when she saw he'd simply hidden the "pants" tab. A man of uncomplicated tastes. Other items were bolded or color coded as he explored.

Over time the arrangement shifted, with explicit renegotiation. (There was a tab in the document for that, too.) She rapidly learned to recognize the colors he liked, or at least liked on her. Pinks, yellows, deep purples. Pencil skirts and blazers passed without a problem. Occasionally a dress was rejected as too shapeless or long. Tights were resolutely rejected until she started investing in stay-up stockings or garters.

It was fun; it was another opportunity to feel close to him.

She had new expensive professional clothes and an excuse to wear them. It *did* feel like he was with her, all around her, when she walked into a meeting in his choices. She went into her performance review in a black and gold Versace shirtdress and another couple hundred dollars in lingerie underneath it, and when her compensation came up, she asked herself what Dennis Martin would say. She walked out with 5% more than she'd even dared to dream she would get.

Later in the summer, when she started sending him a picture of her outfit every day, the limit went up to a thousand dollars per week, although she rarely touched the maximum. By fall, he would be giving her instructions every other day or so, and the prepaid card would be replaced by one of his credit cards. They fought for a week about that before she agreed.

The card, not the instructions. As she had suspected she would, she found the instructions…fun. They texted and communicated endlessly. His expectations and affirmations; her fears and fantasies. It was pretty much always sexy, being dressed up by him, and sometimes it was extremely hot, wearing lingerie under her work clothes or being pushed, just slightly.

The night before their two-month appointment, before her next opportunity to orgasm, he texted her:

Dennis: You bought some bathing suits recently, right?

April: yes Sir

At that point, she'd only made a few purchases. It was simple enough to use the card and send him the links to her purchases for approval. He'd been sparing with the veto, and she was still trying to detect his taste. Nothing too kinky. So far.

Dennis: I want to see how they look on you. Send me pictures.

She wondered where this was going. She'd bought the bathing suits on a whim, but she rarely felt confident enough to swim in public. She'd gotten three suits; a staid black one-piece with a ruffled skirt, a sunny yellow two-piece tankini with matching shorts rather than briefs, and a green bandeau top she could wear with the same shorts.

She thought about shaving—it was after work and her five o'clock shadow was ticking—but she'd have to remove her makeup first and then either reapply or take photos barefaced. She didn't want to keep him waiting too long. She took a deep breath, put the worries aside and let herself drop into the submissive headspace. Starting with the most conservative suit and ending with the bandeau top, her self-consciousness was forgotten as she modeled for him. By the end her arousal meant she could barely manage her tuck anymore. She was stroking herself as she sent him the pictures, although she'd already checked off her edge for the day.

Dennis: I can't believe I didn't veto that black thing. Can you still return it?

April: i think so Sir

Dennis: We're meeting tomorrow for your one-month deadline. I want you to wear the bandeau top and cut off shorts.

April: i dont have any cut off shorts!

Dennis: You have scissors, don't you?
I want to be able to see your tattoo.

Her stomach did a slow lazy roll. She had never once gone out in public in anything that short, let alone as revealing as the top. Her brain immediately thronged both with wordless, giddy glee—it was such a fantasy!—and a thousand unanswered questions. She took a deep breath, tried to resist—tried to hold on to her headspace and just obey—then typed in a rush:

April: where are we going to go dressed like that Sir?

Dennis: You're going to show me your favorite barbecue spot.
It's supposed to break 100 degrees tomorrow, I want you to be comfortable.

April: im not sure ill be comfortable like that Sir!!

Dennis: What color?

She bit her lip.
She could veto this. She absolutely could. And this was… This was close to the red. She was still in the top, and she looked in the mirror on her bathroom door. Right now, she felt sexy, liked the look of the simple scrap of green around her slight bust, liked the shorts hugging her hips, but how would she feel when she wasn't aroused?

April: yellow

Dennis: Thank you for telling me, lovely.
What would make it more comfortable for you?
I had a vision of you as a summer goddess.

Well. Shit. That was sweet. Her heart swelled, and she looked in the mirror again.

Dennis: What if you wore a blouse over it?

April: buttoned or unbuttoned?

Dennis: How about tied off?

April: i could do that Sir
thank you for working with me

Dennis: Of course.
Do you have sandals?

April: yes Sir

Dennis: any with heels?

April: Sir I dont wear heels, I'm already so tall

Dennis: My sister is the same height as me and she wears heels all the time.

April: really?

Dennis: She says she would still be tall if she didn't wear heels, so fuck 'em.

April: ☺
does this mean you want me to get heels Sir?

Dennis: Just one to grow on, I guess. Your regular sandals are fine.
I don't need to always be pushing your boundaries, doll.
Thank you for indulging my whims. You're a good girl.

She shivered and squeaked as she brought herself to the edge of orgasm, then stopped abruptly, squeezing her eyes shut against the sudden flood of regret and longing. The impulse to continue warred with the impulse to be a *good girl*.

There was nothing stopping her but her word. With Marie, there'd been a padlock in the way, at least. But it was the moments like these that held her… Moments where she felt his intoxicating control, more exquisite than any orgasm. She'd gone a month. What if she went further? How depraved would she feel then? How desperate? She realized she was halfway to another edge and pulled her hand away.

April: thank you Sir
youre wonderful to me

And in the morning, she got up earlier to buy sandals with three-inch cork wedges before she met him at the food truck. The truck was located in the parking lot of a bar, right out on the boiling blacktop, and he was there already when she parked, sitting at a rough wooden picnic table soaking up the July heat like a lizard in a tank top and basketball shorts. It was by far the most casual thing she'd ever seen him in. The lean muscles of his arms and legs were on display, and his dark skin glowed with copper undertones highlighted by the glaring midday light.

He was wearing sunglasses—the blazing sun was nailed to a blue-white sky, they both were—but she could *feel* his eyes moving over her as she approached, and she tried to put a little extra sway into her hips. Combined with the unfamiliar heels, she stumbled, and he leapt from the table to catch her before she hit the scorching asphalt.

"Oh dear, oh dear. You're such a good, obedient doll. Come on." He helped her to the table, her face flaming and her brief spark of confidence doused. "Hey. You're all right." He lifted her chin and kissed her thoroughly.

"I'm a clown," she whispered ruefully, but she was able to say it now like a joke and not a confession.

"You're learning. I'm so pleased with you for trying something new." His dark hand stroked her tied-back hair, and for a moment she floated shamelessly between the heat of the sun and the heat growing inside of her.

Gradually, she regained consciousness of herself and her position, and she bit her lip. "Will you…"

"Yes, pet?"

"Will you order for us both? I don't…" She came here all the time. The thought of looking the owners in the face and asking for a lunch special dressed like this felt…impossible. She'd never be able to come back.

He kissed her hand. "Absolutely. What do you want?"

They settled on splitting a three-meat plate, which came with two sides. She had misgivings about eating barbecue when an orgasm was supposed to be on the menu—post-barbecue sex didn't sound like a great idea—but damn it, her honor was on the line. He had to see. "Get the chicken," she said. "Most barbecue chicken in Texas isn't worth a damn, but theirs is fantastic."

"Yes, ma'am," he chuckled, and stroked her hair one more time. It was *too* good. It didn't feel like a scene, or even like a date, exactly. It felt like a dream. It felt like a normal Saturday morning with a (*don't say it*) boyfriend.

Dennis seemed as cheerful and relaxed as she'd ever seen him, trading daps with Roger and laughing as he loped back to the picnic table on his long legs. If she kept looking at him, she was going to keep falling for him. She studied her nails instead—they were new, French tips with metallic gold edges instead of white—and tried to remind herself of her place. That this was a scene, with a beginning and end, and when it was over, he would just be her *very good friend* Dennis.

He was watching her intently as he returned and tore the paper bag down the middle to create a tray to spread out the goods. "Did I tell you that you look fantastic?" he asked.

"Thank you, Sir," she said quietly, lifting her head to smile at him. She shook off her inconvenient feelings and focused on the task at hand. "So—brisket, sausage, and chicken," she said, pointing to the three heaps of meat on the table. "They smoke it in that truck for at least twelve hours. We got a good cut of brisket here, off a new slab, so we've got some of the crispy end and then some more towards the middle. See that smoke ring?"

He tilted up his sunglasses. "I do, Professor Barbie-Q. I do indeed."

"Shush and eat this." She held up a piece of meat that was barely pink at all, mostly crispy outside. Instead of taking it from her he snapped it out of her hand. It made her blush.

"Smoky," he said. "Hm, that's good actually. Takes a lot of chewing, though."

"They call those burnt ends, and they're my favorite part," she said, aware she sounded schoolmarmish but unable to stop. "Try this now." She tore off a hunk of a wider slice, keeping the crust at the top as well as a juicy marbleized streak of fat.

He took this from her hand, too, and she could feel arousal uncoiling in her stomach, a sensation she had never before associated with barbecue.

"Wow," he said, wiping his lips. "That's...it's like butter. It's *so* tender. If I were a cow...and I had to go..."

"See?" she said. "Do you concede the Midwest doesn't know shit about barbecue?"

"I dunno," he said, smirking. "I might need more convincing." He looked down at the rest of the meal with anticipation.

"Have a pickle first," she said, grabbing a piece of brisket for herself. "It clears the palate. Otherwise it's just grease on grease after a while."

As they worked their way through the brisket, the sausage, the chicken, the potato salad and the mac and cheese *and* the cobbler, April relaxed enough to take off the overshirt. It was too damn hot for modesty, even in full view of the busy zip of traffic on Lamar. Dennis looked across the table at her.

"Hey—those shoes. I really didn't mean anything by it. You put up a boundary about the outfit, the last thing I wanted to do was guilt-trip you about something else." He kept gathering up their trash as he spoke, a deliberate casualness to his face and motions, but she sensed a tension there.

"Dennis." She put a hand on his bare upper arm, where the heat baked off his dark skin. "I did it because I wanted to. They're cute shoes. Thank you for telling me about your sister. I think that'll stick with me. No amount of making myself smaller will ever make me *small*, so I might as well..."

"You might as well shine as bright as you can," he said,

and lifted his hand to touch her face. It left a smear of grease, and he swore and patted it off with a paper towel, laughing at himself. Which gave her time to pull her emotions under control again.

"I didn't know you had a sister," she said, for something to say.

"I got three," he said, holding up fingers. "But Kat and Keisha are shortasses."

She broke into laughter. "Oh, okay."

"What about you?"

She shook her head, "Just me and my folks." And suddenly she didn't want him to ask any more, didn't want to talk about her family, because for about an hour she'd forgotten altogether there was any reason for them to be estranged. There were benefits to having only a present with a lover, only short scenes with clear boundaries, and one of those benefits was that she didn't have to talk about her mom.

"Hey," she said, mostly wanting to change the subject. "You tricked me again."

"What do you mean?" he asked, tilting his head.

"I'm all bloated and greasy and gross. I was supposed to orgasm today."

"Oh, was that today?" he said, hand on his chin in an obviously theatrical pose. "Whoops."

She stuck her tongue out. "Thank you for this," she said. "It was great. Even without an orgasm." It really was. Her chest felt tight with it; like her heart would burst, that silly saccharine cliché. She felt full of something she didn't dare to name. And barbecue, of course.

"I'm glad to hear you say that," he said. "When's your birthday?"

She blanched; she could *feel* the blood rushing out of her face. "Dennis…"

"Hmm?" He beamed at her, eyes hidden behind his sunglasses again, and the part of her that liked feeling powerless felt very, very good indeed.

"It's…in September. Sir," she said, very carefully. Watching him intently.

He nodded. Then he leaned across the table to kiss her.

"Let's try again next weekend then. I don't want to jinx it," he said ruefully, "but I'm supposed to be able to move into my house. We can christen it after the Shibari workshop. I'm sure we'll be inspired."

He was, in fact, able to move in—the master bedroom was finished, even if nothing else was. And they were, in fact, inspired. He tied her down and edged her himself six times. By the end she'd thought for sure he'd lose control and push them both over, but he'd pulled out at the last second and finished in her mouth. She cried that night, but when the scene was over, he showered her in aftercare. When she left in the morning, she felt happier than she could remember being. Even if somehow, she'd agreed to her birthday as the next deadline.

I'll never come again, she whispered to herself on the way home. *Just let this keep going. It doesn't have to change. Just let it keep going.*

August

Unfortunately, at work there was no safeword. More and more, development work was being peppered into her schedule, and she was hating it. She'd always worked with the websites and products the development team built, but in truth she knew very little about the process of creating them and hadn't thought about it too much. Now she was expected to be the representative for her ops team in their meetings and she was scrambling to catch up. It was frustrating work, in part because the project management was badly organized, but she suspected she would loathe it even if it was done properly.

She didn't like gathering and documenting requirements, the infuriatingly meticulous level of detail required, and she didn't like the constant meetings with developers, either. Working with the consultants was like having internal clients; the development team were more like hired experts, but fractious and dissatisfied ones. Maybe they had good reason

for being cranky. At the end of July, the entire Help Desk
was let go, and she knew from Fatima it had caused a lot of
unrest in the technology division. The mass layoff made a
certain kind of sense—the Help Desk was a shit show, had
been as long as she'd worked for the company—but it was
still kind of terrifying to think that her...her *Dennis* had fired
so many people.

So maybe the developers weren't their best selves. Most of
them worked remotely, which meant mostly phone meetings,
which meant their impression of her came from her voice and
not her achingly curated appearance. She'd never had voice
training—she honestly felt that the saccharine artificial "trans
woman" voice they taught in those classes was worse than her
natural voice—but for the first time she regretted it. There
were a lot of accidental "him"s, and increasingly sour voices
when she corrected them.

And of course, she couldn't talk to Dennis about it.
Couldn't breathe a word, even as he increasingly vented about
his troubled data migration and the backstabbing bastard she
recognized in his stories as Leo Graham, her boss's boss. Every
smile-and-nod took her further away from the truth; every
time she didn't talk about it, it became more impossible to
ever talk about it.

It broke down like this: if she told him, he'd be angry. That
was a given. And it seemed impossible things would just go
back to normal. Things would change, they would have to.
They would be thoroughly entangled in each other's lives,
and this would either become a relationship or it would end.
And was it going to become a relationship? Was it really?
Who was she kidding?

Towards the end of the summer, he had to go to the East
Coast for a solid six weeks, and in a dark, disappointing way
it was a bit of a relief. At least it was easier to keep the lie

going. But when he wasn't around, things got harder. She fell behind on the required edges and then had to catch up. It was the opposite of the way pain could blur into pleasure with impact play; pleasure blurring into a queasy ache from too much frustration, and no one to hold her and gently laugh at her until she laughed, too.

She missed him, though. That was the truth. If she'd fooled herself this was casual, part-time, practically long-distance dominance, she was now acutely aware of all the evenings or weekends they'd spent together with no more sign of kink than the comforting weight of his hand on her skin or a coy duck of her head.

She found herself spending more time at Frankie's, for the first time all summer. It wasn't that she hadn't been in at all. She had planned the Shibari workshop and made sure everything went smoothly, then worked with Vic to coordinate their contingent in the Austin Pride Parade. (For reasons that surpassed understanding, Austin held Pride out of sync with the rest of the country and in the hottest month of the year. They'd attended together, although she'd had to neglect him for logistics several times. As it turned out, it was her last weekend with Dennis for several weeks.)

She'd even come in for drinks after work and to catch up with friends a few times through the summer; to help Caroline with her OnlyFans or Vic curate the bar's social media presence or to commiserate with Max about his latest breakup. The life of a trans-masculine dom and a trans-feminine sub ran in depressing parallels. But she realized there were a lot of new faces, all seemingly getting along without the welcome wagon. She hadn't been with anyone else all summer. She'd been approached only once, and he had turned out to be a creep worth putting on blast in the submissive whisper network.

Even if someone less shitty had hit on her, she wasn't sure it would be…worth it, to get Dennis's permission. She wasn't sure she had *room* for anyone else, for any more emotions or complications.

It was a few weeks before her birthday when she ran into Mistress Sandra. She was as gorgeous as ever, all big breasts and soft round belly and generous ass poured into a cotton dress; even the most hardcore gave up on leather and latex in an Austin August, when the temperature rose to triple digits for weeks at a time.

"How have you been, my darling?" Sandra asked, cozied up in a two-person booth with her. "It's been months."

"I'm doing all right… I love this haircut." She fingered the domme's short-cropped black hair. "How's Grace?"

Sandra clicked her tongue. "Oh, back home for the break. This is the first chance I've had to come to Frankie's all summer, though. So busy."

She smiled at Sandra. "I'm sorry, ma'am. Could I take your mind off it?" For this, she didn't need to ask for permission. Sandra dealt in impact play, not orgasms, and tonight that held a deep appeal.

Sandra didn't usually take her women home unless it was serious, but she and April were old friends. Her style was gentle but ruthless, and in a tastefully appointed playroom she tied April down and went over her thoroughly with a flogger.

"I can't—I can't—" April panted, dripping with sweat, and Sandra's beautifully cruel face appeared over the bench.

"That's not a safeword, sweetness."

She gritted her teeth and screamed through them, but she didn't use her safeword.

As the flogging continued, she began to take herself away from the situation, bit by bit; like pulling plugs. The longer the sensations went on the more it felt like she must have done something to deserve it, and Dennis's face floated by. Then her ex-wife's.

Marie had loved to do this, to stretch her out and gently torture her for ages. She'd learned to love so many different types of impact toys that way…

(…and sometimes, later, when things had begun to go sour, she'd leave April there and bring in one of her other lovers. She called it a flogging of the soul and swore it would bring them closer together. Like sisters.

Sisters. That's what they'd said on Facebook, when they split up. *We just feel like we're more like best friends or sisters now. We'll always love each other but—*April didn't have any sisters, but she suspected sisters didn't normally do *that* to each other…)

She was almost completely unaware of her body when suddenly, she felt the bindings on her feet release. Then her wrists. Sandra was helping her from the bench, putting her into the bed tucked in one corner of the playroom.

"I—I didn't. I didn't say it," she pleaded.

"I know, darling. You did so good. You were so, so good. Just lie in here in my arms like the good girl you are." Sandra was stroking her hair, and as she returned from numbness, she realized how sore she was. She couldn't remember the last time she'd been flogged so thoroughly. It didn't normally hurt so much—a paddle usually hurt worse. It was sensation, impact, *intensity* rather than pain. But she'd definitely been put through her paces tonight.

"I think I… I don't think I was in a good place," she realized slowly.

"No, you weren't, love," said Sandra. "But it's okay. Sometimes these sessions can bring out old pain we need to heal. It's my job to know when to quit, and your job to be good and let it happen. Let yourself feel it."

She wanted to burrow into the other woman. They were both nude, but April realized she didn't feel aroused at all. She felt wrung out. She let herself drift as Sandra took care of her.

She woke up eventually, disoriented. It was the middle of the night. Sandra was still there. "I was thinking about my ex," she admitted, drawing her knees up. "I mean. Before."

"Ahhh. I thought I recognized the fingerprints of that woman," said Sandra. "I'm so sorry if I made you think of her."

"No. I don't know why I... I've done things like that plenty of times. She doesn't own flogging. I just kept feeling like..." She exhaled. "I felt like I was cheating."

"That must have taken you to a bad place." Sandra knew all about Marie. Sandra had, perhaps, saved kink for April. She hadn't known where to turn except the community when she came to Austin, all alone, but she hadn't really known if she could ever trust it again. Sandra had redeemed it.

But Sandra was married, and her boundaries were clear. She came with an expiration date. It seemed all of April's relationships did.

"Who did you feel like you were cheating on? That woman?" Sandra had a particular way of saying *that woman* that sounded worse than any curse word April had ever heard.

"No. There's... It's ridiculous. I've got...a crush. On a dom I met."

"There's nothing wrong with that," said Sandra, laying a hand on April's tensed arm. "Isn't this your space to do those things? Let your feelings run wild? If I had known, sweetie—"

"No," she said quickly. "I wanted to. It's an open relationship. I mean, we're just friends."

"How long has this been going on?" Sandra asked.

"Since May," she said quietly.

"Three or four months." It was a simple observation, with no judgment in the inflection. "Are you sure it's not more serious than a crush?" Sandra asked.

"It isn't for him," she whispered.

The domme sighed heavily, and rubbed April's back, pressing the constant knot that formed between her shoulders from trying to shrink herself. She knew Sandra would never suggest that she needed to take some space away from Dennis; she wouldn't interfere that way, especially if it might be construed as trying to pry April away from another dominant.

April almost wished she would. She felt the simple submissive ache for someone to please tell her what to do. That was the trouble with playing power games; eventually they had to end, and you were, inevitably, responsible for yourself. While the game with Mistress Sandra lasted, she took her comfort there.

September

And then it was her birthday. Well. The Friday night before her birthday.

I'm going to tell him it has to stop, she decided, as she waited for the video chat to connect; he was still out of town. *The clothes, the denial, the texting. I know how to be alone, but I can't deal with a boyfriend who isn't my boyfriend. We made it to the deadline, and now I'm out.* She'd already insisted he not buy her anything additional for her birthday.

Instead before she knew it, she found herself begging. Not begging to come. He had an idea. A wonderful, awful, despicable idea, and it vaporized every other thought in her head.

"Beg me not to let you come. Convince me you want to live without orgasms. If I find you believable, I'll let you come. If you seem like you're pretending, another month." His face was stoic through the video connection; his eyes were black.

"You're evil," she breathed.

"Happy birthday," he said, and *grinned* at her.

She begged like a maniac. She promised him depraved things, things she never intended to deliver and he never intended to ask her to follow through on. It was just so hot to hear herself say it.

(*"Please don't let me come. I'll tell everyone how good your control is. I'll tell every sub in the bar. I'll tell my friends. I—"*)

She was either too convincing or not convincing enough. It didn't really matter. Some games you don't play to win.

Virtual aftercare was hard, but he didn't hop off, although it was late and an hour later on the East Coast. He sent her videos of bunnies and maniacal hopping little goats. He told her jokes and silly puns. She asked about the ongoing data migration, which she knew only as the reason email was down twice that week. Talking about *his* work was safe. He asked about her other birthday plans.

"Nothing too exciting. I had a call with my mom. Usual happy birthday stuff...plus she wants me to come home for Thanksgiving."

"You going to go?"

"...I don't know. My grandma doesn't know about my transition yet. So I'd have to—"

He got it, and winced. "That's really tough, doll."

"Yeah." She shook her head. "Anyway—other than that, uh, the girls are getting together tomorrow for D&D. That should be fun."

"You've mentioned D&D before," he said. "Who do you play with?"

"Oh!" Had she not explained this before? "It's a bunch of trans girls I met in a support group. I don't really go anymore, but this is how we stay in touch. We aren't really great at it—Melissa doesn't really keep track of her spell slots, and

Beth usually makes up something cool and waits for Elena to tell them what to roll. But it's fun."

For a moment, she wondered if they would like him—if he would like them—all the routine fears of introducing a partner to friends. But that wasn't going to happen. He wasn't a partner. She'd let herself be seduced away from her decision, but he wasn't her boyfriend.

Before the call had started, she had been ready to end it, and then he reminded her of all the reasons she couldn't walk away. Not just by being impossibly hot—oh, but he *was*—but by caring about her as a person. Caring about her birthday, her friends, her family.

But she knew there was a limit. There always was. Always had been, before. And she didn't want to find it. That limbo zone between *hookup* and *girlfriend* suddenly seemed more appealing. Sweeter than nothing. Safer than asking for what she really wanted.

Dennis gave her an appraising look that broke through her incipient megrims. "I bet you've memorized the handbook."

She colored. "I don't mind if they don't take it seriously. It's just a good time. We meet maybe once a month or so. It's just nice to be in touch with other trans people. Does that sound weird?"

He shook his head. "No. You get sick of being the only person like you in the room, I get that. I definitely get that. Did I tell you I was in a Black Greek letter organization, in college?"

"No!" she said, always interested to learn more about his past. He wasn't a closed book, exactly, but it didn't come up much, and she was reticent to initiate those kinds of conversations, for fear of pushing into any no-go zones. Lord knew she had them. "Like a frat?"

"Well, like a frat, but it's not a frat. They're very firm

about that." He flashed a grin. "It was cool. I grew up in a *really* white little town, so it was nice to finally have that community."

"Do you miss it?" she asked. "Austin is…pretty white, and what's not white usually isn't…"

He nodded. "Isn't Black. But we're around. I finally found a good barbershop. And no place could be as white as Seattle."

She laughed, and then he asked:

"You gonna go to Frankie's after your game?"

"Yeah," she said. She had no intention of playing, after her misbegotten night with Mistress Sandra; there was just another event Sunday she had to set up for. She left it vague, though, and she saw nothing in his eyes but understanding and happiness for her.

Do you want to see jealousy? she asked herself. No. Very much not. Jealousy terrified her. But… She had told him about Mistress Sandra, too, and he'd taken it the same way. Was he really not territorial like that? Or was she just…not his territory?

"Have a great time. With both," he said, pointing a finger. "That's an order. Night-night." He disconnected.

"Yes, Sir!" Her smiled faded with his image. Before the call had started, her mind had been made up. Now she had traded her certainty for a squirmy ache in her gut and at least a little longer as his. His…something. And being his something was better than nothing, even if it wasn't what she really wanted.

Dungeons & Dragons was in her apartment this month. She pulled out the collapsible table she kept in storage and lugged it up to her apartment. It was worth it, though; the tiny studio always felt full of love and estrogen after one of their get-togethers. The game took place in Elena's home-brew fantasy-Regency setting, and they called their crew Pride & Progesterone.

Elena had led the support group where they'd all met. She'd come out in the '80s, survived the AIDS epidemic and twenty years of front-line activism as a trans woman of color, and somehow held on to her job and her marriage through it all. She was comfortable with herself in a way that April envied. Maybe when she'd been out for longer than she'd been closeted, she'd be that way, too.

When the dice were back in the bags and they were settled into the second half of the meetup, everyone was gently ragging Beth for missing the last session. They'd gone out of town with a girlfriend, another trans woman the group all knew and who Melissa had also dated.

"We had a great time and that's all I'm going to say about it," said Beth, their skin darkening even further under their blush. They were Black, the youngest in the group, and the one who had transitioned youngest. They were transfeminine nonbinary and beautiful.

"That means she brought the strap," said Melissa in a stage whisper. "Better you than me, boo, I can't be on the bottom like that. Lesson learned."

Joanne predictably turned as red as Melissa's hair and studied her drink. She was a white professional of about April's age inching her way out of the closet and easily flustered.

"Can we *please* change the subject?" Beth said coolly. As the two under-thirties, Beth and Melissa had a bewildering relationship that ricocheted between best friends, rivalry, teasing and occasionally making out.

"Aw, they're shy." Melissa looked around the circle for another topic. "Here's a good question—April, what the fuck, babe."

April's eyes widened. "What?"

"You going into the wholesale business?" Oh. Right. Over time, Dennis had taken over her closet. And her dresser. She was running out of space. She'd just recently bought a couple of cheap clothes racks online and tried to find space for them in the corners of the room.

"I got a bunch of new stuff lately," she said, coloring slightly. "Promotion and everything."

Melissa jumped up and started going through a rack. She was like that, all id, all reaction. April only wished she could be as shameless. She looked around the circle and saw Melissa wasn't the only one who wanted to, though; Joanne looked especially wistful. "Go wild," April said, and waved her hand, which was all they needed.

"*Wow,*" said Beth. "Is this Alexander McQueen?"

Elena raked her eyes over the collection and back to April. "I've never seen you wear heels, either."

She cleared her throat. "Those were a gift from a friend. Obviously I don't wear them to play D&D. They're mostly work clothes."

"Are you sugaring?" asked Melissa. "You didn't tell me." Melissa had done sex work before, when busking didn't bring in enough money, and didn't make any bones about it.

April felt uneasy; for a moment she wanted to tell them to get out, to mind their own business. But why? They were her friends. Everyone joked about how many kinky trans girls there were, and everyone knew it wasn't that much of a joke.

Maybe I don't want to be a joke. "It was... A guy friend. Yeah."

Beth dropped onto the bed with their mouth open. "You never said."

"I'm a-a private person," she stuttered, which sounded, frankly, ridiculous; these were the people she'd called about having her testicles cut off. If anyone would understand the terrible hope and dreadful fragility of the situation she'd created, it would be them. And if she didn't tell someone soon, she was going to explode.

"That means she needs a drink," said Melissa, and raided the tiny pantry for the vodka.

She texted Dennis, late that evening.

April: i told them

Dennis: Excuse me?

April: i told my friends what a dirty little pervert i am

Her phone was ringing immediately. "Hello?"

"April." His voice sounded urgent. "Did you not know that was a fantasy? When I asked what you'd do, I never meant—"

"No," she said, and laughed softly. "No, I wanted to. I don't talk about my kinks much but... I can tell them anything. I know that. I guess I knew it all along."

"How do you feel?"

"Good," she admitted. It had been good to talk about it. She hadn't realized how much she had been aching to talk about it, how much more solid it would feel in the light of day. "I gave away some of my old stuff." Beth was too petite, and Melissa wore jeans pretty much always, but Joanne had almost cried. "And Elena has a contact at the clothing exchange, too."

"Oh." There was something weird in his voice, but before she could push, he went on. "Well. I guess you earned your orgasm, all right."

"I don't want to," she heard herself say.

"You don't—"

"I want to do it when you want me to," she said, and realized it was true. "And I don't want to do it alone."

"You're a very very very good girl," he said, in a low voice that flooded her with need she had just promised to do nothing about. "You're my best girl."

That carried her into the rest of September on a shimmering cloud that rivalled any orgasm. She would need it.

Maybe the event on Sunday should've been an omen for the clusterfuck of the next several weeks. It should not have been a difficult event; she had helped Vic find the performers, and they had excellent reviews and hadn't tripped any red flags when she'd spoken to them beforehand. They were a het couple who did a sort of burlesque-inspired magic act, and they had seemed like a good answer to the requests Frankie's had gotten for some more low-key entertainment mixed in with the practical workshops and more overtly kinky performances. She'd even invited her friends.

She was intensely thankful that only Melissa had taken her up on it; Melissa had a thick skin to rival a rhino. Still, she'd thought this would be a soft introduction to her favorite place, not a barrage of microaggressions. The magician's patter probably hadn't been considered offensive twenty years ago, but it clearly hadn't been updated since then. At best it was painfully unfunny; at worst it was veiled homophobia and not-especially-veiled transphobia.

Vic, the bar manager, was great on matters of security—no one who had ever been thrown out by Vic had bothered to try again—and fine with the vendors, but he lacked any kind of fine tuning. Vic was all about macroaggression. So somehow it had become April's job to talk to the magician during intermission. She had finessed him, targeting first his wife/assistant as a necessary ally and then mounting a full-scale charm offensive. The second half was largely quiet, and they would surely never be invited back, but some of the tricks were actually pretty good. He crowned it by referring to her as a drag queen on his way out.

She felt good about it afterwards, though. A couple of people, who had noticed her set expression and her charge backstage during the break, approached her later with thanks. One of them was Jason, who had somehow comped her and Melissa's drinks for the night.

Mama April strikes again, she thought ruefully.

As she and Melissa walked—her to her apartment, Melissa to a late performance at a Music District queer bar—she apologized again. "Sorry, I feel like you saw more of Aerith than me."

"Nah, it was rad," Melissa said, waving it off.

"Was it what you thought?" April asked, morbidly curious.

"Kinda? You weren't," the redhead said.

"What do you mean?" She felt a hot ache in her stomach; she couldn't see how this could be good.

"Well to be honest, from what you told us I thought you'd be a simpering bimbo in there," said Melissa, always one to pull the Band-Aid off. "But you were...like...in charge. Hey, you think you could get me a gig there? Everybody likes live music, right?"

"I don't... I don't work there," she said, coloring. "I'm just...helpful."

"Well, you rocked it. I still want to see you in full whips-and-chains-excite-me mode with your hottie, though." Melissa grinned salaciously; she'd had some comments about April's photos of Dennis, and even about April in her new lace dress.

She blushed. "It's not really like that. I'm normal when I'm with him. Mostly."

Melissa looked sidelong at her. "Okay, so... I know you said it's not serious with this guy, but who are you kidding here, bud? I mean, I wasn't going to say anything, but... C'mon."

"It's not serious," she said firmly. "He's free to play with anybody he wants. And so am I."

"That's not the point, though," said Melissa. She paused under a streetlight. "The point is, do you *want* to play with anybody else? I mean, if it's just fuckin', cool. Good for you. But do you feel something for this cissie? Because when you talk about him, you look like you're talking about the guy who invented the orgasm-flavored cheesecake."

April scrubbed her hands over her face. "I feel everything," she moaned. "How could I not?

"He's smart—like *really* smart, smarter than me. He's funny and dry and quiet, and he can turn on a dime to be in charge and sexy and he doesn't do it by getting loud, he just does it by being *there*, like there's more of him packed into the same space. I don't know if you get how hard it is to be dominant without being a tool, but Dennis is...is *graceful*. And he's watching all the time, careful all the time, and he never makes the same mistake twice.

"He loves people and he takes care of the people he loves and he's just...good at it. At love. When he was in high school his best friend came out as gay and Dennis went with him to PFLAG meetings for six months because his parents wouldn't. His family basically adopted the guy, they're still friends today. Nobody ever—" She broke off.

She didn't have anyone to talk to about Dennis, so she didn't. She didn't know these feelings were in her. She'd known she had it bad, but this was...this was something else. Something terrifying and impossible. She bit her lip.

"I never knew anybody so good at loving people. He's just so good at it, it makes me think silly things sometimes."

Sometimes. Not often. Not thoughts so much as images;

when she was falling asleep, mostly, Dennis loving her right out loud, not just in the club but everywhere. Meeting the family he spoke of with such affection. Living in that ridiculous cursed house of his. Fantasies. Just fantasies.

"What if they aren't?" said Melissa gently. "Silly."

"They are! He would have said something by now. He would've told me." She shook her head. "He's just...kind. And good. And solid. And I'm lucky he's my friend. If he really knew me..."

"It sounds like he knows you better than anybody, April," said Melissa, her voice still gentle, like she was talking April off a ledge.

April thought about Dennis, working six floors away, and shook her head again. "He's just my friend. And I'm lucky to have that. I'm not... I'm not blowing it up for a daydream." The lie had gone on too long. There was no coming back.

"But if he wanted to?" Melissa asked, still pushing. Damn her.

"In a second," April said. "In a heartbeat."

The conversation made her blush, but it also changed her perspective. She had the best and hottest dominant in the club blowing up her phone nightly; she had no business feeling like the only Lost Boy who didn't get to play anymore. With the pang of feeling left on the sidelines set aside, it was easy to remember how much she enjoyed her support role at Frankie's. Putting the event back on course had been an unpleasant but necessary job, well within her capabilities, and she knew when it was done, she had done something positive and that it was appreciated.

Unfortunately, she did *not* feel the same way about the increasing amount of development work being shoveled on her plate at work. It had started with a trickle, which she had done as conscientiously as she could, despite her distaste, and only increased. She'd talked to her supervisor about it, but John had blamed the new CTO, new requirements being enforced for development that required a product owner for every project.

Which meant this was actually Dennis's fault.

Over the next few weeks, the trickle became a flood, and she felt like she was being swept away. The current eventually deposited her on Fatima's doorstep, with a halal casserole and a bellyful of grievances. Fatima was still on maternity leave for a few more days, but visitors who brought food were always welcome in the tidy two-story house south of Slaughter.

"Let it out, hon," Fatima advised, digging into the food. She wasn't wearing a headscarf over her dark hair, with just her and April and the baby in the house, and that touched April's heart.

"I just fucking hate this development shit," she vented. "It was just a little bit at first but it's eating up more and more of my time every week and I fucking hate it. I've been reading about… Agile, and Scrum, and Waterfall, trying to catch up, but it's like they just use whichever method makes their lives easier on a given day."

"That does sound like them," said Fatima. The database and development teams didn't necessarily get along.

"I run around gathering requirements, just so they can kick me back to get new ones. We set priorities for sprints and then the lead developer—do you know this guy Bob? Bob Flowers?—talks down to me about why they couldn't do it. So why ask me to do it in the first place?"

"Oh, I know Bob," sighed Fatima. "Good ol' Born-Again Bob. He tried to file a complaint when I changed my schedule for Ramadan. You should just thank God he works remote these days."

Oh, she did. Not only did she not want to have to look into that asshole's face, have *him* looking at *her*, but she did her best to avoid the fourth floor, even while Dennis was stuck on the East Coast. She wondered sometimes if Dennis had figured it out by now. She was in the directory... No. She was fooling herself. If he knew, it would be over. The lie-of-omission had gone on too long.

April gestured with her hands, drawing shapes and lines on the tabletop. "I like helping people. I'm a people pleaser, that's who I am. And now somehow, it's my job to run around trying to balance everybody's needs and come up with a plan that pisses everyone off equally. It's like I'm collecting requirements just so I can piss off the developers and disappoint the stakeholders. I hate it."

Fatima shook her head. "I'm sorry, April. I knew from your texts you were struggling but I had no idea..." She sighed. "I shouldn't have pushed you."

"It's not your fault. I didn't sign up for this Product Owner bullshit when I took the promotion, anyway. It just kind of happened." She sank back in the chair. "I guess I can do it. I mean, it's not like I have a lot of options. Most jobs in Texas don't cover my meds, let alone surgery."

Fatima patted her hand. "Do you want to see the baby? She's good at cheering people up."

April smiled weakly. "I'd like that."

It was a cute baby. April found the whole subject of babies confusing. She'd never wanted kids when her designated role was *father*, and now that her options had changed, she wasn't sure what she thought. Maybe the concept of surrogacy or adoption just fucked with her anxieties about being second place too much. But all that to the side, it was a damn cute specimen of the species, with enormous dark eyes and a light dusting of coal-black hair.

"Hello, tiny person," she whispered. "I wrote a letter to

my grandma." Two weeks ago. No response. She jiggled the infant up and down gently. "What do you think?"

The baby made a noise.

"You're right, probably a bad idea."

When she got home and checked her phone, she had a voicemail from Dennis.

Good news, doll. I'm heading back to Austin finally. I want to see you this weekend. Frankie's?

Yes. Please.

October

And then they were together again at last, on the roof of Frankie's, on a weeknight. Now that it was October, the heaters were up and running. He had put her in a bodycon dress that wasn't warm enough, and he had made up for it by giving her his jacket. It was a romantic gesture, but the hateful part of her wasted time wishing she could drown in it the way Caroline would have.

(Caroline had stopped them downstairs so she could show off a new purchase from Kendra Scott. "What do you think, sir?" she asked, tossing her dark hair to show how the earrings matched the necklace half-buried in her cleavage. "Did I do a good job?"

"Absolutely," he'd rumbled, and she'd thanked him in an especially subservient way, and that was *fine*. That was completely *fine*.)

All in all, her mood wasn't great when she told him about

making another drop-off at the clothing exchange and his face clouded. It was nonverbal, but definitely there, and she found she couldn't let it go.

"Why are you always weird about that?" she demanded. "Anytime I talk about getting rid of clothes you get weird. It's not like you ever wanted me to wear those, anyway." In truth, they were clothes she rarely wanted to wear herself anymore. You buy a lot of stuff when you're first working out your style, and she had had to do it at thirty instead of thirteen.

She didn't know why she was picking a fight about this, except it was just one too many topics they flinched away from. His insistence she hang on to her old clothes felt like one more way for them both to keep one foot out the door.

"I don't want you to feel like you have to get rid of your own things just because I give you a present," he said. Evasively, in her opinion. She felt frustration rising, an itch in her throat.

"Well, I do, because I don't have the *space*, Dennis!" she sighed. "And you know I feel weird spending so much on clothes when other people *live* on that much. It helps my conscience."

He looked stung by that. "I'm aware of how lucky I am to have what I have. I try to use my money responsibly and that does include charity. But I do set aside a certain amount for an entertainment budget. If I'd rather see you all decked out than... I don't know, buy season tickets to the Spurs, then so what?"

She gestured at herself. "Well, are you not entertained, *Sir*?" She had never been like this with him—sarcastic and outright disrespectful—but the whole thing just seemed so... ridiculous. "What's the problem with me making space in my own apartment?"

His frown deepened. "You're in a bratty mood tonight. Did I make you edge too much today?"

"Don't do that," she snapped.

"No?"

"No. Red, if you need that, okay? Red. I'm not bratting and I don't want comments about how long it's been since I came. I want to know why you're shitty when I give away my clothes. They're my damn clothes."

"If they're your damn clothes then why do you care what I think?" He looked away, off into the cityscape beyond the rooftop.

"Uh, maybe because of this—" She gestured to include him, and her, and the entire club. "—whole fucking dynamic where I'm trying to get your approval all the time, maybe? It's not fair for you to not tell me what I'm doing wrong."

"You're not doing anything wrong, and I'm not disapproving." Then why did it feel like he was receding from her, out over the horizon of the city?

She shook her head. "I know you don't like it. I *know* you don't."

"It shouldn't matter."

"But it does! We can draw lines around the games we play but if you can't help showing your opinion all over your face then they get pretty damn blurred, okay?" There were tears in her eyes; there was a time when she'd been thankful for the ability to cry, to feel real emotions, but right now it seemed like a sucker's bet.

"I'm sorry if our game isn't giving you pleasure anymore," he said, still staring over the rooftops, and she felt an awful twist in the pit of her stomach.

"Please tell me," she said, deflating. "Please just tell me."

"I told you I did this once before," he said, eyes still on the hotel lights. "When she left, she didn't take anything I bought her. And because she'd gradually replaced everything, she had nothing when she left. I begged her to pack a bag at least, told her I didn't give a damn about it, that she didn't *owe* me anything, but she said they were mine and..."

She waited.

"...and she wasn't anymore." He let his eyes return to hers, and what she saw there hurt her so much *she* wanted to avert her gaze. "She left our home like a runaway, with nothing. She went home to her family, and God knows what they thought of me. I would've given her anything. I would've given her the whole damn condo. But she didn't want it, didn't want anything that reminded her of me. I failed her and she wanted to...delete me from her life, and if that meant losing everything, she was willing to do it.

"I don't ever want to fail someone like that again. But what if I do?" His eyes continued to bore into her; she didn't look away. "If I ever do, I don't want you to be in the same position. Okay? Is that okay, April? Is it okay that I feel that way, or does it spoil the game?"

"I'm sorry," she said in a tiny voice.

He covered his face with his hands and drew them down slowly. "You don't have to be sorry. You didn't—you were right to call me out. *I'm* sorry."

"No, I mean... I'm sorry that happened to you, Dennis. I'm sorry." She slid forward and put her arms around him, and for once it didn't bother her that they were the same height. It felt good to wrap him up. "I don't know the details and I'm sure she had her reasons, but that must have been devastating for you."

"I can tell you," he said quietly.

"You don't owe me that," she said. (And something whispered, *And what if it's terrible? What if it changes everything?*) "Thank you for telling me as much as you did. It helps."

"It's not exactly the image I'm trying to project," he said, in a choked voice.

"Maybe you're overdressed," she said, and let herself stroke the tight coils of his hair, palm the stubble of his cheeks. And he closed his eyes and let her, turning towards her and her kiss.

"I promise," she said solemnly, "not to throw all the beautiful things you gave me in the trash. No matter how mad I get at you. Does that help?"

"You can't be sure you'll feel that way."

"I'm pretty sure." She fished her own necklace out of the neckline of her dress. "My ex-wife gave me this as a graduation gift. For when I need direction."

"It's a compass. Does it work?"

She nodded. "I've had to walk away from a lot of my past. I keep everything I can. If we stop playing together, Dennis, I hope we're still friends. And even if we aren't, I'm always going to treasure the way your gifts made me feel. Like I was worth it."

She'd made her peace with it now; someday she would be nothing but a memory to him, and she just hoped she'd be a good one. It was impossible to stay angry with him, when he was just hoping for the same thing.

"You are worth so much, April. So much more than I can give you."

And there it was, wasn't it? Everyone agreed on that; every person who rejected her or didn't want to take things deeper. She deserved love. And they couldn't give it to her.

"You give me plenty," she said in a rough voice, and tried to believe it was true.

He began to rub her shoulders silently. She sighed and relaxed into his touch. "Thank you," he said.

"For what?"

"For telling me. And for using your safeword when you needed to. Good girl."

She smiled and dipped her head towards his, forehead to forehead. "My ex-wife…" she said.

"Mm-hm?" He was hardly breathing. She never talked about this, she knew.

"She got mad when I would safeword sometimes."

"I'm so sorry. That's awful." He sounded horrified.

"She wouldn't say, but…when she was pissed off, she had ways to let you know."

If he asks, I'll tell him, she thought.

But he didn't ask; not about that. "I'm sorry." He pressed a kiss to the top of her head and shifted away slightly. "Is everything okay, doll?" He held up his hands. "I was out of line. I admit it. But you seem wound up. In a bad way."

She looked away. "It's not a big deal."

"What happened?"

Hm. Would she rather talk about work stuff or family stuff? She didn't usually talk about work stuff with him, it was safer that way, but her grandma had read the letter and all hell had broken loose with her parents. "Just work stuff. I… I don't know that I told you about it. I've been getting stuck in this lousy Product Owner role at work, right?"

"Hey!" he said. "You're talking to a certified Scrum master, lady. Product Owners are important. It's been like pulling teeth to get my company to designate them."

Oh, so it's your fault, she thought. Guilt flooded her stomach. Maybe this was a mistake. "Well anyway there's a new developer on the team and he misgendered me."

"What?" he said, in a voice like a whip crack.

She avoided his eyes. "Yep. We were wrapping up the call and he called me Mr. French."

"That mother—"

"It's not like he could tell from my voice," she said quietly, and he lifted her chin and kissed her thoroughly.

"I love your voice," he said. She had absolutely no idea what to say to that. It had to be a kind lie. It *had* to be. She moved on quickly.

"Anyway, I called him on it and later he phoned me to apologize. He said…" God, this was humiliating. "He said he thought I was Mr. French because that's what the lead developer always calls me." Good ol' Born-Again Bob.

Dennis didn't say anything, but she could *feel* the anger baking off him. "He forwarded me some emails to prove it. Fuck, just when I thought I was finally making some headway with them." She shook her head ruefully. Then she looked up. "Hey."

He looked like he was about to come undone, but not in the way she liked. "Don't be so upset," she said. "It happens."

"It shouldn't happen." It shouldn't feel this good to soak up his anger, should it? She shouldn't be fantasizing about Dennis rolling up his sleeves and beating the shit out of Bob Flowers, of Dennis *defending her* with bare knuckles and that look in his eye. It shouldn't turn her on.

"Well it does," she said briskly. "What do you think about taking me downstairs and dancing?"

"It would be my pleasure," he said. Calmly. But there was still a gleam in his eyes that she was glad wasn't aimed at her, for once.

And on Monday, Born-Again Bob was fired.

Part III: Dennis

At the beginning of the same six months, Dennis Martin had a lot of goals. He would finish his house. He would work hard to become a better dom. He would overhaul the Technology division and make it work no matter how many people he had to piss off. He would figure out where Austin was hiding all the Black people. He would make friends with the chief operations officer, Leo Graham, if it killed him. He would show April French that he wanted her and no one else.

Two of these things did not happen:

*His house was not finished.

*He did *not* make friends with Leo Graham.

May

When he woke up in April's apartment the morning after she told him she didn't want a relationship, Dennis's first instinct was to bail. He woke up ahead of her. It would be simple enough to dress, press a kiss to her cheek and be out the door before any further conversation could happen.

That's what he would've done with any of the hookups he'd had since things with Sonia ended. He kept them at arm's length, and nobody got their feelings hurt because everyone knew what was up. It felt like it was already too late for that with April.

He looked sideways at her sleeping form. She really did have a lot of hair, halfway to her waist when it was down (right now it was shoved up above her like a cloud so she didn't sleep on it) and thick. The desire to comb that hair, to braid it or wrap it in a delicate bun like she'd had last night, appeared in his mind. He was not by any means a Daddy

Dom—Lord, once you started looking, the gradations of kink were endless, weren't they?—but he liked to pamper women. He used to paint Sonia's nails.

He rolled away from her and groaned quietly. Every time he looked at April French, he thought *long-term*, he thought *plans*, he thought of ways to wind their mutual kinks around them and make their entire lives a playground. And that train of thought led, inevitably, to Sonia, and train wrecks.

His phone was on the floor by the bed. Dead, because he hadn't charged it. He tried to imagine what Jason would have said in response to his late night text..

Dennis: You were right.

Imaginary Jason: Always. What was I right about this time?

Dennis: She doesn't want a relationship.

And what would Jason say then? Something funny and scathing, something that would make him feel better and stop taking himself so seriously. Certainly not the imprecations his own brain filled the gap with.

Imaginary Jason: So you know you're ready for another serious relationship. That probably doesn't mean you have to wife up the first person you meet after you're ready.

Was that it? Was she just…here, when he was ready? He turned again to look at her, at her sleeping profile, free of makeup. The high cheekbones, the full lips, the faint shadows under her skin that made her so self-conscious. There was a pang when he looked at her, not of ordinary desire but of what was for him the very foundation of desire. Of care.

What did he really even know about her? Well…she was tough. She had to be, to have gone through what she did and still be so vulnerable. To not be jaded. She took care of other people. She played games with the best of them but with a spark in her eyes that said, *aren't we having fun?* Some subs could be so serious, almost morose in their obedience. Sonia had been.

Especially towards the end, he thought, *and you know why, don't you?*

Enough. Enough of that.

She stirred in her sleep and he realized he needed to make a decision about a question much more immediate than *why am I drawn to this woman?*

He slid out of the bed and maneuvered through the studio. When he looked back at the bed her eyes were open and they didn't look surprised or hurt. They didn't look relieved, either. There was just bleak acceptance there, that of course he was going to sneak out now.

"I'm gonna take a shower," he said as gently as he could. "You can sleep."

She struggled up on her elbows. "I can get you a towel."

"I know where the towels are," he said with a wry note, and it made her laugh as he hoped. "Do you have stuff for breakfast, or do you want to order in?"

He knew he'd read her right when she brightened. "I've got some stuff."

"Have you got eggs?"

"Mm-hm."

"I make great scrambled eggs."

In the shower, he had a brief window to think. She said she didn't want him to be her boyfriend. That could mean a few things: she didn't *want* a boyfriend. She didn't want *him* to be her boyfriend. She didn't think he was *able* to be her boyfriend. She didn't think he *wanted* to be her boyfriend and was trying to get out first.

If she didn't want a boyfriend, he was out of luck. If she didn't want him, same. So he needed a way to test those waters ASAP, because he would jump off the roof of Frankie's before he forced himself on her. But if she thought he wasn't up to it? That was a challenge, and Dennis Martin thrived on challenges. If she wanted him, too, he was confident he could be what she needed...but first he had to be sure she did.

They cooked breakfast together. He fried bacon while she cut up some fruit and tidied up in his wake. Then he had to test his memory of Gordon Ramsay's perfect scrambled eggs recipe while she watched.

When he tempted her to touch herself while he cooked, he didn't have a plan yet, beyond watching the color mount in her cheeks and listening to the noises she made while she did it. She was self-conscious, which was understandable. She was obedient anyway, which was wonderful. It was an exercise in self-control not to burst out of the front of his boxers, but since that would be bad for the scrambled eggs *and* his dick, he managed it.

The idea came together as they ate. She was squirmy, blushing, staring at him hungrily, her self-consciousness about her body and her desires out the window. He liked her like this. *I want you like this all the time*, he thought. And he wanted a way to stay in her life, to not let the discomfort of last night's conversation scar into an awkwardness that separated them.

"What if you couldn't come without permission?"

Her reaction was subtle, but definite. "That could be fun." She pretended to study her food before she went on. "Your permission or just anyone's?"

"What would you be more comfortable with?" That took a lot of restraint, but the alternative was impossible, wasn't it? They'd just agreed not to be a couple, and they'd known each other a week. If she promised him exclusive control it would be hard to believe her under the circumstances.

But when she said she'd be comfortable with that and framed it as a *project*, an experiment in submission—he knew he had her. She was comfortable playing with someone long-term; comfortable submitting to *him* long-term, with no specific expiration date. She wanted him, too, but he'd have to prove he was worth it. Well that was fine. That was just fine.

He was desperately hard as they cleaned up, but then she fished for permission to please him, and he realized he couldn't let her. Denial had simple rules, but they were iron-clad: *give her what she wants but not what she asks for.*

He could take care of it himself. And he would, as soon as humanly possible. But she didn't need to know that. Her cry of outrage (and running underneath it, arousal), told him he'd made the right call.

When he made it back to Jason, his old friend was awake, hungover and rooting through the fridge. They grunted at each other in a traditional masculine greeting, and then Jason peered blearily at him. "So what was I right about?"

"Nothing important," he said swiftly. He no longer wanted Jason's advice; he was pretty sure he wouldn't like it.

Monday morning, he turned up early to his new job. He wanted to take the lay of the land before meeting new people. In his experience, on your first day in any office there was someone who wanted to take you under their wing and show you everything in a specific order they had in mind and wouldn't rest until they had. He was all right with that—it was human nature, and you got valuable context that way—

but he also wanted his first impression to be his own and in his own time.

He looked around the building. There was a gym, which was great, and no restaurant on the premises, which was a mixed bag but shaded towards good. If there was a restaurant on-site, he'd eat there more often than not out of convenience and miss the chance to get out of the building. Security seemed attentive to an unknown wandering around at 7 am, but not *overly* attentive to an unaccompanied Black man. Well, at least one in Gucci. He gave them only provisional approval until he saw how they dealt with him in his workout clothes. But for now, they were cordial and helpful as they checked his ID and provided a temporary visitor badge.

He knew the company had offices on both the tenth and fourth floors, and that he would be spending most of his time on the fourth. He looked around there first, where they had only a small space, a bullpen of cubicles and a row of offices along the back. So many of the developers were remote, and the call center had their own space north of town. It was empty right now, and he left his bag in the office already marked with his name before venturing higher.

Surprisingly, the tenth floor was *not* empty. They had the whole floor, unlike their limited spaces on the fourth, but what he could see of this room was largely a dark field of cubes. Offices were arranged around the walls, and there was one lit up; through a glass door he could see an extremely tall white man practicing his putt while he talked on a Bluetooth headset.

Surely this was the elusive Leo Graham? He was thin as well as extremely tall, the kind of person who looks like they've been stretched out on a table, and his hair was black thatched with silver. He looked about the same age as Dennis; maybe a little older.

Dennis couldn't make out any more of the conversation than a mumbled drone, but as he walked through the offices, Graham's head jerked up and skewered him, as if Dennis had walked in on him in the toilet. He seemed to end the call and beckoned to Dennis through the glass office door.

"So. You must be Dennis Martin. Leo Graham." He had a broad Boston accent—*Mah'en*—and didn't sound particularly impressed by what he saw. "Sorry we couldn't meet up the other night. Howarya?"

"I'm good," Dennis said, and before he could say anything else the COO plunged in.

"Just get into town?"

"No, I've actually been here a week or so, I—"

"Great town, great town. You got a house yet? Where you looking? Travis Heights is nice, pretty neighborhood, close to downtown, expensive—but from what I hear you can afford it, huh?"

"I'm renovating a house now," he replied. He wasn't flustered by Graham's attempt to control the conversation by steamroller, but he was annoyed. He reminded himself that if he wanted to achieve anything, he would need to work hand in glove with this man. "You're in early."

"You got to get up pretty early to beat me, yeah, yeah," Graham chuckled. "Well, you're here, I'm here—shall we get into it?"

Dennis had hoped he could draft up some kind of orgasm control agreement for April sometime today—weren't first days supposed to be a little light on the scheduling to give people time to settle in?—but he didn't have a chance to even think about it. It turned out that Graham had presentation after presentation lined up for him, mostly on the theme of all the important revenue-generating work Operations was doing and how Technology's biggest responsibility was, in short, to get the fuck out of the way.

Somewhere in there he also had to meet his own team. He managed to find a few moments for each of his lead developers (mostly by phone, since they were predominantly remote), the frazzled head of the Help Desk (who was clearly terrified of him), and the data services manager who looked after their massive Medicaid claims databases (a Santa Claus–looking gentleman who seemed sleepy and hard to stampede).

His first impression was that they were mostly competent, mostly white (some of the devs were people of color, but he had yet to meet another Black person), and mostly very worried about what his hiring meant for their futures. He'd tried to reassure them, but he hadn't had much time to earn their trust, and to be honest some of them probably should be worrying. The Help Desk was in shambles, and the developers had no real process or procedures. He had a lot of cleaning up to do.

There were still more people to meet, but it would have to wait until tomorrow. Surely, hopefully, most of his team were themselves home by now. He stifled a jaw-cracking yawn, just in time for a very pregnant woman to knock on his open door.

"Hi," he said. "What can I do for you?" The knocker was a pretty South Asian woman in a colorful headscarf, who looked at least eight months pregnant and thoroughly over it.

"I just wanted to see our new overlord in person," she said cheerfully. "I'm Fatima Nayeem, I work under Alvin in Data Services Management. For a few weeks longer, anyway."

"I can see that," he said, moving quickly to shake her hand. "Are you coming back to us after your maternity leave?"

"Oh, yes," she said. "You won't get rid of me that easily."

"Good, glad to hear it." It wasn't the world's most challenging conversation; in his head he was already ordering dinner.

"You know Leo Graham hates you, right?" she said, still in the tones of a casual observation.

Well. Time to pay attention again. "I might have picked up some vibes," he said carefully.

"A CTO was not part of his master plan. He wanted us to work under him. I believe he still does."

"Well, you don't," he said. It was the first day, and none of the politics were clear to him yet. What did she have to gain by this? True or not—and he was pretty sure it was true—what was the point?

"I don't know you yet," she said, "but I know him and all in all... I think we're better off. Good luck, Mr. Martin."

"Thank you, Ms. Nayeem, and—hang on. We met before, didn't we? You were in one of my interview sessions."

"Oh, you remember that? I was a lot..." She sighed and caressed her stomach. "Smaller then."

"Of course I do." She'd been sharp. Good questions. Didn't waste words. He mentally filed her advice several rungs higher than he had initially intended. "I appreciate you dropping by to say hello to the new guy, and I look forward to seeing you around the office."

She was almost out the door when she asked, "Is it true you're a millionaire?"

He looked up sharply. "Who said I was a millionaire?"

"Oh, you know, people say things."

"Fatima, I appreciate people who are candid and speak their mind. I also appreciate—"

"—when people know to shut up?" She tapped her nose, and for good measure, winked at him, then waved goodbye. So everyone would know by the end of the week, he interpreted.

He sighed and grabbed his laptop bag. On the drive back to Jason's he called his contractor.

The man's name was Reggie Douglas, an older Black guy

he'd found online in the spirit of supporting local business. He was well-reviewed and was painstakingly polite with Dennis; Dennis had seen him loosen up with subcontractors and his employees, but Dennis was A Client and got the Client Voice no matter what. Dennis didn't think the delays were Reggie's *fault*, but he was running out of patience.

"Well…" said Reggie, when Dennis asked for a status update. The longer the ellipses went on the more money it was going to cost, and this one set a record. Reggie outlined the issue with city code inspection and the delay in redrawing the floor plan again; the shipping delays on the flooring; the subcontractor who had had to be fired and who Reggie swore had been stricken from his Rolodex, a punishment just short of beheading in the contractor lexicon.

"But here's the big thing, Mr. Martin. About thirty years ago, the homeowner replaced the pipes here with clay pipes. Pretty fashionable at the time."

"Uh-huh," said Dennis, who didn't like where this was going.

"People don't use this so much anymore because, well, it turns out that after about thirty years, they, ah…"

"Reggie," said Dennis. "I'm a man who's wounded in love. Lay it on the line for me." It was a flip comment, delivered with a wry grin that Reggie couldn't see, but in truth it startled the hell out of him. He had a picture in his head of exactly how he wanted this house to look, always had, but when exactly had April French slid into all those pictures? Perched on his kitchen island, tangled up in his bed, laughing on his couch?

"Well, they pretty much disintegrate," Reggie said. "We're digging up the lawn and replacing those now, but obviously it pushed things back. If we don't get too much rain in the next couple weeks, it should be okay and then we can circle back to the interior."

"Reggie," said Dennis, his grip tight on the steering wheel. He was a patient man, he *was* a patient man, but it was maddening to have all the money in the world to throw at a problem and not be able to make traction. It wasn't Reggie's fault, but it was maddening.

"I am sorry," the man said, and he sounded like it. Or maybe that was just his Client Voice coming through. *This is why he doesn't treat you like one of the guys*, said his inner critic. *At the end of the day, you aren't.*

He counted to ten and exhaled slowly. "I know you're doing your best."

As he turned onto Oltorf, the first drops of rain hit his windshield. Life certainly does come at you fast sometimes.

Tuesday went by in a flash—a flash of rain and lightning— and it was Wednesday before he could get his document to April. It was a bit more formal than he wanted it to be, too close to the self-important submission contracts he had scoffed at before, but it was hard to pivot from writing a charter for the Technology division without bringing a little of that chilly precision with him. When she joked about code switching between formal business writing and her soft-on-soft submissive persona in text, he knew exactly what she meant.

The email banter was fantastic, actually; exactly the palate cleanser he needed after two days of holding his temper and letting Leo Graham bodycheck his ego in the name of teamwork. When she replied with a half-teasing, half-serious capitalized *You* it might have felt silly, over the top, but in that mood it felt great.

Then he fucked up.

He'd tried to be careful; give her space to bail out, to say no if she had to.

If you can, I'd like you to edge right now to seal our agreement. I know you're at work...

He thought there was a reasonable chance she'd do it, and
if not, it would still come off as playful. Her response hit him
in the stomach like a two-by-four:

Like in a public restroom? Like me, a trans woman, masturbating in the women's public restroom in the building
where I work?

When she put it like that, it sounded like a monstrous thing
to ask her to do.
Damn it, he'd been careful!
But not careful enough.
He grabbed his phone and called her immediately, knowing he was panicking, not able to stop himself. But she was
at work, and unlike him, she probably didn't have an office
door to close. Almost as soon as she picked up, he realized
that by pushing her to talk to him he was making it worse,
and when she hung up on him, he tossed his phone on his
desk and swore wearily.
He covered his face with his hands and when he looked
up, he had sixteen work emails. Self-flagellation was going
to have to wait until after hours. He made his way through
the rest of the day with his mind mostly on his actual work,
but a significant fraction dedicated itself to the puzzle of April
French as he worked, as he drove home, as he made a meal
for Jason and himself in a desperate bid against scurvy.
When she'd said she didn't want anything exclusive, he'd
been frustrated. He understood it, of course, but just as surely,
he wanted to be enough for her all by himself. He wanted

to be everything she needed. Up until now, on some level, he'd felt like he just needed to prove that he could and things would be all right.

Now he didn't know. Did he really not know enough to be with a transgender woman? Was she right to assume she couldn't trust him with her whole heart? He'd had a relationship like that in college, a white girl who thought her Black boyfriend gave her a pass to call things "ghetto" and sing along with *all* the words to Nicki Minaj songs.

Sometimes being dominant felt simple—easy, natural, liberating and celebratory. His parents were progressive folks, for suburban Illinois anyway, and they'd raised him to be aware of his own power and the power other people had over him. It could be paralyzing to be a man and to be aware of all the ways he could make a woman feel unsafe, the ways his attraction and sexuality could be weaponized. Not to mention the way his Black body especially was seen as inherently dangerous, inherently violent. Kink had been revelatory, a way to put those truths on the table and acknowledge them and make them into a game that could be halted anytime it went too far.

Then Sonia had made him all too aware of the ways those safety mechanisms could fail. The ways *he* could fail. He'd hurt her; by mistake and naivete, with errors on both sides, but at the end of the day he was responsible. He was the man he'd never wanted to be. He had made her feel trapped in her own home, unable to escape a situation that had palled for her without escaping him.

So did he really want to try again with someone whose risks were so many times greater? Where his capacity to do harm was so much more?

But he had to try with *someone*, someday. Did he really want to start over? He'd been approached by a few subs from his club in Seattle while he was still recovering from Sonia, and yes, he hadn't been ready. But they hadn't been right, either. The worst had fetishized him, and even the best hadn't charmed him the way April had. The right energy, that *click*, with a sub was lightning in a bottle. He didn't want to throw it away. He didn't want to throw *her* away. Wasn't that exactly the worst thing he could do?

"Hey. Earth to Martin. You okay, man?"

He blinked up at Jason; became gradually aware that he'd housed his dinner without really tasting it and hadn't been listening while his best friend talked for the last ten minutes.

"Yeah. Um. I was somewhere else. What were you saying?"

Jason squinted at him. "I was saying I thought I might hit up Frankie's tonight. You in?"

"Yeah," he said slowly. "Yeah, I'm in."

Another Wednesday at Frankie's, and this time he knew enough to change into jeans and a polo, although he couldn't look at himself in a mirror without thinking *these are my dom jeans* and snickering. Frankie's was about as low-key as last week; no DJ, just piped in music, but this time more people were dancing. April wasn't there. Some drinks were.

Her friend Caroline was. She asked him to dance and he couldn't think of a reason why not, so he did. She was fun. Young, giggly, warm and curvy. Not especially interesting to talk to, he considered, but through the filter of inebriation that wasn't a problem. She suggested they do some shots then head over to a dance club on Red River. Jason was down and so, he decided, was he. Why not? Why the fuck not?

His phone was ringing. He glanced at the screen, then hastened to pick up.

"April?"

She wasn't saying anything. Caroline nudged him, said his name, shoved the shot glass at him.

"Is something wrong?" He didn't know why he jumped to that, but he was worried, suddenly. "April?" She'd hung up.

Caroline made a face and downed his shot for him, before wandering off. He barely noticed. He was still staring at his phone as a text came through, assuring him the call was an accident.

I don't believe that, he thought, in the slow, swimmy way of the profoundly drunk. No, he didn't believe that at all. April had called him but then she had decided not to talk to him. He didn't want that. He wanted her to call him when she had something to say. He wanted her to call him when she had nothing to say so he could hear her breathing.

He didn't want to be here. He didn't want to drink with Caroline Burris or go anywhere else. He didn't want to meet anyone else.

Very slowly, in the haze of Jack and Coke, he came to a conclusion.

He realized Jason was staring at him, and Dennis grabbed his friend and pulled him away from the crowd. Jason came along, his eyes on the clouds forming on his friend's face.

"You know how you basically warned me off from April?" he demanded.

"Yes."

"Well, it didn't work, and I'm in love with her."

Jason blew out a breath. "Yeah, sure, of course. Makes sense. Sounds like you."

"I'm going to have to up my game for her. And you're going to help me."

Jason rolled his eyes, but said, "Come with me."

They moved through the crowd to some of the rooms in the back that were locked during the week, and somehow Jason had keys. He opened the door to a smallish office with a desk and a couple of chairs and some filing cabinets jammed in it carelessly. Rather than sit behind the desk he perched on it and gestured Dennis into one of the chairs.

"Why do you have a key to this office?" Dennis asked.

"Because it's my office," Jason said curtly. Dennis considered the curtness to be uncalled for, since there was no reason to expect Jason had an office here. "Look, what are you talking about, you're in love with April French?"

"I'm in love with her."

"You're not, you met her a week ago."

"You can fall in love in a week," he argued back immediately. He'd fallen in love faster before.

"Absolutely not."

"I wouldn't say I *loved* someone after a week, but I could be *in love with* them."

"What is wrong with you?" Jason demanded.

"I feel like this is just semantics," Dennis muttered. He felt like there had to be a way to just reach past the words and pour the certainty he felt into Jason's head, but he couldn't find it.

Jason sighed deeply and tilted his head backwards to stare at the ceiling. "Why do you think you're in love with her?"

He stopped for a moment to consider this. He didn't think; he knew. He knew because of the great inchoate *no* in his chest when he realized she was hurting; he knew because he was restraining himself from going to her right now. He knew because his house would never be finished without her in it.

"Ever since Sonia," he said slowly, "I've been scared to have a woman in my life. Really in my life. But I can see it with her. I want it."

"So suddenly you're not scared," Jason said, pivoting back forward to look at him.

"No, dude, I'm scared as balls! I'm *so* fucking scared I'm

going to fuck this up. But I…refuse, man. I fucking refuse to fuck it up. I refuse to give up on her."

"You refuse," Jason repeated.

Dennis made eye contact. "I refuse."

Jason took a deep breath, and for a golden moment, Dennis thought he was going to help. They were ride or die for each other, had been for twenty years. Surely Jason could see that this was the next adventure, the next thing.

"You're drunk," Jason said. Dennis *was* drunk, but he could hear every layer of weariness and disgust in his friend's voice. He could hear himself tell Jason he and Sonia were experimenting with kink, and Jason asking if they had a safeword, and himself saying *hey man, it's not like that. We love each other.* He could hear the U-Haul pulling up outside his condo in Capitol Hill to drag his heartbroken ass out of Seattle, and had he been drunk then? Yes, he thought he had been.

"So it's like that," he heard himself say.

"Yeah," said Jason, in that same tone of voice. "I guess so. Let's talk about this later."

It was an awkward breakfast in the Beaumont homestead. He left that same day for a trip to New Haven; the company was privately held, and O'Reilly wanted to introduce him to all the shareholders. He also got to meet the heads of the consulting teams, who worked with clients and relied on Operations and Technology to support them.

The trip itself was fine, a grip-and-grin nothing, but he'd grimly observed Leo Graham's chummy status with all of them. A white room; a very white room.

Over the weekend he had his first check-in with April, and it was…fine. Fine wasn't what he wanted. *She* was what he wanted. *More* was what he wanted.

June

Step one, once he was back in Austin, was lunch with Caroline. He asked her to meet him at the diner down the street from his office, and he was a little anxious about how she'd take the invitation, although he'd been as clear as he could. He was relieved when she showed up in a jogging suit and sneakers. He thought she might not have ordered the cheesesteak fries on a date, either.

"It's a cheat day," she said earnestly. "Well. It can be."

Dennis laughed. "I'm sure you earned it." He had no room to judge; he'd ordered a Reuben that was practically sending death threats to his arteries.

"I have to watch my figure 'cause, y'know, other people watch it, too. I'm a hostess at a restaurant," she explained. "I'm also on OnlyFans if you want the link."

"I think your figure could take some fries and be all the better for it," he said mildly, and she rolled her eyes.

"Oh, like you care. You're all about April, right?"

"Yes. I know this might be a little awkward..." Even if April wasn't in the picture, he couldn't see himself with Caroline. She was ten years younger than him, and when they talked, sometimes he felt every minute of that decade.

She shook her head. "Nah, I'm the one who grilled you about being good enough for her. I'm down to help. What do you need?"

"I want to dress her up," he explained. "I want to give her money every week to buy clothes, to start with. But the specifics are the hard part. How much is too much?"

"No such thing," she said immediately.

"For April." Patiently. "Not for you."

"Hm. Yeah... I'm not actually sure how much money she makes?" Caroline said, frowning in concentration. "But it can't be less than I do, and I can spend a hundred dollars without thinking about it. Two fifty would make sense maybe."

"Hm."

"So you should do five hundred," she continued, stabbing into her fries. "It should feel extravagant but not sinful. Use a prepaid card. April wouldn't do anything too wild with a real one, but she'd think you were being reckless. And cash feels icky, very *Pretty Woman*."

"What do you think about this idea?" he asked. Point blank.

"I think if she turns it down you should call me," she said. "But for real? I think it's really sweet. I don't think anyone's ever done anything like this for her before. Not just the money, but like...thinking this hard about it. April's played with a lot of shit doms."

His expression must have slipped, because she covered her mouth quickly. "Shit, I shouldn't have said that."

"It's fine," he said. "I mean—it doesn't make me like her less. I'm...sorry to hear it, for her sake." Those felt like safe things to say. They sounded better than asking for names and addresses.

He didn't want to hurt anybody. He just wanted to go door-to-door and ask them what was wrong with them. Maybe shake them a little.

"I guess…maybe it's better to say that she tends to be approached by doms trying to build their confidence. And like, sometimes that's for a good reason and she kicks them to the curb and sometimes they just need a little time and then, like… they move on. But for whatever reason nobody really sticks."

And now she doesn't even want to try, he realized. *So step one—I show her I'm not going anywhere. Because I'm* not.

After work, he made his way down to Jason's dank basement lair. "Hey. I had lunch with Caroline today."

Jason flicked him an appraising look, just for an instant. "Yeah? How was that?"

"It was good." He paused. "She told me a lot of the doms April's played with before have been trying to build up their confidence before moving on to other people."

Jason nodded. "I don't know her that well but speaking as someone who sees a lot of what goes on at the club, yeah, sounds about right."

"That sucks," he said. Jason nodded again. He waited a little longer and then put it on the table. "Is that why you wanted me to stay away from her?"

Jason didn't look away from the screen. "Yep."

He flinched. "You think I'm like that?"

Jason sighed and pushed away from the desk to look at him straight on. "Like what? Like someone who would fall into the arms of the first person to show him a little genuine vulnerability alongside the sub games? Like someone who might not be ready to get into a long-term relationship right away? I know you, man, and I know the last thing you want to do right now is hurt anybody. And I looked at the two of you together and I thought, here's a *real* good chance for these two people to fuck each other up."

"I know I've fucked up a lot of stuff lately," Dennis grated out. The more it sank in, the more crushed he felt. Jason was protecting *her* from *him*. "I don't want to fuck this up. That's why I wanted your help, man. You've been doing this a lot longer than me."

Jason shook his head, then met his eyes again. "You still refuse to give up?"

He nodded. "I refuse."

Jason flicked his attention back to the computer just long enough to close things out. "All right. Let's talk strategy, then."

Relief shot through him. "Yeah? You're in."

His friend threw up his hands. "What else can I do? I'm ride or die, man. You know that."

He spent some time catching Jason up on events so far. "So this is how I see it," he concluded. "First, I have to be a better dom. What happened with Sonia can't happen again. Ever."

Jason nodded. "You ever think about mentoring?"

"Dom mentoring?" Dennis raised an eyebrow at that. "How does that work?"

"It's a pretty normal thing in the scene actually," said Jason, and Dennis was reminded again that his friend had been sneaking into kink clubs since he was sixteen. "I can try to find someone for you. I know a lot of the doms at Frankie's."

"Shit," Dennis said. "If I had done that when I first got plugged into the scene with Sonia..." It was such a private thing, though. "I'll think about it, okay?"

Jason nodded, eyes shadowing as he turned inward and made mental notes. Dennis was deeply familiar with his friend's expressions after twenty years, and this was Jason in problem-solving mode. "Okay. Yeah, okay, what else?"

"All right. Be a better dom, check. But more specifically, I have to be *her* dom, and that means learning what I don't know about being trans. I don't want her to ever have to explain to me why what I just said puts her at risk or insults her again."

Jason gave him a Look. "That's an ambitious goal, Den."

"Yeah, yeah, I know I'm not going to be perfect, but I need to be smarter. I need to at least know what the fuck I'm talking about. There are ways to get educated about this stuff. You think PFLAG would work for this?"

"…huh." In high school Dennis and Jason had attended PFLAG together. Eventually Jason's mom had started coming, too, but for a while it was just the two of them. "That's… smart, but at the same time, it's kind of weird to go spy on a support group, man."

"No, I know that," said Dennis. "But I figure I can talk to some people and figure out where to go from there."

"Yeah, maybe," Jason said. "There's one more thing, though. And this is non-negotiable for me. If you're going to put yourself through self-improvement boot camp for a girl you just met—which is ridiculous, by the way, this is ridiculous—then you need to go to therapy."

"Oh, fuck you, you're always trying to get me to go to therapy."

"Yeah, because: you need therapy."

"I'm fine." *Not this shit again.*

"What happened with Sonia traumatized you, Dennis. You're not fine."

"I am fine. I am not traumatized. I am not the victim when it comes to me and Sonia, Jason. I'm the bad guy." He tried to use his tone to convey that this subject was closed, but Jason was annoyingly immune to his dom voice.

"Dennis, what I'm about to tell you may come as a shock, but in therapy? They don't like to talk about bad guys."

That, Dennis thought, was exactly the problem. Sometimes there *was* a bad guy. He didn't need excuses; he didn't need to love himself more. He already thought he was pretty cool. But he couldn't allow himself to hurt someone again. Period.

That said...

He was not at all convinced he needed therapy, but on the other hand, he *was* convinced he needed his best friend on his side in this. If it would make Jason feel like Dennis was handling his shit, that this campaign for April's heart was a good idea, it wouldn't hurt to try. He smiled wearily. "Okay. It's a deal. Thanks, brother."

Jason ducked his head and pivoted back to his laptop. But he called after Dennis as he ascended the stairs: "Just don't fuck this up!"

His new therapist was a kink-friendly older woman recommended by Jason's own shrink. She was expensive, and—although he was reluctant to admit it—she was good.

She set aside a couple of hours for the first session, to "get the full download." He told her about Sonia and braced for her to tell him it wasn't his fault. Or maybe to tell him he was an incurable misogynist and throw him out.

Instead she laid down her pen, looked at him over her glasses, and said, "Wow. You fucked up big. What did you learn from that?" in a voice of calm compassion.

For a long moment he didn't know what to say. "That's not what I expected you to say," he said, with a touch of a chuckle in his voice.

"It strikes me as the only thing that matters, don't you think?" she said simply. "Making amends and doing better next time. What else is there?"

He gaped like a fish for a moment. She was stealing all his

lines. "I learned I don't want to hurt people," he said, with a wobble in his voice that embarrassed him.

"Did you not already know that?"

He swallowed. "I learned I can hurt people even if I love them. Maybe sometimes because I love them. I don't want that."

In response to her gentle follow-up questions, he revisited the terror and guilt; the sick helplessness of a situation that could not be fixed, could only be walked away from. The pit that had opened up in his life, and how it seemed to be centered in their condo, in the space they had shared. As he described the slow collapse of his confidence, of the aching void a walk-in closet could become, he lived through it again, with Cordelia at his elbow taking notes and asking gentle questions that flipped things upside down. The second time through it seemed smaller; like something he could live with.

They moved on to talking about April. Cordelia did not think his plan was ridiculous. "If, in the end, she still doesn't want to be with you, what's the worst-case scenario? You're a better dominant, you're more informed about transgender people and transphobia, and you went to therapy. What a waste of time that would be, huh? If you don't think you're ready for a relationship, become ready. If this ends up not being the relationship, another one will come."

She also didn't disapprove of his idea to buy April clothes, although she resolutely refused to speculate on how it would go. "You'll find out soon enough, won't you?" she said. "Your job and your role require you to anticipate things—live in the future. That's allowed you to be very good at what you do. But it can also create a lot of anxiety. Human beings were made to live life in the present, one second at a time. What if you just tried to do that for now?"

One second at a time, life gradually carried him forward. The city code enforcers weighed his architect in the balance and found him wanting yet again. The summer rains not only finished off the clay pipes but also revealed a hitherto-undiagnosed problem with the roof. The flooding forced them to tear up the flooring that had just been laid and for days fans and dehumidifiers ran at full blast. Reggie swore that despite everything, he would get Dennis into the house by July. He also diffidently invited Dennis to a Juneteenth cookout.

Work continued to grind forward, as he remade the Technology division from the ground up. He fired the entire Help Desk staff. He had to—there were items in the backlog more than a year old that had never been addressed. He hired someone new to manage it, gave her a budget and set her loose to rebuild.

Natasha Bledsoe was a charming and competent Black woman in her forties, a referral from another tech executive he had met at Reggie's cookout. She'd run a Help Desk before but stepped back to raise her kids for a while. She was ready for a new project, though, and she took control of the chaos easily, sieving through the old staff to find a competent quarter or so and making them managers for the brand-new folks, and establishing firm turnaround requirements and customer service standards.

While the fear of God was in everyone, he issued his own edicts for the developers, trying to corral them into a unified project management approach and well-defined goals. After the first few stubborn holdouts were put on Performance Improvement Plans, they seemed to realize he was serious. He also began to lay the groundwork for a major data migration; predictably, Graham hated the idea, which was an added bonus, really.

And he and April were talking constantly. At least once a week if nothing else, but really, they touched base most days. Even as the intensity of work picked up and sent him bouncing back and forth between Austin and the East Coast, her place in his schedule was sacrosanct and always a blessing. One check-in she tentatively asked if they could call the week a wash because she'd had some painful electrolysis. He didn't tell her he himself was wrung out from yet another red-eye flight; they just played *Mario Kart* until he was falling asleep at the Switch.

It was by far the most G-rated memory they had made together; yet it was the one he replayed in his mind falling asleep every night. The sleepy burr of her voice and her unguarded laugh. The hope it gave him was dizzying.

He and April had been playing together about six weeks when he launched his big new game. They agreed to meet at her apartment to discuss—he wasn't going to fuck things up over email again. He needed to be able to see her face. He'd asked her to wear something very simple. He didn't know why—his attraction to dressing women wasn't something he was in a rush to unpack with Cordelia, and that went for why his subconscious made certain choices, as well.

But whatever the reason, she was breathtaking, in a white summer dress with a raw hem. He watched the threads shift over her thighs as she led him to a charming little space she'd created in one corner of the room, coaxing a reading nook out of the unbroken floor plan of the loft with a couple of armchairs and some shelves.

God, I really like her, he thought. He liked her poky little apartment and how she made it work, her walls lined with books and her tiny tidy kitchen. The light in her eyes, excited and wary and intoxicating. He liked her honey-colored hair—how long had it taken to grow out like that? Had she cut it since her transition?—and he liked the shadows of her breasts in that dress.

"I… I should say, I dressed the way you wanted, but I really think we need to talk about this out of role."

His mood dropped immediately into the pit of his stomach. She was right, of course. The text about her outfit had been a last-minute thought, trying to set the stage and control the coming conversation, and he'd fucked up. *Score one for Cordelia.*

As the conversation progressed, he tried to climb out of the hole and regain his dominant vibe. It wasn't easy. She had a lot of questions, and he felt rusty trying to explain this game to a new person. It all made a certain sense in his head…he hadn't wanted to tell her he'd done it before, but obviously knowing that made her feel *more* comfortable, not less. He'd rehearsed and anticipated this conversation, but he obviously hadn't done it very well. Talking about Sonia didn't do his confidence any good, either.

April bit her lip, and her soft grey-green eyes found his. "I need you to admit something first. It's at least a little about the money, isn't it? I mean…you have more money than me." She had no idea. God, was this a terrible idea? "That's a fact. That's power you have that I don't. And this is all about power exchange, taking those imbalances and making them sexy, but…we can't do that if you don't admit it. We absolutely have to be ruthless about admitting it."

He took a deep breath. She was right, damn it. And wasn't there something appealing about that ruthlessness? She was so brave to lay it out like this, so smart and careful to guard their hearts, and he cherished that about her, and there was no way to honor that except with his own courage and care.

"I didn't grow up with…the kind of money I have today," he admitted. Being as honest as he could. As ruthless. "When I got my first big bonus, I paid off my parents' house. And I could do that, not because it was *so much* money, but because my parents' mortgage in Illinois was that small. But they would've been working on paying it off the rest of their lives.

"I like that power. I like not having to think about whether or not I can afford it when I want to do something or solve a problem." The words were a flood; not an outburst, but something unlocked from deep within, coming out of his mouth fast and unplanned. "Having options.

"So I like having money, and yeah, I like to show it off a little. Not excessively, and not for its own sake, but because it protects you. It makes things easier. I've heard that Black men have trouble getting into some of the fancier bars on the West Side around here, but I haven't. Not when I'm dressed up. It's not...a perfect defense," he added quickly.

God forbid she think that it was, or that he imagined it was. Racists with power could humiliate a rich Black man like anybody else. Cops killed rich Black men just like any other Black folks.

This conversation was making him vulnerable in ways he hadn't expected, in ways he hadn't even considered before today. But the more he thought about it, the more foundation he found for the fantasy in himself; the more he realized that *was* how he felt when he got up in the morning and put on an expensive suit. Maybe Jason wasn't the only one with baggage about money.

"But that's...that's the fantasy," he finished.

"No, I get it," she said quickly, eyes brightening. "I think I do. It's like... I work...really hard. I work really hard on how I look. Because I feel like if I've done everything I can to send the message that I'm a, that I identify as a woman, then even though I don't pass, I... I did my best. It's probably a little fucked up...but it makes me feel better, and I can face the world as my best self."

"*Yes.* And the money just makes it easier." His eyes locked

on to hers. "I want to share that with you. Yes, I want to retain some control of how it's spent. And yes, I want to see
you in the kind of things you can't usually afford. It *is* about
power—and I want you to feel my power head to toe when
you walk out the door in the morning. But I never want you
to feel trapped by it. I want you to wear it like armor."

He let his eyes bore into hers; let some of his hunger slip
out. Hunger for her, yes, but also his hunger for this to go
well. Not just the kinky hunger for power and control, but the
longing to bring her more fully into his life, to build something with her, to be with her even when he was far away.

He could see it hit her, like a shot of strong alcohol, and
he liked that; felt his feet on surer ground again. There were
logistics to sort out, but he had her; he *knew* he had her, and
when she met his eyes again and said "Yes, Sir," something
inside of him crowed.

"Terrific." He could feel his grin tugging his cheeks. "Can
I see your closet? I'm not going to pass judgment, and I won't
tell you to get rid of anything. But I'd like to know what I'm
working with." It was practical, it was necessary, and it was a
fig leaf to stop himself from ravishing her immediately. It held
right up until they came to her lingerie—just a few pieces,
tucked in the back of a drawer with obvious care. He drew
out a filmy babydoll nightie and whistled.

She colored. "You like that?"

"I'm not sure," he said. He absolutely did. "Let's see it on."

She nodded, hands already moving to the ragged hem of
her dress. "Yes, Sir." She turned away slightly as she peeled it
off, perhaps self-conscious in the bold daylight, and he moved
closer and let his hands settle on her hips to show her she had
nothing to fear.

She melted back against him and his hands grazed up her
smooth, soft skin to her breasts. She turned her head back

to meet his mouth and groaned into his kiss as he began to touch her nipples, small and pink and tightening under his touch. "What about the lingerie?" she murmured.

"Shhh." He ran one hand back down to her hip, to test her arousal, and found her ready. He brushed his fingers over her clit and then settled lower, following her cues from having watched her pleasure herself several times now. He nudged her feet further apart to slip his hand between her thighs more firmly.

"Did you edge yet today? Just nod or shake your head." She shook her head, tossing her loose hair.

"I'm here to help," he chuckled. "Arms up."

She stabilized herself away from his arms and lifted hers over her head. He skimmed the nightie down over her shoulders, carefully adjusting the hang and seams. "Beautiful. Let's lay you down on the bed."

She seemed to be picking up the vibes he was laying down. She let him guide her, pose her, watching him from under hooded lids. "Am I a dolly, Sir?" she asked, in a half-teasing voice.

"Shhh, dolls can't talk." She giggled softly at that, but compliantly let him put her arms above her head. He slid between her legs, lifting the skirt of the nightie, and began to kiss and lick, letting his hands roam over her body but always gravitating back to her core. In accordance with the rules of the game, she tried to be still and quiet, but he didn't make it easy for her, and in truth he wasn't so deeply into this kink that it bothered him.

It was exciting to watch her ability to play the role slip away as he teased her, her hands writhing and clasping together as she fought to keep them over her head without real restraints, the muscles of her thighs tensing and jumping as she struggled not to press against his face. When she let slip a single cracked, "Please," he lifted his head.

"Good girl," he said, kissing her thigh. "Was that weird?"

She smiled at him. "Not too weird. I've...done weirder for sure. Anything else you want to do with your doll, Sir?"

"I'm not sure yet." He was, but he was putting it off for now. "How's denial treating you?"

She let out a shaky laugh. "A lot harder suddenly!"

"Just think about how bad it's going to be when you're covered in things I gave you...feeling my touch from head to toe."

She made a plaintive noise, and he pushed himself up the bed to kiss her. They kissed for some time, as her hand began to explore and unzip his jeans, and then she slithered lower and returned his attentions. After a few moments he felt her growing focused and still, picking up the threads of the game, and he gathered her hair in his hands and guided her strokes as he used her mouth like a kinkier kind of doll.

He gathered her up and hugged against his chest afterwards, still panting. "That was hot." It was such a terrible, incomplete word for what that had been, but he wasn't sure what else he could safely say right now. He just wanted to hold her.

"I'm glad you liked it." Her expression was dreamy and slightly glazed. She snuggled against his linen shirt and fidgeted with a button. "You were more casual today."

"Yes. Do you like it?"

"I like you however you dress. I think that kink only runs one way." He laughed, and she said, "Would you have enjoyed it more in a suit?"

He had to think about that. "I'm not sure. Maybe."

She kissed his neck. "You should wear one next time. I want you to feel like your best self."

He squeezed her, suddenly emotional. Dom drop was a

thing, too. He usually kept a pretty even keel, but he hadn't realized how badly he wanted this to work, how much he'd invested in it. "That's what I want for you, too. That's why I want to do this."

"I know," she whispered against his chest. "I'm looking forward to it." He held her for a long time, squeezed her close and murmured to her what a good girl she was.

After a few minutes, she exhaled a long breath, and stiffened just slightly. "Hey," she said in a low voice.

"Hey," he echoed.

"I'm real, right?" she whispered. He relaxed his hug so he could look her in the face. Was she disassociating?

"To you, I mean," she said. "I'm a real person to you. I'm not just something you can buy so you can dress me up and squeeze me when you want someone to hold and leave me on the shelf when you don't. Please?" Something jagged wobbled in her voice.

"No," he said instantly; his urge was to gather her back in his arms, but maybe she didn't want that, from what she said. "No. It's just a game." He made a mental note to take her out more often between check-ins; she shouldn't feel like a dirty secret or a side piece. He didn't know as much as he wanted to, yet, but it didn't take a PhD in Queer Studies to realize realness was a loaded topic for a trans woman.

She took a deep breath. "Okay."

"We don't have to do the doll thing again if you don't like it. We don't have to do any of it." Panic was tugging at his sleeve, but for now he had it under control; sub drop was a part of a lot of scenes, even ones that went well. He was more than willing to take her through it; to make sure she felt real and cherished, seen and appreciated inside and out. "You're very real to me. You're the realest thing I've got right now."

She looked startled, then her expression settled. "Right

now. Right." She took a few more breaths, then let herself slide back into his arms. "Sorry, I... I did enjoy it. I just had a second afterwards..."

He nodded. "No need to apologize," he said. "Holding you like a teddy bear probably isn't the best aftercare for that kind of scene, on second thought. Do you want to talk?"

"Talking is good," she said, her voice tentative.

He thought for a moment. "Tell me something real. You have any pets growing up?"

She relaxed against him as she nodded. "Yeah, cats. My mom loves cats."

"Does that mean you don't?"

She shrugged. "I don't like them as much as she does. I used to have one, but my ex-wife got him in the divorce."

"Sorry, lovely." He kissed her temple briefly, but she shrugged again.

"It's okay. What about you?"

"Oh, I was a soft touch for every kind of stray. My parents thought it was funny until I brought home Jason."

She snorted with laughter, then quieted. "Is that what I am?"

"No," he said, with all the gentleness he could while still making it firm enough to imprint her bones. "You're not a doll and you're not a pet." *But whatever you are, you're mine*, he thought. *Lord, I need you to be mine.*

"Then what am I?" she said. Her tone was playful now, not keyed up like it had been. Good.

"A very good girl," he said. It was a fairly rote bit of praise, was truly what he was thinking in the moment, and he didn't expect the brightness in her eyes as she slid close again. Only after a moment did he realize the gendered aspect of what he'd said. An accident for the good this time, but damn it, he didn't want any more accidents.

July

It turned out the local PFLAG had a meetup for trans people and their partners; they met in the rec room of a Presbyterian Church. He'd already planned to leave a large donation, but the coffee was so bad he doubled it immediately. He did indeed feel voyeuristic sitting in on the support group, so he spoke instead to the facilitator, an older Latina trans woman named Elena; she told him he was sweet and gave him a few places to start his research. In the way of the Internet, each led on to more and more.

He learned that in Texas, a transgender person could be kicked out of their apartment or fired from their job because of their gender with no legal recourse, and he wondered if he had any employees living in fear. He learned about Texas's failed attempts at bathroom bills and successful attempts to target trans youth. He learned about high rates of suicide, and high rates of intimate partner violence and murder, and for the first time really understood the kind of risk April was taking inviting him home that night. He learned about TERFs (trans exclusionary radical feminists) and chasers (people who pursued trans women specifically because of their status), and it resonated with his own experiences with people in kink spaces who saw his race as a fantasy.

He watched, listened to, and read stories from trans individuals. Stories of stunted youths spent pretending and always watching to see who was noticing and stories of young transitioners tentatively asserting their truth with their parents behind them; stories of relationships that couldn't take the strain and stories of the ones that did; stories of humiliating questions from HR directors and crushing assumptions by store clerks, and stories of inclusive policies and how they made people feel.

After just about every story he wanted to hug April and never let her go. Microaggressions and concepts like psychological safety weren't new to him, God knew. But now he was learning a whole new register of them in addition to the ones he'd experienced all his life and the ones he'd learned to notice for Jason's sake, the last time he'd attended PFLAG meetings.

He was down one of these YouTube wormholes when his phone rang. "Hey, Bubba," said the cheerful voice on the other end of the line.

He paused his laptop and leaned back in his chair. "'Sup, Peanut?"

"Ugh, I hate it when you call me that."

"You *just* called me Bubba, you think I love that nickname?"

"That's what I call you, 'cause you're my big brother. I've called you that since I could talk."

"And you're my little sister and I call you Peanut."

"No, you call *all* of us Peanut and it sucks. At least give me a personal nickname."

"I'm gonna be real with you and tell you you're all in my phone as Peanut. I don't really know which one of you this is." This wasn't true—well, they *were* all in his phone as Peanut, but he had recognized Georgia's voice immediately. But part of being a big brother was driving a bit into the ground.

"Asshole. This is Georgia."

"Ohhh, the *tall* Peanut. 'Kay. What's up?"

He could *hear* his oldest little sister shaking her head down the line.

"Just calling to catch up," she said. "I haven't heard from you in a while and you went and deleted Facebook, so I was just curious." Oh. Right. He'd nuked most of his social media earlier in the summer, in order to resist the temptation to peek at Sonia's life without him.

"Yeah, sorry." He closed out his browser and prepared to focus on an old-fashioned family catch-up. It had been too long. "I've been talking to Mom often enough and I guess I just assumed it all got circulated." Not that he told her everything.

"Well, I'm not saying she hasn't told me plenty." Their mother *always* had plenty to say. "But it's different hearing it from you."

"Maybe you just miss me," he said.

"Nah, can't be that," she said. "I've got enough family here, with Mom and Dad and Kat and the cousins and all that. Who cares about Bubba off in Austin?"

"Well shit, I thought you guys might want to come down for Austin City Limits, but I guess I see how it is now." The weeklong music festival was coming up in October, and Dennis and Jason already had wristbands; but he had indeed considered bringing his family down for at least one weekend.

Or at least Georgia and Kat. He'd like them to meet April; even if he wasn't exactly sure how that introduction would go. Maybe, once they met her, he could talk to them about the trap he'd caught himself in.

"Now I didn't say all that…"

He laughed. "Nah, it's okay. I'll keep all this good food to myself, too. I was going to teach you about barbecue."

She snorted. "You can keep that Texas shit. I'm a vinegar-based girl."

"Wait a second, you know about different types of barbecue? I thought I'd been missing out all this time because of being from the Midwest."

"I don't know about Seattle, but there is perfectly good barbecue of all different kinds here in Illinois, Dennis. You just gotta find it."

"How did I not know about this? The only barbecue I knew about was Grandma's."

"See, that's your problem, though. If you don't like something you just don't ever try it again instead of learning something."

"I do not," he protested, although inwardly he was registering a direct hit to his ego. Nobody could rival their mother when it came to seeing right through people, but all of the Martin girls had inherited a little bit of her X-ray vision.

"Mm-hm."

He rolled his eyes. "So how are you doing, though? How's work? How's Ray?" He liked Georgia's husband, a big, quiet and self-possessed guy she'd met in college at Urbana-Champaign. They'd been married several years by now.

"Ray's good," she said. "We've been talking about kids again, but I just don't think it's time yet. I've got one more exam for my CPA and then hopefully I can move up next year. I can think about getting pregnant after that."

Kat and Georgia both had good careers, although neither had hit the jackpot like Dennis; he had been in the right place at the right time, and there just weren't that many right places to go around.

"Yeah, you got time. How is Kat?"

"Katrina's good...you oughta call her, too, you know."

"She still living at home?"

"You think Mom would miss a chance to tell you if she moved out?"

"I genuinely don't understand why she doesn't want her own place," he said, shaking his head. Living in the attic of their old family home had made sense while she was getting her graphic design business off the ground, but she was doing fine now. And she worked from home, which meant she was with their parents *all the time*. Dennis loved his family, but...

"She says she likes it there. She takes care of the dogs."

"It couldn't be me," he said, shaking his head again.

"You know it won't be long until we might be glad to have somebody living with Mom and Dad," Georgia said gently, and he winced.

"I don't want to think about that."

"Bubba, we both know when Mom and Dad can't live on their own anymore, it's going to be you paying and Kat on the spot."

"What are you and Keisha going to do in this equation?"

"I'm management," she sniffed, and he chuckled at that. "And I don't expect anything from Keisha." Unlike the previous comment, that wasn't a joke. It was real bitterness.

"You hear from Keisha at all these days?" His third sister, and the one most distant from the family. Dennis had moved away, but he tried to stay in touch and came back for Thanksgiving at least every year; Keisha was a permanent maybe.

As the baby, Keisha was the only one who hadn't grown

up in a house where debt collectors were calling night and day. Maybe that was why her ambitions were less practical, or maybe there wasn't a pat explanation for it. Whatever the reason, Keisha had dropped out of college and gone west to be a movie star. It hadn't gone great, but she was hanging in there.

"Nah, she's still dating that guy and she doesn't want to hear from me right now," said Georgia wryly. Reluctantly: "I heard from Kat she needs money."

What Keisha *did* have in common with her siblings was the intense personality they had inherited from their mother. Only Katrina had their father's gentle peacemaker gene. The rest of them were slightly too prone to making sure their opinion was known. It didn't always promote family harmony.

He exhaled. "I'll call Kat soon. I don't know why Keisha doesn't just call me when she needs money."

"Yes, you do," Georgia laughed. "She's too proud. She tells Kat because she knows Kat can't help. Just putting it out there and letting word filter around to you is just about all she can stand."

It was true. After a beat, Georgia pointed out: "You know you didn't answer, right? About how *you're* doing?"

"I'm good," he said, dragging his mind away from the puzzle of his baby sister. "Everything's good. I just don't have a lot to talk about, I guess. I'm in Austin, I'm eating well, having Jason down the street is like being back in high school, in a good way. House still isn't finished."

"Dennis, the fuck. How is your house not finished?"

"That's what I keep saying," he said. "How is this not finished? Mostly we're dealing with city code stuff. Maybe in the next month or so."

"You need to talk to your guy."

"Reggie's doing his best. He's a good contractor, this house just has a lot of surprises in it. We had some leaks and they had to rip up the floor and start over once they fixed the roof."

"Mm-hm," she said again. The two syllables were an impenetrable wall of knowing better, and it frustrated him. Now he was feeling like it was a good thing she didn't know about April. There was nothing like family for putting you in two minds about everything.

"He's nice," Dennis argued. "He invited me to a cookout for Juneteenth."

"Oh, well if he can *grill*, then that's okay," she said, dripping sarcasm. "Y'have a good time at least?"

"Yeah, it was great. I've been wondering where Austin was hiding all the Black folks. I met some cool guys." There'd been a lot of people at the cookout, a pretty wide spectrum of Reggie's friends and clients and younger people invited by his kids. He'd found a pocket of tech guys and settled in. "I'm supposed to do some trivia thing with one of them actually."

"Good job, Bubba, you found the Blerds."

"You're an accountant, you can't say shit about Black nerds."

"I'm not an accountant *yet*." Georgia had not started out to be an accountant, but a job as an office assistant had carried her sideways into an unexpected career, and she felt that set her apart from people born with a pocket calculator in their hand. "Nah, I'm glad you made some friends. You said you met some cool guys…what about the ladies?"

"Subtle."

She snorted. "It's not supposed to be subtle, it's a straight question."

He didn't say anything for a moment, and she continued. "We all liked Sonia, Dennis, but you broke up and that's it. I worry about you down there in your leaky-ass house all alone."

"I'm not all alone," he said. All right; here it was. His chance, if he wanted it.

The problem was, he didn't know *how* to explain about April; anything about April. Their relationship was officially nothing official; he didn't know if he was allowed to tell people she was trans, and he absolutely didn't want to discuss kink with his sister. He certainly hadn't explained anything about his relationship with Sonia or what ended it, and so the breakup had come out of left field for his family. He didn't want to go down that road again with something that, despite his best efforts, might never solidify into a real relationship. "I keep plenty busy. I'm barely in this house between work and everything else."

"How is work? Mom says you're dealing with some clown who wants your job."

"Yeah, I don't know," he said, sighing. Work was definitely a headache right now. "Things have been going all right, but I knew sooner or later I'd hit something me and the COO couldn't settle on. We need to do this server migration, but he's being a tool about it. He thinks it's going to fuck everything up and no one's going to be able to find their files."

"Okay, translate that for some with a slightly lower Blerd quotient, Bubba."

"All right, so this company keeps all their data on servers, right? And all the different teams have found their own solutions to this so there's a bunch of different ones, run by different companies. Different services. We can save a lot of time and money by putting it all in one place, but Graham is a stubborn son of a bitch. We were giving a presentation to the shareholders about our plans for the quarter and he deleted my slides from the deck we had put together. I had to just freestyle on the spot."

God, he'd been angry. "I can't help feeling like a couple

years ago I would've pushed this guy out already," he said. "Or at least shut him up. But I don't know, it's a new company, I don't have the social capital I did before...he's been there a long time and all the other East Coast big shots know him and they don't know me."

"Mm-hm." There it was again, and the most frustrating thing was her skepticism was warranted; it sounded like excuses to him, too.

"But that's not even it, really. I mean. I guess if I really wanted to, I could finesse him. But I just...don't want to. I wanted this to be easier."

"Well, that makes sense," she said. "If I had your money, I wouldn't be working at all."

"I like working," he said. "I just don't want to have to be a dick to do it. But I don't like getting pushed around, either."

"Look, Bubba, I know you don't want to talk about whatever happened with Sonia. But anybody who knows you can tell that you're different than you were."

"Thanks," he muttered in a dry tone of voice.

"I'm just saying...that doesn't have to be a bad thing. You remember when we were kids and you read my diary? And you found out I was dating a guy in your grade and you beat seven kinds of shit out of him and got suspended? Is that still what you'd do today?"

"I stand by that beatdown. Any high school senior dating a middle schooler is trash, Georgia."

"I know that now, Dennis, thank you. But is that still how you'd handle it? Or, since we're all adults now, looking back, was that the *right* way to handle it?"

He closed his eyes. "I mean, I still feel pretty good about hitting him, but it shouldn't have come to that. In a perfect world I wouldn't have read your damn diary, Peanut." Life as a Black man in a white business had taught him to keep his temper under control, and Sonia had put the seal on that lesson. Sure, he got angry. Everybody got angry. But you could care about solving problems or you could care about taking your mad out on someone's face. They were—mostly—mutually exclusive.

"Exactly," Georgia said, as if she had scored some tremendous point.

"Exactly what?"

"You grew up, Dennis. People grow up. If I could have that talk with Keisha again, I'd sure as hell handle it different."

"Yeah, but I'm…"

"But what?"

"I might not get what I want this way."

There was a long pause, in which he could sense Georgia restraining a record-breaking fourth "Mm-hm."

He rolled his eyes. "Yes, I heard how that sounded. Love you, Peanut."

"Love you, too, Bubba. Call more often."

"I'll try." And he would definitely call Kat. But first he shot Jason a text message. He was ready to swallow his pride and work with a mentor. You could care about solving problems or you could care about holding on to your pride. He was going to do this right, and maybe, if he was lucky, he could get what he wanted, too.

August

As the summer went on, April grew gradually more comfortable using his card, and he grew gradually more comfortable giving her directions. April grew gradually more desperate and invested in her denial and he continued to find new ways to tease and torment her. They attended the Shibari workshop together and came away with a million filthy ideas, then went back to his house to try them out. Reggie had kept his word; the house was still mostly uninhabitable, but the master bedroom and en suite were ready.

He watched in admiration and managed to mostly stay out of the way as Natasha stood up the all-new Tech Support call center, only intervening to keep her path clear of meddling from the COO. He managed to prevail in his own battle with Leo Graham, too—the data migration was on, although he knew he'd spent just about all his capital with O'Reilly. Hell, he was in debt up to his neck, to tell the truth. He'd made promises and he would just have to deliver. When the tension started building in his neck and he felt like he was forgetting how to smile, he blew off steam shopping online and sending more mysterious packages to April. (He was becoming an expert in finding the rare sites that sold lingerie for trans bodies.)

He preferred to have his arguments with Graham on his home turf when they had to be face to face, and the COO's quick temper made it easy to tempt him into stomping down to the fourth floor to Dennis's office. On one occasion when he had been forced to come to the other man's territory, he'd seen a flash of sandy hair go past the glass door and thought for a moment April was there. That was when he knew he was far gone. The situation had to change. But he had to be ready first.

In early August, he joined Jason, April and a handful of others from Frankie's on a float in Austin's Pride Parade. While April ran around herding cats, Jason introduced him to Tony Bulsara, an older olive-skinned man, well-built, with grey in his moustache. "Jason says you're looking for a mentor in the lifestyle," he said in a gravelly voice.

His eyes flicked to Jason, who seemed uncharacteristically subdued. Did he and this guy play together? "Yeah, that's right. I'm...mostly self-taught. The Internet, stuff like that. Whatever I've picked up hanging around the scene. It doesn't have to be anything too formal, but I've made mistakes and I...don't want to make any more."

Tony nodded. "I can make time tomorrow. Jason, you can come unlock Frankie's early so we can get in?"

Jason eyes darted back and forth between his friend and the older man. They waited. Finally, Jason said, "Yes, Mr. Tony," as *sotto voce* as he dared and then looked away.

Dennis blinked. Okay then. Anybody who could make Jason act like *that* was worth learning from.

"I have to warn you," Dennis said the next day, as they faced each other across a table in the empty bar. "I may have to go out of town soon. I was hoping we could do this mostly by phone…"

"We can," agreed Tony. Jason had let them in, then scurried to his office with the bar manager, Vic. "But some things it's better to do face to face." He waited a long beat. "What did you do?"

Dennis cleared his throat. "Excuse me?"

"You said you made some mistakes. You're carrying it around with you, and that's the easiest way to make more mistakes. If I'm going to help you…" The older man opened a hand. "What happened?"

Dennis took a deep breath. It was an easy question to ask. It wasn't an easy one to answer. He'd told Jason. He'd told his therapist, now. "I just met you," he said quietly.

"Trust. It's all about trust. None of *this*—" Tony gestured to encompass him, Dennis, the whole bar. "None of it works without trust."

"I know that," Dennis snapped. The air-conditioning wasn't on outside of business hours, and the bar was sweltering. His T-shirt was sticking to him. "But I'm not your sub."

"You want my help." It was mild.

"What's the worst thing you ever did in *the lifestyle*?" growled Dennis, harsher than he meant to. "How about you?"

Tony looked at him like something stuck on the sole of his shoe, and said flatly, "Punished someone when I was really mad at him. You can't do that, in case you don't know. Fucks up the lines in your head. Theirs, too. Even if it's a real punishment, you've got to be in a place of calm and love, or you shouldn't do it. End the scene and have a fight, if that's what you're spoiling for. It's a mistake I still think about every time I touch a paddle or a belt."

"What happened? After," Dennis asked, in a smaller voice. It wasn't a problem he'd ever wrestled with—not too much, anyway—but the pain on the other man's face was real and it was hard to maintain his bluster in the face of that.

"The trust was gone," said Tony, with a shrug of great finality.

They sat together in uncomfortable silence. Part of him hoped if he just didn't say anything, Tony would move on, but the older man wasn't budging. Patience, Dennis reflected, was something you had to have to be a dominant.

"Sonia was the one who wanted to try kink, but I got really into it," he said, in a low voice. If the old man couldn't hear him, too damn bad. "It was like what I'd always been waiting for. It made sex make sense, the way other people talked about it. I knew about BDSM, from Jason and TV, movies, whatever, but I'd never tried and I always thought I wouldn't like it, but I liked it a lot."

Tony waited.

"So we started doing it. A lot. We didn't know what we were doing. No real safewords. No clear distinctions in role. No way to negotiate outside of the games. We were 24/7 from the word go, except we didn't even know that was the term for it. Eventually we found our local kink scene and we learned a lot and we could look back and laugh. Except we still hadn't really..." He looked off into a corner of the bar. "Fuck, man."

He'd been rattling it off at a good clip, just trying to move past the storytelling phase, but there was no easy way to speed past this part. There were land mines buried in that road. And still Tony waited.

Dennis's voice was quiet; hushed with bottled-up grief. "I

like control. I don't like to hurt, I just like...control. I like pretty dolls. It...ate her life. Both our lives, I guess."

Except his role was still being Mr. Big Alpha Businessman. And her role became Obedient Arm Candy and Obedient Housekeeper and Obedient Sex Doll, and... "And then she stopped wanting that, and we didn't have any way for her to say that."

Maybe she never wanted it, he thought. Maybe it just closed in around her and she couldn't stop it. He didn't really believe that—had to believe her initial enthusiasm was real—but it was a bleak and terrible possibility, however small. He drew a ragged breath.

"And then one day she just left. She didn't have a way to say it, so she did it. She just left, and she didn't take anything I had given her, so she had nothing.

"I was so...lost," Dennis said. "I loved her. I had no idea how toxic the game had become. I thought we were both... I thought it was love. I went after her, to apologize, to ask what I could do. I showed up at her parents' house."

"And?" Tony said.

"And she was afraid of me. She thought I was going to *make* her come back; that I was coming to *drag* her back," said Dennis. "I will never forget how she looked at me. Never." It was as unvarnished a retelling as he'd given anyone, even Cordelia, and he felt again the blistering pain of her dark eyes on his face.

Tony held out a hand in an acquiescing gesture. "Now we can start. So, tell me about what's been happening with April."

Dennis's hand tightened on his glass at the sudden change in gears. He spoke slowly at first, as he packed his pain from losing Sonia back away. He explained about his games with April and about the distance he always sensed in her; about her fears and his unwillingness to close the gap. "I need to know she really wants to be with me," he said. "That I'm not just bulldozing her into it. And I don't want to hurt her. I don't want to make mistakes."

Tony nodded. "I understand that. But you *will* make mistakes. It's inevitable. And it's a pointless, preening kind of masculinity that thinks its power lies in always being right."

Dennis's jaw winched tight again; he wanted to argue that point. There was a world of difference between being careful and being arrogant. Wasn't there?

The other man continued: "The question is, when you make a mistake, how quickly do you acknowledge it, and how much will you sacrifice to make it right? That's something everyone should care about, but as a dominant, it's the measure of your quality. That's what I believe."

They both sat with that for a long moment. Dennis had no argument with anything Tony was saying. There was just a part of him, something in the core of him, that believed if he tried hard enough, he could avoid making the mistake in the first place. No matter what Cordelia or Tony said, it was hard to accept that that pain was inevitable. The stakes were too high.

Weren't they?

"You said you're going to be travelling?" Tony asked.

Dennis sighed. "Yeah. There's a work thing that…yeah, I'm going to be on the East Coast for a few weeks." He had to meet with the people at the data center and finalize the contract.

"Okay," Tony said. "We can talk on the phone, but I'd also like you to do some reading. 101 stuff. Some of it I'm sure you've picked up, but if there's any big holes in your knowledge it will help you identify them, and we can talk."

"Thanks," Dennis said, after a long and ungracious pause.

Tony nodded again. "I know it's not easy to ask for help. You're working hard to do the right thing. That's admirable. And I admit I was pushing your buttons a little, to see what your reactions were."

"Are we done with that part?" Dennis said, with a humorless smile.

"We are for now," the older man said serenely.

September

His trip to the East Coast lasted longer than he anticipated, as the data migration he'd fought for and staked his name on developed into a solid-gold nightmare. He'd contracted with a small but seemingly well-regarded company in New Haven, near corporate headquarters; when he arrived at their office to sign the final agreement, he found them glumly packing up their desks. He would later find that they'd been quietly acquired, loaded down with debt and then jettisoned by a larger competitor. The bankruptcy announcement had surprised the people he'd been talking to as much as him.

By dint of furious effort and a lot of legal threats, he managed to keep the time his company spent without email or network connectivity down to a couple of days, staggered a few days apart while he found a replacement to take the load while he looked for a more permanent solution. From then on, he handled everything personally until the migration was achieved, and that meant staying in New Haven.

He missed April.

Horribly, in the shuffle a large quantity of data just flat disappeared. None of it was necessary for active projects, thank God, but by federal statute they were required to keep it on file for ten years.

Dennis knew, but could not prove, that Graham's best buddy on the management team had left it on the wrong server despite numerous warnings *and* hadn't been making the required backups. It took every trick he knew to bring it back from the data netherworld with only minor losses.

Despite the chaos, he couldn't unplug totally to focus; he had too many other responsibilities. He gave O'Reilly and Graham regular updates and made sure to stay in the loop with Natasha. Outside of work, he managed to stay in touch with Tony Bulsara, his therapist and, most importantly, April. He didn't miss a check-in. It wasn't another responsibility on his endless list. It was his only respite.

It wasn't the same as being there in person, of course; the sex without smell or taste, the aftercare frustratingly distant, like trying to stroke a cherished pet with a plastic hand on the end of a stick. And most of all he missed the moments that were neither foreplay, action nor aftercare. The movies they didn't see together, the meals he ate alone, the bad jokes he saved up for text messages.

Her birthday was coming up. She flatly refused a birthday present, and he could tell she meant it, so he resignedly sent the jewelry to Caroline to thank her for her help and told her to exchange it for whatever she wanted.

But April's September birthday was the deadline for her denial, had been set for months, and he was determined to make it a good one for her. He'd had no intention of extending beyond this point, but there was no way he could fly back to Austin right now. Fixing this mess was like trying to untie a knot made out of snakes, and the first rule was to never take your eye off the snakes.

The least he could do was make this call memorable.

He dressed up for it, in the best suit he'd brought on this trip. Ironically, most of his time at the data center was spent in khakis and polo shirts. But for her he wanted to gleam. He didn't send her any instructions for her wardrobe this time—he genuinely hadn't had time to plan an outfit—and she turned up wearing a surprisingly sober denim shirtdress. She seemed low-key, as if there was something on her mind, but his initial conversational probing didn't give him anything. To tell the truth, he was pretty excited about his own idea and moved past the preliminaries quickly.

"I thought we'd try something different this time," he said offhandedly.

Her eyes narrowed in suspicion, and rightfully so. "Oh?"

She'd told him about her encounter with Sandra Barreras, although she'd been sparing about the details; it was within the rules of their arrangement not to tell him beforehand. Hell, it was within the rules not to tell him at all. They weren't exclusive and orgasming had never been on the menu. But he felt...*motivated* to show her Sandra wasn't the only one capable of delightful sadism. He wanted to be everything she needed.

He tilted the camera forward and leaned in, trying to spear her eyes with his over two thousand miles. "Beg me *not* to let you come. Convince me you want to live without orgasms. If I find you believable, I'll let you come. If you seem like you're pretending, another month."

"You're evil," she breathed. Whatever distractions she'd

brought to the call were long gone now; she looked absorbed, aroused and a little horrified.

"Happy birthday," he said, and grinned at her. He had her, he knew. Even over the distance, he could feel the energy beginning to swarm between them. Beyond his own arousal and engagement in the moment, he felt a giddy pride as he waited for her to start. He'd wanted to give her something special for her birthday and he'd nailed it.

"Um…" She swallowed. "I don't…really even, want to. I mean, it's only been four months. Who cares?" she said with false brightness. "I'm fine. Please don't let me come, Sir." She smiled at him.

"Hm… I find it hard to believe you. Why don't you edge for me and try again?"

She seemed to laugh despite herself as she reached off-camera for her Magic Wand. "Of course, Sir."

As she unbuttoned her dress, he opened his fly and began to stroke himself. "I miss your body," he said, and she ducked her head. Under the dress she wasn't wearing a bra, only delicate pink panties with lace panels over the hips. "Pinch your nipples, lovely." She did so, and he shook his head. "No, do it like I would if I could." This time she cried out, and her legs fell open. "Perfect. You're perfect."

She lifted the wand and switched it on. "You can't keep saying things like that, Sir."

"Why not?"

"What if… God…what if I believed you?" Her eyes kept flickering; wanting to close, wanting to watch him on the screen. He slipped back his foreskin and brushed his thumb over the sensitive skin.

"What if you did?"

"I might…mm…get a big head." She was still in her panties, rubbing the vibrating wand over herself through the fabric. "I might get the idea a hot number like me can... Fuck! Come whenever I want."

"Hm, but that's fine," he said. "Because you don't want to come, do you?"

She swallowed. "Oh no, Sir, not a-at all." Her voice broke a little on that. "Fuck," she whispered.

"Let me hear you moan," he said. "I want to hear how bad you...don't want it."

She was half-sitting on the knob now, the switch flipped to the more intense setting, rocking back and forth. "God, I don't want it *so bad*, Sir. It's all I can think about."

He laughed at that. "All you can think about is not coming."

"Yyyyes," she panted. "How I'm not coming for you. I walk around all day thinking about that, how I'm not allowed to come. How you won't let me. How lucky I am that you won't let me."

She squeaked and lurched away from the vibe, gasping. "Too close. Toooo close, too close."

She took a moment to recover before she gingerly reached for it again; he slowed down accordingly. It was too hot, otherwise; he was going to explode. "I think I almost believed that. Perhaps I will let you," he said, but her eyes told him she knew a test when she saw one. Clever girl.

"No, please, Sir. I'm in the groove now. I could go..." She winced. "I could go forever."

"Really? What will you do for me, if I let you stay under my control?" he asked, his voice sharper than he meant. God, he was getting close himself.

"I'll—" She got a wild light in her eyes as she began to tease herself more. "I'll do whatever you want."

"Not nearly specific enough..."

"I'll spend all your money!" she gasped. "On frilly, slutty

things I can't even wear out of the house." She leaned forward on the wand again and yelped. "But I will. I'll wear them wherever you want. You can show me off." She was rocking again, her eyes staring through the screen, a perfect picture of desperation. Perfect. Perfect.

"You can put a collar on me and lead me through Frankie's. Through downtown. Through our work. Ah God!" She winced but held on. "Please!"

"Please what, dolly?"

"Please don't let me come," she said, and it was almost a sob. "I'll tell everyone how good your control is. I'll tell every sub in the bar. I'll tell my friends. I— Ohhh!"

She yanked the wand away and shuddered; at the same moment he spilled over, semen exploding all over his hand and into a hastily snatched Kleenex. He closed his eyes for a long moment as his orgasm crashed through him and she whimpered, watching. "Oh, that's my good girl."

When he opened his eyes, she was drinking bottled water like it was going out of style. "You were perfect," he said. "What a nasty imagination you have. Are those the things you fantasize about when you're all needy for me?"

"Maybe," she giggled. "Maybe sometimes."

"Well, I won't make you do anything like that," he said. "But I will grant your wish. You may go without coming for a little while longer. We'll revisit when I'm back in town."

She groaned inwardly and said, "Thank you, Sir," from behind a wobbly smile.

They talked for a little while after that, about her plans and his ongoing headaches. He made sure she was grounded and cheerful and fluttering her hands adorably again before he relaxed.

She was going to Frankie's that weekend; he tried not to let that bother him. He wasn't a jealous person by nature. It did rankle him; but he had no right to jealousy. He hadn't told her that he wanted to be her lover, not just another friend to play with. And a Zoom call wasn't how he was going to do it, either, so he summoned the grace the situation required. Once he was sure she wouldn't sub drop, he put her to bed; she had D&D in the morning.

The next morning, he headed for a fun-filled Saturday at the data center. But he was making headway, he was certainly making headway. He was typing up a status update for O'Reilly when a text appeared on his phone.

April: i told them

He snatched up the phone.

Dennis: Excuse me?

April: i told my friends what a dirty little pervert i am

Jesus Christ. He dialed her as quickly as he could, almost fumbling the phone in his anxiety.

"Hello?"

"April. Did you not know that was a fantasy? When I asked what you'd do, I never meant—"

"No," she said, and laughed softly over the line. "No, I wanted to. I don't talk about my kinks much but... I can tell them anything. I know that. I guess I knew it all along."

He took his first breath in a minute. "How do you feel?" he asked. In truth, he'd never told anyone outside of the kink world but his therapist.

"Good," she said, and sounded like she meant it. "I gave

away some of my old stuff, and Elena has a contact at the clothing exchange, too."

"Oh." He was glad she felt good about it. His own feelings were…mixed, but he wasn't sure he was in the right to feel that way. It wasn't fair to project his guilt about Sonia here, but if anything, this felt worse. At least Sonia had had family to turn to when she left their home with nothing left of her old life.

He didn't want April to ever feel that way about him. But if she ever did— Well. It was certainly something to save for a face-to-face conversation, if he brought it up at all. Maybe he should just keep it to himself.

"Well. I guess you earned your orgasm, all right," he said, trying to smile. It was disappointing, he really wanted to be there, but he'd asked what she'd do for an orgasm and she'd sure the hell done it.

"I don't want to."

He realized his jaw was open. "You don't—"

"I want to do it when you want me to. And I don't want to do it alone." She sounded astounded at herself, too.

"You're a very very very good girl," he said, suddenly wanting her more than he ever had before. Her faith and confidence in him, her sweet trusting obedience, felt like cool water on a hot day. It was a tremendous responsibility, and he should have felt the weight of it; instead, he felt like he'd been given wings. She was everything he'd ever dreamed of in a sub and in a woman. "You're my *best* girl."

He couldn't get back to Austin soon enough. He needed her, not just for a night or for a scene. He needed her and he needed her to know.

October

When he got back, he and April saw each other at Frankie's about as soon as humanly possible. Unfortunately, they'd had a bit of a fight—she'd called him out for being insecure about her giving clothes away, for projecting his past with Sonia onto her. She'd seen right through him, God.

He thought it had resolved cleanly, though. He'd apologized and explained, the most he'd ever told her about Sonia. She had relaxed and talked a little about the things on her own mind. She'd been having a nasty time at work, something she almost never spoke about, and he thought he'd been appropriately sympathetic.

Next time, he told himself. Next time there would be no fight and no ugly work drama, and he would tell her he couldn't go on without her any longer.

But since that night, she hadn't responded to email or text. Well—that wasn't quite true, was it? He had a text from Sunday, a response to a meme he'd sent her. If "lol" was a response. But nothing since then, and most of a week had passed. He'd even sent a couple of follow-up messages, which wasn't usually his style. Nothing. Dread began to nibble at his toes.

It wasn't a great week, anyway. He didn't enjoy firing people, had almost entirely lost his stomach for it after the Help Desk bloodbath, and he'd had to fire one of the lead developers when he got back. He'd warned them that he wasn't joking, that they were going to have to start using proper Agile project development with real two-week sprints and daily Scrums or he was going to lay down the law. They'd had months to get it together.

Bob Flowers had been on a Performance Improvement Plan, and at this point was openly defying Dennis's direction. He'd had to go. It hadn't helped Flowers's case that his file was full of warnings for both inappropriate behavior and technical mistakes, even by the rather lax standards of the pre-Dennis era. But he'd been well liked by some of the developers, and Dennis had picked up some grumbling.

Fatima Nayeem had brought him cookies, though.

He'd seen Graham and the man had been gruff, if not openly hostile. He'd made an oblique reference to Dennis rescuing his project data, but Dennis couldn't tell if it was meant to be a parting shot at the migration for putting it at risk in the first place or a rather clumsy attempt at a thank-you. It certainly hadn't stopped Graham from fighting viciously for more than his fair share of the budget in the 6Q budget planning meetings.

He'd had to leave the contractors unsupervised at his house for six weeks. He had come back to the wrong cabinets and other projects on hold until he could give his opinion about one meaningless thing or another, most of which he'd already specified somewhere in the endless correspondence. Sometimes he had fantasies of burning the place down and buying a prefab McMansion in Leander.

Mostly it was April, though. He'd followed up a few times, with no response, and he was beginning to genuinely worry. Thursday morning his phone buzzed with a text, and he snatched it. It wasn't her; was an unknown number. He almost didn't read it, but the teaser line from the app caught his eye and dragged him. If you don't know it, April is...

He opened it.

Unknown Number: If you don't know it, April is getting electrolysis in Dallas today and she's having a pretty bad time. I imagine you don't know because she's stubborn as a mule. Someone should be there with her.

He froze for a long moment, then texted back.

Dennis: Who is this?

Unknown Number: I don't want to get in the middle of it, but I thought you should know.

Didn't want to get in the middle of it?! He called the number. And very faintly, heard a phone ringing nearby.

What the fuck?

He followed the sound out of his office, and whoever it was hung up, but he just called them again. He could hear it better now, and followed the ringtone to—

"Fatima?" He was not normally a fan of appearing over

the wall of people's cubes like an angry giant, but there were times it was called for.

"Shit," she said, and dropped her phone. Cleared her throat. "Good morning."

"What the fuck is going on?" he asked. He was honestly pretty proud he kept his voice under control.

"Maybe we should talk in your office?" she said.

"That's probably wise." His mind was racing. Was he going to have to fire Fatima? How in hell was she texting him about April? How did she even know April, and how did she know he and April were connected?

What the fuck was going on?

In his office he closed the door, settled behind his desk and exhaled. She'd been back more than a week, but it was still odd seeing her not-pregnant; she'd practically been pregnant as long as he'd known her. Without ten pounds of baby she was tiny. She looked embarrassed but not afraid.

"Fatima," he said again, meaningfully.

"April is a good friend of mine," she sighed. "She didn't tell me you two were an item until a few days ago, though."

"I don't know what she told you," he said, wincing, "but I doubt she said we're an item."

"No, she's silly that way, isn't she?" Fatima agreed. "I think she just can't believe anyone would ever choose her."

"…how much did she tell you?" he demanded. This could be…disastrous. He was struggling to process it, to even absorb the fact that someone he saw every day was also in April's life. What were the odds on that? It didn't quite seem real yet.

"Not very much," said Fatima soothingly. It did not soothe him. "But enough to make it clear you've been a big part of her life these past months."

"April's not answering my calls, Fatima. I'm sorry if she's

having a bad time with electrolysis, but if she wanted me there, she'd tell me."

"No, that's the very last thing she'd do." Fatima shook her head. "You tipped your hand, you know. She knows you really care about her now and she's scared. Now she's in Dallas having a very bad day and she's stuck there overnight, and the one person she wants to help her she thinks she can't tell."

He barely heard the second part of her statement as darkness descended in his head. She was scared. She ran away. April had run away from him, was trying to escape him. "If she doesn't want to talk to me, I won't force myself on her, Fatima. I don't chase women." *Not anymore.*

She shook her head at his foolishness, at the foolishness of all men. "Well. I tried. Am I in trouble, Mr. Martin?"

"You're not—" He pinched the bridge of his nose. "No, you're not in trouble. How the hell did you get my cell phone number?"

She shrugged. "It was on your resume." Ah.

"Please go," he said wearily.

She looked like she had more to say, but for a blessing she held her tongue and left. A moment later, though, his phone buzzed with the address for the clinic.

He wanted to put his head down on the desk and scream. This was the third of these appointments since he'd met April and he knew approximately what went into them. The only clinic in the state that did all-day, full-face electrology was in Dallas, a short flight away, so April got up at 5 am and flew to Dallas and usually came back the same day. She didn't usually complain about it, but he knew it was painful.

Was today worse than usual? April had never hinted she wanted him there—had in fact been adamant he not see her before or after. She had to grow out her facial hair in advance and for days after, she said, her face was a mess. He'd always respected her sensitivity around it.

He had to do that now. He wasn't going to chase her. He didn't chase women. He was cured of that.

He tried to take deep breaths. He tried to center himself back in the present, not in the past or the future. He tried to remember what Tony had told him.

The thing about making mistakes is they teach us lessons, but they aren't always the right ones. Every sub is different and if you're always reliving the last mistake, you'll make new ones.

Was that what he was doing? She didn't want him there, did she? What if she did? Damn it. Damn it.

He had another budget meeting at three o'clock.

His phone told him there were hourly flights to Dallas on Southwest.

Damn it.

Between driving to the airport, waiting for the flight, flying, renting a car, driving in Dallas—all told it was 4 pm before he walked into the clinic. Lots of time to stew and stress and fret and wind up back at the same decision.

The lady behind the front desk looked up when he entered and asked if he had an appointment. He could hear someone sobbing in another room.

"No," he said. "I'm…here for someone. I'm her ride."

Part IV: April & Dennis

April

When April got to work on Monday and discovered Bob Flowers had been fired, her first reaction wasn't one that made her proud. It was brief, flaming, vindictive joy, a primal feeling of victory. *You fuck with me, my man will fuck you* up.

Except that was barbaric, and regressive, and anyway, he wasn't her man. And a person, a real flesh-and-blood person, was now out of work because of something she said to a third person, and in fact maybe she kind of wanted to throw up.

I shouldn't have that kind of power! No one should have that kind of power, but especially not me! Yes, Born-Again Bob was awful, but...maybe he had kids. Maybe he did prison ministry or...or something. And even if he was just as awful as he seemed and deserved to be fired, he should be fired because of a policy or a rule, not because he pissed off a powerful man by causing problems for his...

Fucktoy, whispered the cruelest part of herself. It was a word it had begun wielding recently to describe her relationship to Dennis. Dennis who dressed her up and played with her and then put her away while he ran off for months. Dennis who could hire and fire regular people like her and Bob Flowers without even thinking about it. It was terrifying. It was...

Kind of hot?

No! No, no, no, no.

And how did Dennis know she was talking about Bob Flowers, anyway? How long had he known they both worked here? Had he been keeping tabs on her work life?

She felt like she was having a panic attack, something that hadn't happened in years. She thought she had some emergency medication at home, but that didn't do her a lot of good right now. She tried to do the breathing exercises her therapist told her to do, but she couldn't remember how it went.

She went to therapy weekly, she loved her therapist, she carefully cultivated a good relationship with her therapist because he controlled the letters that determined her access to health care, and only now was she realizing that maybe she should have told him about Dennis, or Frankie's, or her kinks at all.

Thank God Fatima was back from maternity leave.

AFrench: I know it's way too early for lunch but I have to talk to you.

FNayeem: What's going on, hon? Is it hot gossip? Please tell me it's hot gossip.

"That," said Fatima, her mouth hanging open, "is some hot gossip. *Damn*, girl!"

It was twenty minutes later, and they were in the windowless room where Fatima went to pump milk several times a day. With no one else to see her, April very nearly had her head between her knees. In her bewildered and numbed state, she'd spilled everything. *Everything.* Fatima hadn't seemed shocked, exactly, but she did seem to have become the physical manifestation of a gif of a woman eating popcorn.

"What am I going to *do?*" April hissed.

"Well, what is there to do? Born-Again Bob is gone—too bad, so sad, no one is sorry—and now your secret is out. He's obviously not mad."

"He could still be mad. He could be mad at me and at Bob. He's chivalrous like that."

"Chivalry is holding the door for you, girl. This is…something else. Still, though. Good for you."

"No!" April said. Almost shouted. "Not good for me! This is the opposite of good for me. It is…scary."

"Why?"

"What do you mean, why?"

"Why is it scary?"

"Because…" She gestured vaguely, clawing the air. "Because if he can fire Bob for upsetting me, what's stopping him from firing me if he gets sick of me?" Even as she said it, she knew that wasn't the real reason.

Fatima rolled her eyes as she switched breasts. "That's silly. Because first, you work for Leo Graham, and those two hate each other. If Dennis wanted you fired, Graham would probably promote you. Second, you really think he's going to do that?"

"Well how should I know! I didn't think he'd fire Bob." She didn't *really* think Dennis would fire her. But everything had just turned upside down. She couldn't think straight. He wouldn't. And he couldn't. So why couldn't she breathe?

"He fired the whole Help Desk," said Fatima pragmatically.

April glared. "How does that make this better?"

Fatima shrugged. "You trust him, don't you? I mean, you let him tie you up and all this, you must trust him."

"I...yes, I trust him," April said, more quietly. "He wouldn't hurt me." Her mind was racing with a lot of paranoid thoughts, but she knew that, really. It wasn't being punished she was really afraid of. It was the inevitable conversation, the terrible admission, the humiliating apology. The impossible wait for him to shut her out of his life. And she'd deserve it this time, wouldn't she?

"Then why would he fire you? You're not making sense, honey. You're spiraling."

"I lied to him," she said, finally spitting it out. "I kept this from him. For almost six months. And now he knows. God, how long has he known? I..."

She shook her head. "I can't face him. And, and...it's not just at the club or in my phone I can't face him. He's *in the building*. Oh my God, what did I do?" Every day for six months she'd painstakingly built this time bomb, and now it had finally gone off in her face.

She drew her hands down her face; felt her makeup smear and cringed internally. She couldn't do this. She had to get out of this situation—and incidentally, wouldn't it be great to never attend a Scrum meeting again? "I think I have to quit."

It sounded incredibly appealing...right up until she said it out loud. As soon as it was out of her mouth, though, she was visualizing walking into a conference room for an interview with someone she'd never met and asserting, yes, my name *is* April, I do use she/her pronouns, no, this isn't a joke. No. No, no, no.

"Except... I can't quit. Because. I can't go on an interview looking like this. And a Texas company won't be required to cover my trans stuff. And…" She was definitely hyper-ventilating.

"Hey. Hey. Hey. Look at me." She trained her terrified eyes on Fatima, who locked gazes and gripped her hands. "Here's what you're going to do. You're going to go home. I will tell John you went home sick. After work, I will bring you your laptop. You were going to work from home most of this week anyway, because of your electrology appointment, right?"

She nodded. She never wanted anyone to see her while she was growing her facial hair out.

"That's the rest of the week. A week from now, you will be able to breathe, and we will find a solution. I promise. You are not alone, April. You are going to be okay."

"Okay," she whispered. She couldn't imagine what that solution would look like, but she clung desperately to the idea that if she got through this week something would present itself.

She tried her best to not think about, to put it entirely out of her mind and pretend life was normal. She tried to ignore the texts from Dennis. She tried to get work done. It was one of the worst weeks in her life.

And then on Thursday, she'd flown to Dallas, into what became the best day so far.

It didn't start that way. It started badly. Extremely badly. By 4 pm she was sobbing in the electrology clinic while the technician stood by awkwardly. That was when she heard a voice in the waiting room.

In a deep rumble, it said: "No, I'm here for a patient. I'm her ride." And it said, *I'm here*. And it said, *You're safe*. And it said, *What if?*

And she said tentatively, "Dennis?"

Dennis

Hearing her voice, Dennis began to walk towards the room, moving at a deliberate pace. The urge to rush to her side was fighting with his fear; he didn't know how he was going to be received, after all. There was a part of him that was certain chasing a woman was never the right decision, that her eyes would hold the same fear that Sonia's had.

In fact, he didn't see any expression on her face, because she was hiding inside her shirt, the neck pulled up over her nose so only her enormous eyes peeked out. She was in jeans and a plain, baggy T-shirt, with ratty sneakers he couldn't remember ever seeing before. Her hair was tied back in a ponytail that also disappeared into the shirt at the moment.

"Dennis?" she said again, still laced with disbelief and a thousand other emotions. There were tear tracks on her face, disappearing into her collar. She looked forlorn and wounded, and it tore something in him. Did she go through this every two months, alone? That was…unacceptable. *Not ever again,* he told himself. Never again alone.

The scrub-clad young technician seemed professionally sympathetic, but also like she saw this kind of thing a lot. Her expression lightened when Dennis entered. "I'll leave you two alone," she said, and vanished.

"Hey," he said, trying to hold his chill. Hoping he was projecting only calm and affection instead of the cocktail of longing and fear he'd been mixing all through his flight. "I brought you something." The pashmina was never going to make the all-time greats of things he had bought her, although since he had grabbed it at the airport the cost per square inch was probably competitive with some lingerie. Its primary virtue lay in the fact that April was able to wrap it around her neck and shoulders and cover the lower part of her face.

"Of course you did," she said, with something like humor in her voice. Her eyebrows, at least, suggested she was amused.

"Fatima said you were having a bad time and could use a…friend," he said.

"She shouldn't have done that," April said quietly.

"You're going to have to stay overnight?"

"Yeah. I…we got started late," she said, in a fragile tone of voice. "And we weren't able to finish. So I have to come back in the morning. Only I'm supposed to be working from home tomorrow and I didn't bring my laptop because it was just supposed to be in and out and I don't have a hotel reservation or my meds or a-anything." Her voice cracked a bit, then evened out.

She took a slow breath, and then another. "I'm really fine. I just got a little overwhelmed."

He nodded. The longer they went without her telling him to get out, the steadier he felt, and the more the eager problem-solving parts of his brain clicked into place. "We'll find a hotel, and the world isn't going to end if you call in sick. I did it four hours ago, and I promise, the sky didn't fall.

"And we'll get you some clothes to wear for tomorrow, if you're worrying about that. You know I'm good at that." He smiled wryly and was heartened when her eyes brightened above the scarf. "I may have to see your face at some point, though," he said.

"No thank you," she whispered, but her eyes were bright with relief. The two-inch strip of her visible to him looked shattered with weariness and gratitude.

This was the right call, he thought, his heart climbing down out of his throat. *No matter what happens, it was worth it for that.* All the anxieties piled up in his chest evaporated, and he felt one hundred pounds lighter as he went to handle logistics.

As it turned out, this kind of thing *did* happen a lot, and the clinic had standing relationships with certain hotels in the area. The receptionist even offered to have a shuttle sent around, but Dennis told her he had a rental car. April was effusive in thanking the receptionist and the technician; he didn't understand why she was quite so over the top until they got in the car.

"I came on the wrong day," she muttered into the pashmina, nudging it up to wipe her eyes. "Just…a pure fuck-up. I always do it on Thursdays and work from home Friday, so I have more time to recover before work. But I guess I scheduled it for Friday this time. They had to call someone to come in on her day off to help. That's why we started late."

"Anybody could make a mistake like that," he said, trying to watch her and drive in the unfamiliar city at the same time. The pashmina had obviously comforted her, but it was making it damn hard for him to monitor her mood.

"I can't believe you came," she said, not for the first time.

She looked battered; not just her face, which he hadn't seen yet, but how she held herself. She seemed...wounded.

His first thought had been that he'd never seen her dressed so carelessly, with so little work put into her appearance, but with more time to think about it he realized that her appearance was as deliberate as ever. It was an outfit designed to hide in, to project androgyny and say *please don't look at me.*

It wasn't working on him. All he could see was the fragile, long-suffering woman hiding inside the clothes, and all he wanted to do was hold her and shield her from the heartless world.

"Let's talk about it in a little bit," he said. "Just rest." She nodded and looked down at her phone.

The hotel was not far away, fortunately. Dennis handled the check-in and let her hang back, but the concierge seemed to realize they were together. "How many in the room, sir?" she said pointedly.

"Two," he said, providing his driver's license.

She nodded and gestured towards April. "I'll need to see his ID, too."

Dennis was having a bit of a long day by this point, and for a moment his vision flashed red as rage reached for the steering wheel. "I'm paying for the room, not *her*," he ground out pointedly.

"Yes, sir, but it's our policy—"

"It's okay," April whispered, and handed over the ID. The concierge's eyes flickered from it to her.

"I'm sorry but I'll need to see—"

"I understand." Her voice was tiny. She unwound the pashmina, keeping eye contact with Dennis. He had a split second to decide if she would rather he look away, but he kept his eyes on hers.

She looked like she'd been through the wars. Her upper lip

especially was red and swollen already, and most of her face was puffy and angry-looking. There were deep blue lines of bruise along her cheekbones. The skin on her lower neck was apparently untouched, and lightly scattered with whiskers.

Without thinking, he moved closer to her and slipped an arm around her waist. The urge to say something acid to the concierge rose up, but he felt like it would only embarrass her more.

The concierge coughed. "Everything seems to be in order here. Have a nice day." April wrapped the scarf back around her neck but didn't bother covering her face as they proceeded to the hotel room.

He tried to be solicitous but unobtrusive once they got there; hung up her jacket and his, before taking a seat on the bed. "I know it's been a long day," he said. "Do you want to take a nap and I'll run out and get the things on the list?" The clinic had provided a sheet of what he couldn't help thinking of as aftercare supplies; icing her face off and on would keep down the swelling, and ibuprofen would help with the pain.

"Yes please," she said, still in that tiny voice from the lobby.

"Hey," he said, wavering, half into his jacket. "Ah... I'll be right back."

"Okay," she said. She was paused in the act of pulling back the blanket, watching him, as if he was about to say something.

Maybe because he was, he realized. He let the jacket slip off his shoulder and puddle in his hands. "I didn't come just because I'm your friend," he said. "I want to be more than that. I want to be the one who comes for you every time. I want to be the first one you call. You're not just somebody I play with, April. You're..."

"Your best girl?" she said, tears in her eyes but a lilt of

humor in her voice. Trying to joke her way away from the tension in the room.

He dropped his eyes, then looked up and found hers again. "What if you were my only girl?"

Almost immediately, he regretted dropping it on her in this situation. It was just unbearable not to say it. But now they were stuck together, and she might feel pressured—

"Yes please," she said softly, her hands tight on the coverlet.

God, he did love it when she said *yes*.

April

She'd never seen Dennis at a loss for words before. So much of their relationship was wrapped up in games of control, where he at least pretended to be unflappable and in control all the time. But now the dynamic was reversed, as a slow giddy smile spread over his face and she vibrated with internal emotion.

"Okay. Okay then!" He laughed. "I'll..." He looked at his jacket, still in his hands. "I'll be right back. Don't go anywhere. Please." Joy was flaming on his face, and when he turned to leave, she could still read it in the set of his shoulders and the cock of his head. For her! He was so happy to have *her*, when he could have had anyone.

April sunk down to the bed, her head swimming. She was exhausted, her face was hot and aching and swollen, and the manifold humiliations of the day hung on her. Yet bliss was welling up inside her, from the very center of her. It seemed impossible.

She waited for the hateful voice in her head to tell her it *was* impossible. But for once it was silent. She felt hideous and miserable. If Dennis could look at her like this and say he didn't want anyone else, she had to believe him.

He hadn't said anything about the six-month omission of their common employer. On the other hand, he hadn't said anything about firing Bob Flowers for her, either. Maybe... maybe those were just things to not be discussed?

She took off her shoes and got under the covers, thinking she had to at least text Fatima, and promptly passed out. When she woke up Dennis was back. He had...more bags than he ought to. Of course he did.

"Hey," she said in a scratchy voice that made her wince. But what the fuck. He was looking at her facial hair right now. All dignity was behind her.

"Hey lovely," he said. He seemed like the cat that ate the canary and made a significant dent in the indigenous wildlife besides. "I got us dinner. I thought cold sandwiches were the best bet."

How long had she been asleep? It was darkening outside now, and she was starving. "Yes please," she said, and his grin widened.

"I think I'll always love hearing you say that now," he said.

She found a spark of mischief in the embers and said, "What about 'Yes Sir'?"

"We can alternate," he said, handing her a wrapped sandwich. Then his expression turned serious, as it could on a dime. "You know it's not just that, though, right? I mean, we didn't exactly spell things out."

She examined the sandwich and carefully removed the tomatoes. She could feel his silent regard and it made her feel

warm and seen; she was willing to bet he'd never bring her a
sandwich with tomatoes on it again. "I guess not," she said.
"Are you my boyfriend?" She tried to make it sound light,
but it stuck badly in her throat.

This was the part where he told her she'd gotten confused, right?

"Yes," he said, definitively.

"And my...oh, I don't really care for Master," she said,
thinking. His expression indicated he was on the same page
about that one.

"We can just say I'm your dom. And you're my precious,
beautiful doll."

She flushed. She didn't feel the least bit precious or beautiful. Except when he said it, it was as if she slipped sideways
for a moment into an alternate life where she was both those
things.

"As well as my girlfriend. Sounds good?"

"Yes please. Sir. Yes-please-Sir," she said, giggling a bit.
"Jesus, this day!"

"I'm sorry it was such a cluster," he said, and she had to
laugh, because he really had no idea.

Did she really want him to know about this? On the other
hand, if he was going to be her boyfriend, that meant she
had to tell him things like this. No—it meant she *got* to tell
him things like this, it meant she had someone to tell when
things like this happened.

"I got groped by the TSA," she said, and his face darkened.
"What?"

"Oh, they have to push a button on the scanner. Like a
male or female button? And I looked," she gestured, "like
this, so they hit M, but of course my bra showed up, so they
did a pat-down. But I really feel like he could've figured that
out without going up front. And then he said, *you can go Sir,*

and I was feeling hoppy, so I said, *ma'am*, and he gave me the get-the-fuck-out-of-here thumb jerk." She demonstrated.

She was trying to keep her voice light, just another fun adventure in transing your gender, but from his expression she must not be doing very well.

"Please don't try to get him fired," she said quietly.

"What? No," he said. "Just thinking. I'm sorry. I'm sorry that happened."

"It's okay. Can't blame him." His face said he differed. She pushed on. "And then I thought I saw my ex-wife."

"Jesus." He shook his head. "Was it her?"

"Oh Lord, I don't know, I ran across the food court and hid," she said, laughing, and again he didn't laugh. "I'm making too big a deal of it," she said quickly. "It was just a lot piling up."

He moved across the bed, and she shifted the remains of her sandwich to make space for him. He embraced her from the side, one arm between her and the wall and the other wrapping around her waist to squeeze, then falling into her lap. "You're not making too big a deal of it. Thank you for telling me." He released her, but stayed close, and she leaned back into him. "I know you don't like to talk about her, especially."

"I can," she said. She put one of her hands over his, and wished it was smaller. Wished and wished. "I'll try to, more." She closed her eyes and let herself melt into the heat of his body against hers. The anxiety of giving up the truth gave way to the relief of not being alone with it anymore. She spent so much time second-guessing herself and minimizing her injuries. His fury and desire to protect her was everything she had ever wanted.

(And if that had cost Bob Flowers his job? Too bad, so sad.)

They sat like that a long moment, and then she asked tentatively, "How long did you want...this?"

"Did I want you?" he asked, his voice close to her ear and sending a shiver up her spine. She'd rarely felt less sexual, but sensual? Sure. She wanted to sink into him like a bath. "Pretty much right away. But you didn't want to be exclusive."

"I didn't say that," she protested, playing with his fingers. "I said being exclusive never worked for me."

A laugh, again huffed right into her ear and making her tingle. "I see I'll have to pay closer attention," he said, and the thought of him paying *closer* attention to her made her feel like she was melting. Evaporating. "Is that because of her?" he asked.

"I guess. The same way you didn't push because of *your* her, huh?"

He made a quiet sound of acknowledgment. "Yes. My relationship with Sonia, it wasn't...safe. I thought she was okay with everything, and when I found out she wasn't, it... wrecked me. I didn't want to take any chances. I didn't want to push."

She drew in a deep breath and shifted to settle further into his arms, letting his body backstop her. "I can tell you why I needed a push," she said. "If you want. You showed me yours."

She prayed he wouldn't ask her to, and then when he said, "Only if you want to. You've had a hell of a day already," she knew that she needed to say it. Her damn brain!

"I married Marie my senior year of college. We were both kinky and she was my domme from the beginning," she said, speaking quietly but trying not to go too fast, knowing she would want to sprint through it and trying to rein herself in. It was just agonizing, to remember how happy she had been, how sure she had been that things were going to work out.

She'd had so many pictures of the future in her head back then, and even if she wouldn't trade her present for that imagined future, it hurt to look back and remember being so blindly hopeful. "And when I transitioned a few years later, she supported me. She was…great, at first. Mostly.

"But after a while she thought we should open up the relationship," she said, willing her voice not to waver. "She said I should have…a full range of experiences, as a woman, and she admitted she missed…a real man." She licked her lips.

"But it was a bad idea. She was…she was jealous. I've known other people with open marriages and plenty of people who are polyamorous, too, but I don't think she was really wired that way. It was something else."

It seemed like every time April got even a little attention, went on a date or got off a call giddy with the possibility of romance, Marie had gotten mad. And when Marie got mad, she got even.

"She would bring in other men, make me see it, and she never dominated *them*. But it was still all about control. Afterwards she would taunt me about it, ask me how it felt to see a real man fuck my wife."

"She was using them to hurt you," said Dennis, squeezing her tight. His emotions were opaque to her again, and for the moment she was glad. Hers felt big enough to take up the whole room. They had been compressed for a long time and now that they were out and full-sized again it seemed impossible she could ever put them back.

"I told her I never signed up for that…cuckold shit. And she…she told me she thought it was what I wanted. With my…my sissy games." Her voice shook there. Damn it. "So all along she had just seen it as…role-play. Kink. Not real. I was still her little subby husband, just in a dress."

She'd been so humiliated. So betrayed and furious. So

ashamed of her anger, which tasted like the poison of testosterone. She'd spent too many years trying not to be the
kind of man who yelled at his wife; being the kind of woman
who yelled at hers didn't feel right. But Marie had had no
such qualms. She'd gone scorched earth, and things she had
said still haunted April. She'd never loved conflict, but those
nights had made her terrified of it.

It had taken her years to assign blame to Marie, and even
now, it didn't come easily. She didn't want to be one of those
people who bitched about their ex-wife.

"I guess, in the end," she said, distantly, "it was my fault.
For letting the…lines blur, like that."

"No," he said fiercely, and hugged her again. "It's not
your fault. It was her job to keep the lines straight, it was her
job to know if it was safe to play that game and to ask if she
wasn't sure."

"Maybe it was just a mistake," she said softly. "People
make mistakes." She wondered if it was cutting too close to
his own issues.

"Maybe. But she's still responsible." Yeah, there was definite projection in that, in the vibrato and terseness of his voice.

"Dennis." She felt exhausted, but she couldn't let this pass.
"You really have to forgive yourself."

"I have," he said firmly. "But if Sonia never does, that's her
right. You don't have to forgive Marie. Frankly, *I* don't forgive her. This is a *responsibility*, damn it. You said before she
punished you for using your safeword. That's not forgivable."

He was right. She knew he was right, and she knew that
it was very possible Marie *knew* exactly what she was doing.
That she was just gaslighting April by pretending she thought
it was consensual. She had a mean streak. April had always
found that sexy until things went wrong. She didn't know if

she could forgive Marie. Could you forgive someone if you never quite managed to blame them?

"I, I… I don't know," she said, and she felt him relax his grip on her. It felt intentional, like if his brain hadn't told his arms to stop squeezing, he'd still be holding on for dear life.

"I'm sorry. We don't have to talk about this anymore if you don't want to."

"No, it's…that's almost the end of it. When she…said that, everything blew up. I moved out. Then after a while, I got sick of seeing her around town, at our places, and sick of everyone at work slipping and using my dead name and I just… left town with my tail between my legs."

He kissed the side of her head. "I think that was very brave."

No, I was weak, she thought. But was that the end of the world? She never promised anyone she was strong. What was so great about being strong, anyway? It felt like the most wonderful thing in the world to have a place where she could be weak and be loved, anyway. She hoped Dennis could understand that, that he didn't have to be fierce and protective and in control all the time. She wanted more than anything to be a safe place for him, and the regret for the six months of lies was something palpable, a lump in her throat.

"Hey," he said, and she ripped herself away from her internal thoughts, wondering what could be next. She never would've guessed, in a thousand years.

He ran his fingers over her scalp and through her hair. "Could I braid your hair?"

Dennis

He listened in mounting anger, quietly keeping it under control. She didn't need him to rage and stomp around, but God damn it was hard! How dare they! How dare any of these people? Her own wife!

He needed to calm down. And judging by her trembling, so did she. "Could I braid your hair?" He'd wanted to for a long time. He hoped she wouldn't think it was weird; he knew many people would.

But she turned to him and blinked, and said, "I'd love that." He got up to grab the bag of stuff he'd bought for just this eventuality as she slithered down in the bed.

"I didn't get you any products because I don't know what you use," he explained. "But your hair is pretty straight, it shouldn't be an issue."

"No, I never really put anything in it for a braid," she agreed, and lay back down with her head in his lap. He brushed her hair first, and she closed her eyes and let out a deep-seated sigh; her battered face began to relax. Her hair was soft and yes, mostly straight, with a sort of gentle wave. The texture was totally different from Sonia's or his sisters', but he could adapt his experience without much problem.

As he brushed her hair and slowly twined it into braids, he felt his temper ease and remembered he was happy. Actually, extremely happy. He laughed out loud, and she smiled and murmured, "What?"

"Nothing. I'm just in a good mood," he said. "You have so much beautiful hair. Have you been growing it out since your transition?"

"Oh, even before. I had a ponytail since high school. It's always been my one vanity," she giggled. "My dream is to one day be able to sit on it." She opened one eye and peered at him. "So is this more dolly kink?"

"Not really," he said. "I mean, I know it's not…that far off. But I just like taking care of people, it's not always kinky. I used to help braid my sisters' hair. Three Black girls take a lot of braiding." This was different from that—very different, since April wasn't screeching that Keisha stole her doll or snapping bubble ties at his nose—but there was the same gentle intimacy to it that softened him in a way that he associated with family and the smell of coconut oil.

"Did your mom teach you?" April asked.

"My dad, actually. He took a lot of pride in being able to do it. He always said a man who couldn't do everything his wife could was just a hired hand." His dad was a quiet man, always ready to go with the flow of the more hotheaded personalities in the Martin household, but there was a lot Dennis had learned from him. He was always there when you needed him, with exactly what you needed to get the job done. Unflappable and prepared for anything.

"He sounds like a cool guy," she said. She sounded adorably sleepy.

"He is. They're both pretty great parents. I was lucky. Jason's mom came around eventually, but he spent a lot of time hiding out at our place when he first came out." It was the gentlest of overtures; he felt confident Jason would forgive him.

"Yeah...my folks took it hard. I killed their son, you know." She grimaced, and he paused to stroke her scalp gently, trying to radiate gentleness and care down through his fingertips. "But my mom and I came out of it okay. Closer than we were, maybe. My dad doesn't know how to talk to me, but he never did."

"You mentioned you might be going home for Thanksgiving," he remembered. Thanksgiving was getting close, now.

"Oh. Yeah," she said, in a flat voice. "That's not happening. I wrote a coming-out letter to my grandma and I guess it didn't go well? I didn't listen to the whole voicemail this morning."

His hand stilled for a minute, and his heart ached for her, as it had for Jason all those years ago. He just couldn't understand families like that. "*Shit* you had a bad day."

She opened her eyes and looked up at him with a quirked smile. "It...got better?"

He resumed. "I'm sorry, lovely."

"It's okay. My mom says she just needs space, and she's probably right."

It was on the tip of his tongue to invite her home with him, but he held off for now. Bringing his white trans girlfriend to an enormous Black family holiday might be more stressful than kind. There would be some steep learning curves on both sides, no doubt, and there was always the Illinois of it all. He had faith in his immediate family and in April, but there were a lot of cousins...

He shook his head and focused on the present. "I'm sure she is. Here, sit up, doll."

He folded the braids up on her head, messily, just to pin them out of the way. "That should hold you through tomorrow, anyway." She leaned over and kissed him softly. He would've liked to go on doing that for hours, but he knew her face was sensitive, and there were still logistics to sort out.

"Thank you," she said.

"I got you some stuff to sleep in, too," he said, tossing her a soft nightgown from one of his bags.

"You're ridiculous," she laughed.

"I'm foresighted. I got you a few T-shirts to choose from for tomorrow." His smugness was partially affected—he knew she liked it—but he took a real pride in being able to think ahead and solve her problems before they even came up.

"Did you get me luggage? 'Cause I didn't even bring a carry-on."

"Oh, we're driving," he said, simply.

"Oh, we are?" She began to strip out of her clothes.

"Yes, we are."

She dropped the nightgown over her head. "What if I was looking forward to getting felt up by TSA?"

His hands wrapped around her hips, settling on her butt. "Oh, I'm taking over those responsibilities, too," he said.

Her lips smiled against his kiss. "Yes *please*."

April

The next day went a lot more smoothly. She only had another few hours of needlework left to go, and her neck was always easier than her face. She fingered the bruises on her chin as they sped along the highway back towards Austin; midday traffic was as light as it ever got in Dallas.

"Does it hurt a lot?" Dennis asked.

"The electrolysis itself doesn't hurt at all, actually," she said. "They numb you first. But they do *that* with a fuck-off big needle, and they have to keep inserting and re-inserting to squirt lidocaine in different directions. It feels like a sewing machine. The bruises are where I flinched." She smiled to show it wasn't a big deal, but she could tell he was starting to see through that one. Learning to let him see her flinch was going to be hard, but knowing he knew, and he cared, and wanted to protect her...that was worth it.

"I can't believe you've done this three times already since we met," he said, shaking his head.

"I'm used to pain," she said blithely.

He nodded. "I can see I'm going to have to take things up a notch."

She shivered pleasurably. "Just no needleplay, Sir."

"Absolutely not," he agreed.

They made it to Austin just in time for the evening traffic to kick in *there*. By the time they made it to her apartment downtown, Dennis was happy to stay there rather than battle the rest of the way south to his unfinished house.

She settled on the foot of the bed and began to ice her face. Dennis approached from behind and rubbed her shoulders.

"Mm, that feels nice."

"You ready for that orgasm?" he joked. He grinned at her when she fumbled the ice pack and almost dropped it.

"Um... I mean, I wasn't...uh, if you—"

He laughed. "Hey, I know you're pretty wrung out. What do you think about ordering in Chinese and watching a movie for tonight?"

"That sounds perfect," she said, and smiled.

"You don't have a TV, though," he pointed out. "Have we ever talked about how you don't have a TV?"

She smiled again. "I don't think so." The only time they'd spent this many consecutive hours together, it hadn't been in her space. "It's not like a snooty too-good-for-TV thing, I just don't have space."

"You do have space for six bookshelves, though."

"I watch a lot of TV!" she protested. "I just do it on my phone or laptop. Honestly, that's how I do most of my reading these days, I just keep my books around for sentimental value."

He gave her an affectionate squeeze. "Millennial."

"Aren't you a millennial, too?" She frowned.

"I really have no idea," he said. "You could mount a TV over there. I could do it for you."

She squealed happily and flopped backwards on the bed.

"Are you okay?" he asked, leaning down over her. She reached up and let her hands clasp behind his neck, drawing him even closer.

"I'm wonderful. I was just overcome by domestic warm fuzzies." Her mind was racing. Dennis was her boyfriend. Dennis was with her. Dennis was going to be here tomorrow, and the next day, and the next one. If she needed a TV mounted she could *call her boyfriend.*

God, did she even know how to be a girlfriend? She'd been a husband and, very briefly, a wife. She'd been a one-night stand, a friend with benefits and a rest stop. But a girlfriend?

Maybe they could figure it out together. They would have things to navigate. About race, about gender, about sexuality, about a full-time relationship that was also a kinky one. But maybe they could figure it out together.

He closed the gap between their lips and pressed a fast, chaste kiss to hers. "I could've hung a TV as your friend."

"No, that's way too intimate," she murmured, and pushed up with her elbows to chase down more kisses. Once she captured his lips she sank back again and pulled him with her. He kissed her more and more thoroughly, lips and then tongue exploring. The joy that had taken root in her chest at the words *my only girl* swelled again at her ribs, pressing against the confinement.

She hadn't felt joy like this in a long time, and it felt out of place now; there was a painful pressure in her chest as her heart swelled against the scars that kept it pinched and wary. There wasn't space for it. He came up for air and looked at her, brown eyes shadowed with concern.

"Does it hurt? Because of your face?"

It didn't hurt too much—no worse than a bad sunburn—but the question made her self-conscious. She bit her lip. "Maybe we should stop," she said reluctantly.

He slid down until he knelt at the foot of the bed, between her dangling legs, and lifted her Wonder Woman T-shirt to press a kiss to the soft curve of her stomach. She felt the rasp of his chin against the tender skin as he nuzzled against her, and she traced her nails over his scalp as he kissed her again and again. His fingers wrapped around the waistband of her jeans and tugged them down her legs, and she braced to lift her butt, letting him.

She didn't know where this was going, but she surrendered to him and the moment, let the feeling of being under his control wash over her again and crack open her chest to let the joy spill out all over.

He kissed her thighs, her knees, her calves, lifting each leg and pressing kiss after kiss against her skin, and she was glad again that he couldn't see her face, this time because she was crying. Again, it was more sensual than sexual, and the most tender thing anyone had every done for her. She wiped her eyes as he stood up and reached out a hand to draw her up from the bed to one more kiss. Then she went to find her laptop in a daze, as he called the Chinese place.

As if it mattered to her what they watched, as long as he kept touching her like that.

Dennis

When morning came on Saturday, they talked about going back to his place, but they never got around to it. He had packed a few extra shirts in his bag for Dallas. They made breakfast, and as he did his trick with the eggs once again, he reflected on the six months between that meal back in May and this overcast morning with thunder grumbling around the horizon.

He'd made a choice then and there that he wanted her in his life; not a commitment, but a decision to try. It had taken so much longer than he expected to gather his courage, and in the meantime, he'd been falling for her more and more. Now that long fall had ended, not in a crash but in her arms.

It didn't feel like starting a relationship, because they weren't. It felt like finally giving what had been growing between them a name.

When he'd woken up this morning, he'd watched her sleep.

By dint of vigilant icing, the swelling had gone down in her face, but her bruises had deepened, and more purple shadows had bloomed on her cheeks and chin. He knew she'd flinch away from his gaze when she was awake, so he soaked her up while her guard was down.

It was such a miracle to finally be with her, to be alone with her. The last six months had been so hectic and stressful, their encounters over-scheduled, his time always running out, his mind always racing and trying to figure out how to get to here. Now at last he'd made it, and his work was no longer eating him alive, and he was ready to slow down and enjoy this victory.

He knew Jason often went to South Padre Island to unwind, about seven hours south. He imagined taking her there, lying on the beach as the sun blazed on the Gulf of Mexico. She'd be self-conscious about the bathing suit he'd put her in, absolutely she would, but he was learning how to help her be brave. Hell, he'd pay for access to a private beach if he needed to.

Money couldn't solve everything, but it could do a lot. He felt again his solemn determination to change her life, to smooth the bumps and keep her safe. He couldn't heal her bruises but she would never have to go to Dallas alone again.

When he thought again about how she'd been treated by other lovers, he no longer even felt angry. He felt like the only person in a coalmine who knows what diamonds look like. And by God she was going to shine.

When breakfast was ready, they sat again at the counter to eat. "Sorry," she said. "I can go grab the folding table from storage, I just really only bring it out for D&D."

"It's fine," he said. "At least you *have* a kitchen counter."

She laughed and picked up a piece of bacon. "What's the latest ETA for your place?"

"It was five days ago, so… I don't want to talk about it," he said wryly. He had a voicemail from Reggie, but he hadn't checked it yet.

"You don't give up easy, do you?" she teased, and he reached over and tilted up her chin, carefully, carefully. Locked eyes with her.

"No," he said simply. She flushed, a tentative smile spreading over her expression.

She ate a little, then asked with a nonchalance he was beginning to recognize as posed, "Do you have plans for today?"

He wiped his mouth. "I've got to take the rental car back. After that…depends. You still want me to hang around?"

Another flushed and somehow shy smile. "You don't have to spend the whole weekend taking care of me."

Which was not, he realized, a no. "I like taking care of you. Hey," he said gently, finding her eyes again. "I mean it. You don't have to thank me, any more than you have to thank me for spanking you."

She had just taken a swallow of something, and sputtered for a second. "I do thank you for spanking me, though!"

He laughed. "Yes, but you know I enjoy it as much as you do, right?"

She nodded, ducking her head. "Well…if you want to hang around for the weekend, we could watch more *Utena*!" she said brightly. "There's still the whole series."

"Does anybody turn into a car?" he asked. Last night she'd selected a very confusing anime that she'd explained was a film adaption of a TV show. He'd bobbed along in amused incomprehension as they ate in bed, and as she gently drifted into sleep. She'd been exhausted, and he'd finished it without her in the vain hope that the story would eventually explain…anything.

"Arguably?" she said. "But not explicitly."

He made a *tch* sound. "Well, that might be a dealbreaker."

They watched the first season; it *did* make more sense as a TV show, or at least the extra legroom gave the weirdness more room to breathe and build. "Is this translated badly?" he asked. "I mean, does that explain some of it?"

"I don't think so," she said cheerfully. "I think it's just like that." They were back on the bed, and she was leaning back against his chest with his arms around her, and he would've cheerfully watched anything like that. She was warm and soft and relaxed, and he was incredibly turned on by the touch of her skin against his. It felt like the tables had turned on teasing and denial, as she shifted gently against him.

Of course, he probably had some fault for confiscating her pajama pants. She was adorable in her T-shirt and panties, but his deferred arousal was a dull ache by now as a result. Soon, he thought. The last few days had been too turbulent to introduce an intense scene, and when he finally let her orgasm, he was determined it would be *intense*. Even if it meant punishing himself as much as her while they waited.

When his head was swimming with magical curry and upside-down castles in air, they took a break to eat some dinner, and then it was his turn to introduce her to something new. He found David Chang's cooking/travel/culture documentary *Ugly Delicious*, and started with the barbecue episode.

"I kinda prefer nonfiction over fiction," he admitted. "Especially cooking shows."

"Do you cook a lot?" she asked.

He laughed. "Not lately. But yeah, I like cooking. Not just eggs. I thought about studying it, but technology felt more practical."

"We're very practical people," she said, so solemnly that it cracked him up.

They spent another chaste night side by side. In the morning they ordered in breakfast, then laid around in bed and did some reading. She was almost finished with a reread of a Young Adult series she loved, she said, and he browsed through her eclectic shelves, organized broadly by genre, until he found something that looked interesting: a collection of New Orleans folklore.

They read quietly together for a time. After a while, he looked up from the discussion of Mardi Gras krewes to ask if she'd ever been there—another possible trip?—and realized she'd dozed off with the book collapsed on her chest. He lifted it carefully, marking her place, and tucked the blanket around her, feeling again the warmth of domestic intimacy and the tender glow of caring for her. He read another chapter and then slipped into the nap with her.

He dreamed of rough surf on the coast and pleasures long deferred coming due.

April

And now they were awake again, as the daylight drained out of her studio and they faced the prospect of separating at last. "I wish you could stay," she murmured, her hand inside his shirt and flat on his strong chest. She could feel his heart beating. "I wish you'd brought clothes for work."

He laughed. "I should have."

Thinking of tomorrow cooled her off, anyway. She sank back on the bed. "I guess we'll need to talk to HR, tomorrow, huh?"

"What?" He sounded confused, and it made her blood run cold.

She froze and whispered, "Fuck."

"Why would we need to talk to HR?" he asked.

She held perfectly still, hoping that if she stopped breathing, stopped time now, he wouldn't figure it out.

He cocked his head, his expression still schooled, controlled. Puzzling it out. She could see the pieces sliding into place one by one. Her mortified expression was probably a clue, too, but her freeze wasn't a voluntary thing anymore; it was a deep icy immobility, daggers of cold reaching for her newly hopeful heart.

"April..." She couldn't stand to look at his face as it clicked. "Do you..."

She'd been so sure he knew.

"Do you work at... I mean do I work...do we work at the same company?"

No. No no no no—

"Is that why Fatima—"

"I thought you knew," she said, in a very small voice, and then silence fell like the ceiling caving in.

"If I knew," he said eventually, tension rippling in every word, his control getting wobbly now, "I would have said something before now. I wouldn't feel...like a goddamn joke, right now." Her anxiety began to spiral out of control. She knew Dennis wouldn't hurt her. She knew that. She wasn't afraid of any physical threat. But he had every right to be furious, and if he had unkind words for her, she felt like it was no more than she deserved. She just didn't know if she could bear it.

He shoved up from the bed and began to pace the confines of her studio, yanking himself away from her.

Her stomach heaved. She'd worried so much about disclosure at the beginning; worried about the wrong thing. The wrong facts. Because while the truth of her transition was ultimately her secret to keep if she chose, this wasn't. This very much wasn't. Shakily, she asked a question she already knew the answer to: "So you didn't fire Bob Flowers because of me?" She was glad for the darkness of the room; she didn't want him to see her face; her tears. She didn't want to be able to see his.

"No, I fired him because he was awful at his *job.*" His voice rose to a peak, and she cringed. Dennis never yelled, and seeing his control slip dialed up both her guilt and her panic.

"I'm sorry," she said, not able to keep the tears out of her voice now.

"Did you—did you know all along?" She nodded silently. "So for… For six months now. You've known. And you and Fatima have been—somebody I see every day—you've been telling her—*Jesus*, April."

"No! I only told her this week," she said. "After…after I thought you'd figured it out." It was, she knew, a really terrible excuse, because even if she'd been right, Dennis had not consented to Fatima knowing about them.

"Do you feel like that's making it better? Do you feel like that's going to make it better? How many other people at work know?" The questions sliced her open, coming hard one after another, and the tears began to flow.

"None. Oh my God, Dennis," she sobbed. "Why would I do that? Why would I tell anyone?" Even as she said it, the guilt and shame crashed over her. Why *would* she do it? Why *would* she go to Fatima and not to him? Because—

"Why wouldn't you tell me?" he demanded. "You 'thought I figured it out' this week? So…you knew, and you knew I didn't know, and you just *lied*?" She wrung her hands together, sitting up on the edge of the bed and watching him pace with wide eyes.

"I knew I should tell you," she whimpered. "Every day I told myself I should tell you. But there was a part of me…a hateful little part…that said, well…what if I don't?"

—because if she told him, there might be a confrontation. It might hurt. But now all her avoidance and omissions had caught up with her and here she was, in the confrontation she never wanted, times a million, and she wasn't equal to it. Everything was falling apart, and she was just standing there, unable to save any of it.

"And what if you didn't?" he said tightly, taking her hands by the wrists as he sat down.

"Then I could keep you," she said, trembling. "For a little while longer." *I never said I was strong*, she thought, the sentence crashing around her skull like a panicked bird in a living room. *I never promised that.*

"Oh, my sweet doll," he sighed. "You had me, though. You always had me."

He let go of her hands, like letting go of a ledge, and stood up.

"Oh God, Dennis." She covered her face with her hands and tried to catch her breath. Afraid of the wrong thing. Of course she was. He wasn't just angry, he was crushed. He wasn't going to yell at her; he was going to *leave*.

"I've—I've got to get out of here," he said. He sounded... furious. He sounded lost. He sounded gutted.

"I'm sorry," she cried out.

"You should be," he said, his voice shaking. "You kept a *huge* secret from me, and without trust we have nothing. Nothing at all."

"Are you—" She choked; she couldn't say it. "Is it over? Already?"

"I think we're worth more than five hundred dollars, April. I think we're worth more than one lie." All she wanted in the world was to crumple against him and feel his heartbeat again, confirming his solidity. That he was here. He was still here. "But I also think," he said, "that this is going to take some getting over."

"You should punish me," she said. Desperation and hope mingled in her voice.

"I can't," he said. He sounded exhausted. "I'm too angry. You...you do whatever you want. Wear whatever you want. Come whenever you want. Red, okay? That's fucking red, for me."

He was halfway to the door and she called after him. "I'm so sorry, Dennis. What do I do? Tell me what to do to fix it and I'll do it, I swear to you." He was in the doorway.

He hung his head. In silhouette, he looked slumped. Defeated. "*Red* means I can't tell you what to do, remember? I don't know what you can do to fix it. When you figure it out let me know, okay?" And the door shut behind him.

Dennis

Dennis drove home, on the way rehearsing the conversation he was going to have to have with Jason. He'd texted him earlier in the weekend, of course, before everything went to hell. Now he would have to take back his good news. He'd have to deal with questions; *how do you feel* and *are you angry at her* and *what's going to happen*. He didn't have any answers.

When he stopped in front of his house, he realized something was different. The contractors had picked up the miscellaneous items that had been strewn around his lawn for as long as he could remember. The porta-potty was gone.

Coming through the front door, the foyer was open up to a gallery around the second story. The railing had been half-finished when he left on Thursday after driving home to pack a quick bag. Further in on the first floor was a large open-concept kitchen that had been waiting for countertops. Some of the facing on the walls had been unfinished and one corner of the flooring had been torn up so fans could blast the matting beneath. Now...

It was a finished house. The furnishings were sparse, because he hadn't dared to move things out of storage, but it was all ready. He walked the house and checked each detail. Two and a half baths. A walk-in closet that had halved one of the guest bedrooms. Hot tub in the en suite, and a connecting door to the remaining guest bedroom that he'd had specially modified.

"How am I going to wake up in the morning without hammers and miters?" he muttered to himself. He pulled out his phone and started snapping pictures. His first instinct was to send them to April, and he froze as his second thoughts caught up and his heart sank.

He opened the adjoining door to the remaining guest bedroom and looked inside. This, too, was done. The playroom had been a part of the plans from the beginning, and thankfully Reggie had chosen not to ask any uncomfortable questions. It was perfect, exactly to his specifications, waiting for his gear to move in. He couldn't think, right now, of anything he'd rather do less.

He called Jason.

"Hey. Yeah, finally came up for air. No... Uh, not that good, actually. Not good at all."

He paced the floors of his empty house while he tried to explain. "I don't know how I didn't notice, Jason. We aren't on the same floor, you know."

There were beers in the fridge, if not much else. That was good.

"I don't know, man. I don't know how I feel. I mean... I'm kind of pissed. I don't know. I don't know why I'm not more pissed."

Because he had no furniture except in his bedroom, he

went out and sat on his front steps. "I don't know what I'm going to do. No, not this time." He listened and shook his head. "This time, Jason, I genuinely have no idea what to do next. I think she beat me." In the distance, over the tree line, he could see the shape of the city.

Monday morning, of course, he had to go to work. Heartsick and hungover, he hoped desperately that Leo Graham would try something today. In his current mood a little bit of corporate warfare sounded more than acceptable.

He saw Fatima Nayeem, who blanched when she saw him and scurried away. It was strange to think April was in the building. Strange to think that she had been for the last six months. She could've sat here in his office. She could've—

He pushed the mental images away. He hurt, terribly, in the helpless bewildered way he'd felt after Sonia left. At the time it had reminded him of when he'd broken his leg sledding as a kid, the screaming claxon of pain that couldn't be fixed or ignored. *I hurt! I hurt!* Now despite all his best intentions he was back here, and it was almost unbearable.

After lunch Graham did come by and he thought it might be his lucky day, but instead the COO wanted to talk budget planning strategy against what he described as "the real enemy: Consulting." Dennis let him talk because it would've been more work to throw him out, occasionally grunting or nodding or saying something meaningless like "let's circle back on that," or "we'll have to sharpen our pencils and see what happens."

Eventually Graham stood up, which must have indicated that whatever this was, was over. Graham stopped in front of his desk and stuck out a hand. "Hey. I realize I never said thanks. You pulled my ass out of the fire when we lost that data back in September. You know, I've been here for ten years and I've put in the work, so I get a little stiff-necked when somebody new comes in, but you showed you're willing to work hard, too, and I've gotta respect that."

"Okay," Dennis said, because he didn't know what he was supposed to do with that and had absolutely no bandwidth for being polite. He shook the COO's hand, though, and that seemed to be all he wanted. "Why the change in mood all of a sudden, though?" Dennis asked, his brain apparently working on a ten-second delay.

Graham looked at him soberly. "Ed told me we had to reschedule the budget meeting last week because you had something personal come up. Hey—" he said, holding up a hand as Dennis began to react "—none of my business. But you're a scrapper just like me. You wouldn't miss something like that without a damn good reason. And you look like shit today.

"Ergo, you're having a rough time. I'm not a fucking animal, Martin." Graham shrugged. "We're both trying to work our own patch and ultimately we're on the same side. We may not be friends, but we aren't enemies, are we?"

Dennis stared at him. "No," he said, still half a beat late. "I guess we're not." He looked at his phone, which was vibrating. "Hey, I gotta take this." Graham nodded and left. Dennis did not, in fact, answer the phone, which showed April's smiling face. He let it go to voicemail, and then immediately checked the voicemail. Then he immediately called April back.

April

Hi John,
I won't be in today or maybe for the rest of the week. Something personal has come up and I have the PTO so I'll be back when I can be.
   Thanks for understanding,
April

April French
Operations Analyst, x1667
She/her/hers

April—
Are you sure you can't work around this? Even work from home would be fine. You know we have deliverables *and*

development deadlines coming up quickly. This is really a bad time.

John Weems
Senior Operations Analyst
x1892

Hi John,
No, it's not negotiable. Maybe Meili can handle the development stuff. The deliverable deadlines are internal, we can push them if we have to.
April

April—
Actually I was planning to start weaning Meili off the development stuff entirely and start transitioning you to be our designated product owner for all our projects, so I think having her take over your stuff would be counterproductive. With that in mind if you want to back off the operational deliverables that makes sense, I just need you on the scrum calls this week. You can take those from home, right? Everything else can wait until you're back in the office.
John

What? I'm not going to be the product owner for everything, I already hate being the product owner for the things I manage now.

 I cannot work this week, in the office or at home

April, this is part of the increased responsibilities we discussed with your new, salaried position. You are still in a probationary stage in that position. We really need to see you're a team player right now.

Hi John/HR:
I quit, effective immediately. You don't need to cash out my PTO, please use it in lieu of my two weeks' notice.
   There is nothing in my cube I want or need. Please give the bamboo plant to Fatima Nayeem. I will have her bring my laptop in.
Thanks for everything!

April French
Operations Analyst, x1667
She/her/hers

"Hey, Dennis. It's April. Please listen to this one, it's... It's important.

   "I quit today. So you don't have to worry about—it's taken care of. I don't work there anymore. That's one less thing to worry about.

   "Okay. I... I miss you. I'm trying to figure it out, I promise.
   "Bye."

She slumped back into her easy chair, her knees pulled up to her chest. Almost immediately her phone rang; just enough time for someone to listen to a message and call her back. Her face was blank as she took the call.

   "April! What happened? Are you okay?" Dennis sounded panicked, like he had when she told her friends. For a moment she felt irritated with him, piercing the blank haze of *what just happened?* Did he really think he could have it both ways? Move into the center of her life and then pull himself out and then wring his hands when it affected her?

"No, I'm okay," she said. She felt not so much okay as numb. She had a suspicion that when she felt things again, she'd feel like she'd cut off a limb.

"April, I know you need this job. Do you need me to help you walk it back?"

The *last* thing she needed. "No," she said, as harshly as she could manage. "Really, I'm—I hated it. I hated my job, and now I don't have to do it."

"April, I'm so sorry. I feel like this is my fault." There was a wheedle in his voice of both guilt and frustration. He was upset with her for throwing gas on the fire, for making him feel bad for her when he ought to be mad at her. That seemed fair when she thought about it, but it was almost unbearable to hear in his voice.

"It's okay," she said grimly. She wanted to hang up, but the part of her that still ached to make things right with him and the part of her that was comforted by the sound of his voice, no matter what it was saying, vetoed that.

"What are you going to do?" he demanded, and for a split second she hated him, because that was exactly the question that she was trying not to ask herself.

In the same dull voice: "I don't know yet. I'll figure something out."

"If you need money to tide you over," he began, and everything in her rose up in revolt at that, from her pride to her desire to the self-loathing urge to be punished.

"You don't have to do that," she said.

"April, I feel like—"

"I said no," she said, a ragged edge of emotion showing through at last. It was like a deep cut that took a minute to start bleeding, but any second now she was going to be lying in a pool of her own blood.

"Why won't you let me help you?" he said, and he sounded wounded, and that dropped her right back into the ice water.

"Because I don't want you to," she said in a low voice. Why couldn't this part be over? She needed it to be over.

"Please. If things get desperate. Please reconsider."

"Okay," she said, because obviously it was the only way off the phone. And he said something else that she didn't ever register. "Okay. Yes. Okay, bye." Okay. That was that.

She went and sat in her nook and watched *Chopped* on her phone until it sank in what she'd done, and then she threw up.

A few days later, Fatima came by to pick up her laptop and tell her how much she would be missed. "But good for you. I know you hated what it turned into. I'll never forgive myself for telling you to take the promotion."

"Well, maybe once I have health insurance again, I'll forgive you," April grumbled. Fatima's face fell.

"I'm sorry."

April bit her tongue, just long enough to let the explosion build in force. "Yeah, maybe you can just remember this the next time you want to get your meddle on. You wanted to help me with my career, you wanted to help me with my relationship? Both of those were one hell of a lot better before your *help*." She swallowed, aghast at what had flown out of her mouth but not willing to apologize. She hated feeling like this, acting like this, but the words were out and stubbornly refused to be taken back.

Fatima closed her eyes and took a deep breath. "I am sorry, April. Please stay in touch." April said something noncommittal, and Fatima left without a hug.

April started and deleted six apology texts, but in the end, she left it on that chilly note.

Snarling at Fatima seemed to shatter her lethargy into restlessness and discontent. That night, she went to Frankie's; half-afraid she'd see Dennis there and half-hopeful. Either way, he wasn't around.

Instead she was cornered by Vic, who was desperate for help planning the club's annual Halloween party. She politely refused but felt bad enough to at least help him manage the bar's erratic social media. It was officially his job, but for the last three years she had handled the newsletter and tweets and FetLife profile for the bar, and all of the accounts needed to be dusted off. She found some messages from the Shibari demonstrators from the summer and took the time to respond before catching up with friends over drinks. Lots of drinks.

Caroline drifted up to her, tight PVC and shimmering lips. April was in jeans. Not even good jeans. She just...couldn't be bothered right now.

"Hey," said Caroline. "I'm sorry about the thing with Dennis."

"It's fine," she said, staring at her drink. "You coming for my blessing before you make your move?" *That was a bitchy thing to say*, said the part of her that watched and criticized all the time, but it was drowning in rum.

Caroline rolled her eyes. "Jesus, April."

"What?" She felt fed up, sick to death, ready to bite. "It's not like it hasn't happened before. I'm just training wheels, right?"

"Hey, dummy, are any of those guys still with me? I forget." Caroline's shimmering mouth pulled into a tight purse. "And you know what else? I asked you, every time, before I played with someone you knew. Every time, you said it was fine."

"Well, what the fuck was I supposed to say? 'Oh, Caroline, please don't take my man?' I have a little more dignity than that."

"Yeah. You've got your dignity, and you've got no man," said Caroline. April absorbed that direct hit as Caroline brushed her hair back and set her jaw. "So I guess you've got more than I do, at least. You know Dennis took me out to lunch—"

"I don't want to—"

"*Took me out to lunch* so I could tell him how to win you over? Did you know that? Has there ever been a guy in this place who took *dom lessons* with Mister Tony to learn to be better for *me*? Did I miss that?" She exhaled heavily, and said in a less combative tone: "I'm sorry if you feel disposable sometimes, but so do I. So do a lot of girls, sometimes. It comes with the package."

"It's not the same," April said in a low voice. She stared down into her drink and shook her head.

"You're probably right," Caroline said, in a softer voice. "But does that mean we can't be friends?"

She closed her eyes. She could feel her anger collapsing like a leaking inflatable bouncy castle, all the proud ramparts of indignation sinking into themselves. As the things Caroline had actually said caught up with her, she felt her anger flushed away by her grief that she'd fucked things up so badly. He'd done all that? For her? And Caroline had known—not just known, had been in on it?

How could you be angry at someone who was part of a *conspiracy to make you happy*?

She cleared her throat of the sudden choke of emotion. "I'm sorry, Caroline. We are friends. At least, I hope so."

"Aw." Caroline gave her a squashy side hug. "Of course we are. Subs before hubs, right?"

"Is...that's not a thing, is it?" She realized abruptly, in a way that she remembered but had stopped feeling when envy really took root, that Caroline was several years younger and slightly ridiculous and despite everything a good friend. A good person.

"I just made it up, what do you think? You know, like hubby?"

"Let's...keep workshopping that," she said gently.

Later, head still gently swimming, she went up to the roof. It was getting colder at night at last and the place was almost deserted, but she sat under one of the heaters and looked out at the lights of the city. *He can't take this from me,* she thought. *It doesn't belong to him.*

The lights doubled, redoubled through her tears.

Dennis

One of the things the contractors had finished was a regulation basketball half-court in the backyard. Work was over and in the tiny rind of November daylight, Jason and Dennis jostled and tried to feel sixteen again.

"So how's recovery?" Jason asked. He took a shot from beyond the three-point line and missed dramatically.

"Is that what this is?" Dennis retrieved the ball. "Feels more like purgatory."

"Nice line. Very dramatic. I'm serious. Are you mad at her yet?" Jason set the world's worst pick and Dennis slid past him.

"Why do you want me to be mad at her?" Dennis snapped. He fired off a shot which also missed.

Jason hustled after it. "Dennis, straight up, is it possible we just suck at basketball? Did we get old maybe?"

"My theory is there's something wrong with this hoop. Does this look regulation to you?"

"Yeah, it definitely is. Look. You didn't tell April off the night that—"

"We didn't break up."

"—the night that you and April decided to fundamentally devastate each other in exactly the way I predicted," Jason said. "Better?"

Dennis shook his head. "You're the worst friend."

"I'm just saying you've got to have some shit you need to get off your chest." Jason took another shot, which dropped through. Nothing but net.

"I did yell at her," Dennis mumbled.

"You did? About lying for six months?"

"Not exactly..." He walked over the back patio and dropped into a padded lawn chair. It was getting too dark to play, anyway. "It was later. When she wouldn't let me give her money."

"Sure, very normal thing to get mad about." Jason tucked the ball under his arm and walked over to him. "Dennis. My man. What the fuck."

"I don't know," said Dennis. "I mean, I am mad at her. I'm fucking furious. I'm just mad about all the wrong stuff."

"Like what?"

"I'm mad that she quit her job because of this, and now it's on my conscience that she's out of work and maybe can't cover her bills. I tried to give her money to help tide her over and she wouldn't let me. Like, what the fuck is all this money good for?" It made him think of Keisha and her stubborn, pointless pride.

He deflated slightly and admitted: "I'm mad that she didn't say anything when I used the safeword." That was bedrock; when someone safewords out, you acknowledge and thank them for communicating before anything else. Dennis took it seriously, like any late convert, and to tell the truth it frightened him to see it go by the board when things got tense. It reminded him too much of Sonia. Maybe hiding behind the rules of the game had been a way to avoid how genuinely devastated he'd been in that moment, but that just made it feel worse that she hadn't followed them.

"I'm mad," he said, "that for six months she walked around waiting for that bomb to go off and end our relationship, and she was fine with that. She thought that was all she deserved. I'm mad because I don't know how I can ever be with her if she thinks that little of herself, and I want to be with her..." He hung his head and muttered, "So goddamn much."

Jason exhaled and dropped into a chair. "Well, shit. You really are in love with her."

Dennis looked up at the purpling sky. "Yeah, I really am. So fuck me, I guess."

"Maybe..." Jason waved a hand and sighed. "Maybe you should just forgive her."

"It's not about forgiveness," Dennis said slowly. He'd been thinking about this a lot. "It's...about whether she's ready to be in a relationship or not. Especially one as intense as ours. I need to know she's not... I need to know. I talked to Tony about it and he agreed, it has to come from her."

"Oh, well if Tony said so," Jason said with an eye roll.

"Hey," said Dennis, sharp enough to get Jason's attention. He smirked. "That's *Mister* Tony to you, isn't it?"

Jason gave him the finger.

"So what are you going to do?"

Dennis shrugged. "Wait. Hope." He was spending a lot of time hoping lately. He couldn't say he preferred it to planning. His every urge was to *do, fix, solve*, but this was something she could only do herself. Tony agreed. His therapist agreed. It was the right play.

It felt like dying by inches, but he knew it was the right decision. He just had to wait. And hope.

April

Elena and the rest of the Dungeons & Dragons crew were supportive. Melissa had pointed out she still needed a new roommate, which was horrifying to imagine but kindly meant, and Joanne had offered to see what positions were available at her company. April knew the closeted girl was taking a risk bringing her two worlds so close together and appreciated it.

Elena had pressed her, very, very gently, about telling the truth to her therapist, and she hung her head. "I know," she said. "I know."

While she still had insurance, April started going to therapy twice a week. She needed the extra time to backfill her personal history. Her therapist scribbled furiously as she rewrote the history of the last ten years to include certain truths. Finally, he laid down his pen.

"Thank you for telling me all of this. I know it wasn't easy." His tone was calm and even, and it pissed her off a little.

"That's not true," she said. "You're mad. Nobody likes it when you keep secrets." Her own voice was jagged.

"I'm not mad," he said. "I'm a therapist. People lie to me a lot, even though they pay me to be able to tell me the truth. Hopefully, eventually, they tell me the truth, and we can talk about why they felt like they had to lie in the first place."

"There it is," she said. "You know why I didn't tell you? You know why? Because this is not a relationship of equals, okay? If I tell you I'm into kink, if you think this is a fetish, then you can say, whoops! No hormones for you! No surgeries! Textbook case of autogynephilia!" She could hear the bitterness and fury in her voice. She felt like someone had torn open a hole to some kind of abscessed pit in her soul and it was just pouring this stuff out all the time now. It made her feel sick, yet the relief was unutterable.

Her therapist smiled crookedly. "That would be a pretty outdated textbook. But your point's well-taken. So you feel like as a transgender person, there's an inherent trade-off between telling the truth and...being taken seriously?"

"Between telling the truth and safety," she snapped. "You don't know how many times I've had to pick a restroom and not know which one will get me beaten up. I told my grandma the truth and I'm not welcome at home now. I told my work the truth and I don't have a job anymore. I told Dennis the truth and he's gone."

"That's very profound," her therapist said. "It sounds like this is a pretty central belief for you."

"It's not a *belief*," she said, her voice ringing in the cozy room. She usually liked this room, although it was small; the natural light and the many plants made a charming, comfortable space. Right now she wanted to start smashing flowerpots. "It's the central fact of my life. Every day since I was born, I woke up and decided if I could stand to keep lying."

He nodded. "And eventually you couldn't."

Her jaw worked. She choked on a sob and put her head down.

"Telling the truth means trusting someone not to hurt you," he said. "And you certainly can't trust everyone. But if you don't trust anyone, sooner or later something has to give. That happened a few years ago. I think that's what's happening now."

She sniffed hard and raised her head. "I know. I'm... I'm out of control. I lost *my job*. I yelled at Caroline and at Fatima." She sounded to herself as if she'd just heard about it and was horrified.

"Your friends don't seem to blame you. And it *was* a job you didn't like."

"A job I need to pay for things! To pay you," she pointed out. Her therapist waved that away.

"We have a sliding scale if we need to use it. I'm not going to abandon you, April. Some people will run away from the truth, that's true. But some people want to help you, and telling the truth can help them do it. I'm just saying, it's not a one-way choice."

"I need your help," she said quietly. "I'm wrecking my life lately."

"I don't think that's true," he said. "You turned down Dennis's offer to help financially. Why did you do that?"

"Because it would..." He waited. She bit her lip. "Because it would mean we could never be together. He'll never let someone be totally dependent on him again. A friend, maybe, but not a lover. And I don't want that, either."

"If you thought you were going to be on the streets, thought you were going to starve, would you let him help? Or would you rather die first?"

"Of course not," she scoffed. "If I had to..."

"So doesn't that mean you haven't given up yet? On finding a job, *or* on getting Dennis back. Part of you—the part that truly cares about survival—read the situation and decided it was okay to take that risk. I know you've got plenty of savings. Part of the point of being a practical person is that you're prepared when things go out of control."

She sat silently for a long moment, and he let her. Finally, he prompted: "What if you leaned into this? What if you let yourself be out of control for a little while?"

She laughed helplessly. "I'm pretty sure this is not what a therapist is supposed to tell you to do. I want to be getting better, not spiraling out of control."

He nods. "Getting better. What does that mean?"

"I don't know, I—I've never been in a relationship like this. My ex-wife was a white woman who never really stopped seeing me as a man. I know I've got a lot to learn and figure out if I'm going to be good enough for Dennis. And right now I'm...really far from being that person. I lied to him for months. I remember thinking, when he came to Dallas... I remember thinking I wanted to be a safe place for him. I didn't want him to have to be strong all the time. But even now he's being strong for us. Let alone..."

She laughed weakly. "He found a mentor. He learned about trans stuff. For me, because he wanted me in his life. Nobody ever wanted me like that.

"I have to match that energy. I have to be a good partner, I have to educate myself. And I have to show him that I can." She let out a long shuddering breath. "Making these kind of shitty decisions is the opposite of that."

Her therapist tapped the pen idly on his notebook.

"Well...counter point. When you thought you were making good decisions, you were stuck in a job you hated because you were afraid you couldn't find a better one, and you were lying to a man you cared about because you were afraid to be honest with him. Given that, maybe it's time for some bad decisions."

She gaped. It was a direct hit, below the waterline, and she had absolutely no idea what to say to it.

"I'm not telling you to do anything specific. And I'm not telling you not to think about…all that other stuff. It's not bad to get educated. It's not bad to learn how to be there for another person or to understand their struggles. I'm just asking…what if you let yourself get mad? What if you just did what you wanted? What if you accepted that Dennis thought you were good enough for him from the start, and all your 'good' decisions only ever got in the way?"

"I could get hurt," she said in a low voice. "Don't you understand that?"

"I do," he said. "But—do you play sports?" She shook her head. "There's a difference between being injured and being hurt. An injury puts you at risk. An injury can end your career. But hurt…lots of things hurt. Getting hurt is the price of admission for some things. And we both know, now, that you've got a hell of a tolerance for pain."

"For physical things, sure," she says. "But I hate hard conversations. I hate *disclosing*. I hate sitting there telling people how I feel and opening up and waiting for them to come back and punch me right where I'm the most vulnerable or peace out on me."

"And then you lost your temper and you did just that," he said. "How's it going?"

Good question.

"Maybe," he said delicately, "getting better starts with extending trust. To the ones who've earned it."

When she got home, she called Fatima and asked if she could come by after work. Her stomach churned with dread, and her first order of business was to apologize for the last visit, but the older woman waved it away. "Forget it. Never happened. Honey, how are you *doing*?"

"I'm okay." She poured the tea she had made for both of them, shaky with adrenaline. She'd been prepared for Fatima to be icy or angry or anything but kind. "I've gone on a few interviews... Nothing so far, but it wasn't as horrible as I imagined. I've got enough savings to make it past the holidays, and I'm hoping hiring picks up after that."

Fatima nodded, took a sip and looked at her sidelong. "So... is it all over with Dennis?"

April shrugged. "I really don't know," she said quietly. "I haven't given up."

Fatima raised an eyebrow. "So this means you still haven't—" When April blushed and shook her head, Fatima clucked her tongue. "And you like this? This withholding?"

"Denial," April said. "Or really, control. Orgasm control, because it doesn't always mean saying no." And added under her breath, "Even if it feels like it."

"I couldn't do it," Fatima says. "I'm not letting this man talk to Samir, ever."

April laughed hollowly. "No, I do like it. I like feeling like someone else is in charge and it's...pretty intense, as far as control goes. And when...if...he does let me, it's going to be..." She wiggled on her stool. "Unbelievable. I might die."

"I'll send flowers," Fatima said dryly.

"I know I should give up, but I don't want to yet," she confessed. "And I'm trying to do this thing right now where I do whatever I want for a while. I feel like I'm ruining my life, but my therapist is actually supporting it."

Fatima frowned at her. "Well, what have you done so far?"

"Quit my job. Yelled at you. Yelled at my friend Caroline for always scooping up dominants. Ate a lot of pasta."

She snorted. "See, this is what I thought. You running wild is a lot less than a lot of people on their best day."

"Well, that's hurtful."

She laughed. "I'm sorry, then. But you really are a sweet girl deep down. A kinky girl, but a sweet one." April tried to decide how she felt about that. She thought maybe it was a pretty okay way to be. Fatima touched April's arm. "Have you talked to him lately?"

"I really shouldn't," April said.

"What *shouldn't*? Aren't you that notorious bad girl April French?"

Dennis

Dennis *had* ended up joining the trivia team created by the other Black tech workers he'd met at Reggie's. They called themselves the Carltons, a name he privately thought was even worse than Blerds, but it had been decided on long before he came along. He'd missed the last several trivia nights, being on the East Coast, and although he had very little enthusiasm for it, he'd decided to go to this one. Friendships died if you didn't put the work in, and this little coterie had been hard to find.

It was a good time, actually. It was a pub quiz format, relaxed and convivial and well-lubricated, and he was a competitive person. It was nice to win. It was nice to hang out with the guys, too. He'd never talked to them about April—he'd thought about introducing them, during that brief weekend of victory, and wondered how it would go, but it had never

gotten that far—and so it didn't come up. For several hours
he didn't think about her at all.

When he got home around ten in the evening and pulled
out his phone—you obviously weren't allowed to look at it
during the competition—that reprieve came to an end.

April: I'm sorry I lied, Dennis
I don't have a good reason
I did it because I felt like we were always doomed so what
if I just put it off a while
And the more time passed the harder it was to take back
I really did think you'd found out by the time you came to
Dallas

She'd sent it a few hours ago. He could imagine how anxious she'd been waiting for him to respond to that, and now,
thanks to the wonderful gift of technology, she knew he'd
read it. He found he didn't have the heart to leave her dangling, and choosing his words carefully he typed:

Dennis: I know. I know all that.
But the question is, what are you sorry for?

Her response came almost immediately.

April: I'm sorry that I was scared to tell the truth

Dennis: You don't have to be sorry for that.

April: I'm sorry I didn't have faith in you

Dennis: Thank you, but that's not it either.

April: Can't you just tell me what I should be sorry for?
I'm sorry for a lot of things so it's probably on the list

Dennis: I wish I could make it easy for you.
You deserve for things to be easy.
But

He hesitated a long time, deliberating over his wording.
He needed to get this right. He needed—

But I need to know you understand this.

April: I get that
And I think maybe I do
But I'll let you know when I get there, okay?

Dennis: Okay.

He felt an ache in his chest, the same one that he'd carried for months after Sonia left. It never seemed far away these days. He wanted more than anything to cure it by going to her and wrapping her in his arms and forgetting everything.

If he did that, though, what would change? If he did that, how long until they were back here?

April: Not to change the subject, but did you get the news-letter about the Oshiros coming back?
It'll be right before Thanksgiving

I know you had wanted to learn more about Shibari after last summer

Dennis: I did see it.
And I do want to learn more.
But it said this is a workshop for couples.
And I don't have anyone to tie up and show off right now.

April: You should take Caroline

He glared at the phone.

Dennis: Don't do that.

April: I'm not doing 'that'
I know I do 'that' sometimes but I'm really not
I promise I won't be psychically screaming Jolene at both of you the whole time
I just don't want you to miss the event and she's a big ol rope bunny
Besides I trust her
I trust both of you

Dennis: I'll think about it.

April: I miss you Dennis

He typed, I miss you too doll. Then he carefully backspaced over the last four letters and typed April; hesitated again, and didn't send it at all.

He put his phone away. After a minute, he took it into the bedroom and left it there before returning to the couch. He didn't trust himself with it. If they kept texting like this, he would be in her apartment by midnight.

No sooner had he sat down with a book—the new Obama memoir—than his phone began to ring. He embarrassed himself half-jogging back to the bedroom, but it wasn't April. He dropped onto the bed. "Hey, Mom."

"So excited to hear from your mother. I see how it is." He clicked the phone to speaker and let the vibrant tones of Angelique Cash-Martin fill up his room. "Who did you think I was, that you were so disappointed?"

He was going to have to be careful. His mom didn't believe in psychic phenomena, but she was the only one in the family, because Angelique could apparently read your mind off the back of your skull, fine print and all.

"Nobody, Mom. What's going on?"

"Just wanted to check if you'd bought your tickets for Thanksgiving yet."

"I am an adult, Mom. I've been making my own travel arrangement for more than a decade now."

"You get those tickets yet?"

"…no, Mom." God damn it.

"Well you better buy them before the price goes up." She knew perfectly well he could afford to fly the same day if he needed to; he could hire a private plane to Illinois if he really wanted to. But she'd already moved on to what family members were coming, which family members were in disgrace and not invited, which family members were possibly too busy (and thus courting disgrace), and all the other hot gossip from an Illinois town of three hundred and fifty people.

Dennis loved his mother; but to be in a room with her, or even on the phone, was to experience a flood of energy that swept along lesser mortals in her wake. When he was younger that had been something he fought, sometimes, but right now he was working on letting go and it felt nice to let all the *her* of her roll over him.

It wasn't like talking to Graham, because he *did* care what she had to say. He just…bobbed on the surface and tried to keep up, contributing the occasional, "She what?" and "I bet you had something to say about that," and "Phew. It couldn't be me."

"Hey, Mom," he said after a while, when the flood receded. "You got HBO, right?"

"You know I don't miss *Westworld*," she said.

"I saw something on there the other day—you remember that documentary you liked, *The Black List*? Same guy made one about transgender folks, *The Trans List*. Pretty interesting stuff."

"Mm-hm," said his mother. Silence reigned.

"What's up?" he asked, when it was too much. She always won these.

"Just thinking about when you brought Jason home and asked me what I thought about *Will & Grace*."

He exhaled. Damn it.

"I told you then, Dennis. You are mine, and I love you. If you aren't what I expected, I love who you are, not the you I imagined. And I will love whoever you love, as long as they are worthy of you. You remember that?"

"I remember," he sighed. "I'm not transgender," he added hurriedly.

"I know that," she scoffed. "You couldn't *wait* to get that first chin hair."

"Jesus, Mom."

"You go ahead and buy those tickets. And get one for your friend." Damn her!

"It's not…she probably won't be coming," he said, wearily. She always won.

"Well you just buy it, anyway. You can afford it," she said. He did not tell her that's not how plane tickets worked anymore.

He let silence back in, for a long time. And then he said, "Mom? What do you do if you love someone who doesn't love themself?"

She was quiet, herself, for a moment. "Well, you can't make anybody love anybody. Not you, not themselves."

"No," he agreed.

"You can make a place for them that's safe," she said. "A place they can always come back to and see how love is supposed to work. But they've got to decide to come back. And sometimes that means they have to change, and not everyone is ready to do that."

"I'm not…good, at waiting," he said. "I mean, I can be patient. But just waiting and hoping isn't my style."

"Kiddo, you were born two weeks early, you don't have to tell *me*," she said. "All you can do is keep busy. Make that place for them even if they'll never fill it. If they don't, somebody else will come along. Somebody ready for all that love."

He shut his eyes. "You're a pretty good mom."

"I know it," she said. He could see her in his mind's eye, preening foolishly to make a joke out of it.

"I'm gonna go," he said. "Still got some stuff I haven't unpacked."

He didn't actually go then, because the next thing that happened was, they talked for twenty minutes about the fickleness of contractors and the upstairs bathroom of the house in Illinois. But eventually Dennis got off the phone and unpacked the boxes in the playroom.

April

April left another interview, finally feeling like she might be turning a corner.

She'd had her bad interviews; the one that wanted software skills she didn't have and the one where she'd registered the split second of disgust when the interviewer clocked her. She'd had her good interviews that never got a follow-up, or the ones where she'd been edged out by an internal applicant.

But today she'd gone on a second interview, and it had been great. The interviewer—an earnest and bearded young man—had called her Miss French and looked her in the eye while he did it.

More than that. He had asked her how to untangle a particularly snarled data set, and she'd launched confidently into her bag of tricks. She even hopped up to scribble on a whiteboard. She realized when she finished, breathless, that she'd forgotten her voice control and was speaking two octaves lower than she usually aimed for.

She'd flushed, and her cheeks had burned even harder when the interviewer asked her, "And why wouldn't you just use the text-to-columns feature in Excel?"

"Because… I didn't know about it. I'm, I'm pretty much self-taught." The interviewer had nodded, and made a small note on his pad, and her heart had sunk into her Louboutin heels. But then something incredible happened.

"Well, your answer definitely shows the right kind of mind for cracking these puzzles, and a pretty good grip on the formulas available. Have you ever thought about going for an Excel Mastery certification? We have a program under our training umbrella."

And the rest of the interview seemed to take place on a different footing, as if they were just sorting out details. As if *they* were trying to land *her.*

"To tell the truth, Miss French, I'm trying to build a new sort of team for our organization, a specialist operations team that would just deal with these kinds of problems. If this worked out, how would you feel about managing a team of people like yourself in a year or two?"

She was speechless for a moment, and then found a very important question. "Would there be development work?"

He looked puzzled. "I'm afraid not, is that something you're interested in? We outsource all our development and their product owners and teams handle most of it."

The job sounded…not perfect, but the ideal version of what it was. She knew she could do it. She wouldn't say she was looking *forward* to it, but she could do it. She felt like they would call her back soon and it would be good news. She could use some good news.

But first she had to go meet with Jason Beaumont, who had

called this weekend and inserted himself into her schedule. She couldn't possibly imagine what he wanted, except maybe to yell at her for breaking Dennis's heart. Maybe something to do with the upcoming workshop? That felt like wishful thinking, though.

At least he couldn't yell at her too much in public. She ducked into the little coffee shop; she'd seen this place but never been inside. The wall-sized mural collaging Italian tourist photos was cute enough, if obviously prefab from the coffee brand. Jason already had a table and was spinning his empty coffee mug from hand to hand, one knee bouncing.

He waited, not particularly graciously, while she got herself a hot chocolate that the November weather barely justified and joined him. She didn't know where this was going, so she waited for him to speak; he was waiting for her, too, then realized it and started abruptly.

"So what do you know about me and Frankie's?"

She cocked her head. "I know you're an investor…"

"I own it," he said flatly.

"You own it," she said, mostly just for something to say while she wrapped her mind around that.

"I invested in a bar and over time, after a while, I bought the other investors out. Changed the name. It's my bar."

She wrinkled her brow. "Why doesn't anyone else know?"

"I don't want them to? I hired Vic to run it because I don't know shit about running a bar. All I do is shovel money down the hole periodically. Why does anyone need to know?" He went to drink from his mug, realized it was empty already and put it down petulantly.

She thought about asking *why do you own a bar?* but realized he would just be obnoxious and evasive, and instead asked, "Why are you telling me?"

His eyes stopped roaming the mural and moved to her face. "I want to hire you to work there."

Her heart skipped a beat. "Like as a waitress?"

"What? No." He scowled at her, a *don't be an asshole* face. "Some light bookkeeping, event planning, social media... community stuff, like better rules and like keeping an ear to the ground for troublemakers. I don't know. All the stuff you already do that we don't pay you for."

She opened her mouth to say that was ridiculous, that it wasn't enough to be a full-time job, but she stopped as her mind turned over the possibilities. It *was* a lot, actually, it was something that absorbed at least several hours from her every week and sometimes whole weekends. And she had a whole list of ideas she'd considered or suggested but hadn't had time to volunteer for.

There was so much they could do—education for people new to the lifestyle on a recurring basis, more guest trainings and events, an official membership roster. Right now she practically was the membership roster; as imperfect as her memory and opportunities to meet people were, they didn't have anything better. The bookkeeping she could probably do in her sleep after all these years of Excel.

"What about Vic? And the other managers?" she said instead.

"Everybody but Vic is part-time, anyway. And what Vic knows is how to run a bar and throw people out so they stay thrown out. He knows the vendors. But he's shit at the math and just about everything else. Vic couldn't have handled those asshole magicians the way you did...he could do nothing or he could throw them out, because those are his two settings, but you've got, you know, nuance and shit."

Some of his cagey intensity receded and he looked downright sincere, if only for a moment. "Besides...you know how to make it the bar I want it to be."

For a moment, she let herself imagine the bar Jason wanted it to be—that they both wanted it to be. A kink bar where queer people of all stripes could be not just safe but at home. A place where no one was overlooked and left to the predators. A hub; a community for people whose identities and desires separated them from their own communities. For a moment, it flared into existence in her mind, and her heart swelled.

She tried to shove herself back to earth. Asked: "Why are you doing this? We're not...we're not friends. Are you just doing this for Dennis?" She scanned his face, wanting this but wanting to be sure it was happening for the right reasons.

"I'm not doing it for Dennis. I mean—it's obvious to both of us that it's going to be easier for you and Dennis to get back together if you have a job, so let's not pretend that's not in the mix. And Dennis is my best friend. Me and him... it's ride or die. So yeah, it's part of it. But this isn't just about him. I thought about this even before he moved to Austin. You're *perfect* for this, French. You're pretty much already doing it. You're..."

"Mama April?"

He gave her a flat look. "You make a joke out of it, but you're the beating heart of that place. You're the only person who cares about it as much as I do. And you've got the time now. You need a job. You need health insurance. Take it."

She stared at him. "Is this a real job, or are you just trying to be nice to me and don't really know how it goes?" Millionaires could be really...frustrating, she had learned.

Jason gritted his teeth. "It can be two things. Will you take the fucking job? C'mon, Halloween sucked on ice without you planning it."

She'd heard that, too. She sipped hot chocolate while she

absorbed. While her head caught up to her out of control heart. "...on one condition."

He sighed and rolled his eyes. "Well. Since you've got me over a barrel here, I guess I have no choice. What?"

"You said you renamed it. Who's Frankie?" She'd always wondered.

He smirked. "Just a guy I met a long time ago. Sometimes the weirdos you meet in shitty bars can change your life, French. Don't you know that by now?"

Dennis

Dennis almost didn't go to the Shibari workshop. He'd considered April's idea of taking Caroline, but he genuinely couldn't muster enthusiasm about tying up anyone else. He was interested in the ornate Japanese bondage tradition—had been since the event in the summer—but his mood was dismal and there were plenty of YouTube tutorials.

It was Jason who forced him to get off the couch and throw on real clothes; Jason who basically frog-marched him into the demonstration room with the stage. Tables were set up in the front for the participants in the workshop, who would be binding their partners under the guidance of the Oshiros—Caroline was there, having found another playmate for the evening—but the rest of the room was occupied by a small crowd of interested observers. It was a beautiful and erotic art. Dennis felt a little weird about standing around and watching others participate.

(He might have been more interested in demonstrating, he realized. Definitely more of an exhibitionist than a voyeur. Well, we live and learn.)

Then April stepped out on the stage, and he stopped breathing. She was wearing a Shibari-inspired sheath dress of watered silver silk. The silk cords webbed over the dress framed her tight waist and generous hips, and exaggerated her bust by wrapping tightly above and below. The halter neckline left her shoulders bare, and the skirt wound in coils around her legs, revealing glimpses of thigh through the binding. The straps of her heels winding up her bare legs followed the theme and her sandy hair hung in two ropes of braids that started at her temples and fell down her back. Even her jewelry was twists of gold rope. She was wearing the cuffs he had given her, stark steel and black leather against the luminous gold and silver.

There was no spotlight—no real light board, just a bunch of gels pointed at the stage. Yet for Dennis she was outlined in light. Everyone in the room seemed to appreciate her; there were yells of greeting and a couple of cheerful whistles.

She smiled at the crowd, coloring. He watched her scan the room, settle on him, and flit away, a nervous quality infiltrating her smile. She had a microphone, and she switched it on with a pop.

"Hi, everybody, and welcome to tonight's event. In just a second, Doug and Madeline Oshiro are going to give us the follow-up workshop to their awesome demonstration, back in July, but I just have a few quick announcements first."

She looked out over the crowd again. "I guess...the big one is, starting tonight, I have a new position as Frankie's community manager. That means I'll be formally handling things like booking events like this, our social media, mediating complaints, and things like that. Some of you know me. If you do, you know how passionate I am about this place and our community."

It sounded like an amazing job for her. She would be great at it, and more than that, he could see how happy she was—not just the radiant smile, but the loose limbs, relaxed posture, spirited gestures. The urge to go to her, to throw aside the past and leap up on the stage and kiss her in front of all these people, was so visceral he had to grit his teeth. She looked ecstatic, and he wanted to be a part of it, celebrate with her, twirl her around.

"For those of you who *don't* know me, I look forward to learning about what Frankie's means to you and how I can support that. We've got some amazing plans for the coming year that I think you're all going to love, but we always want to stay in tune with what's going on with you."

"If any of you are here for the first time tonight...welcome, virgins!" There was a titter of laughter and some hooting and hollering. "I hope you discover just how special a place like this can be, where you can live your truth among people who won't judge. How life-changing it can be."

She hesitated.

"Six months ago, I met someone here who changed my life. And I felt like, because I was me, it wouldn't last, couldn't last, so I made some choices to make *sure* it would crash and burn. And I did that because I thought it was impossible that someone could love me." The room was silent now, and her face dipped down into shadow, before she raised it to the lights again. It felt like the whole room was holding its breath. Dennis knew he was. It felt like everything in the last six months, everything in their entire lives, was coming down to this moment; this time and place and these words.

"But it turns out someone can love me. It turns out someone does. I made a mistake. I did it to protect myself, and

I don't apologize for that. But I see now it was a mistake. There is love in this world for me, and for all of you, and it's a mistake to live without hope because you think it will hurt less when the crash comes. Because the secret is, sometimes it doesn't."

She looked down again for a moment.

"So get out there and love each other, folks. Make mistakes. Get hurt. Trust your friends—and I'm telling you right now that I'm your friend, ride or die—to pick you up, dust you off, and make you laugh about it. Because love is real, and it happens everywhere. It even happens here. So what if you gave it a chance?"

From the groups of couples in the front, Caroline shouted, *"Just say it!"* April lifted the mike again.

"I love you, Dennis Martin."

The room was applauding. Dennis was stunned. He didn't know half of these people. He realized April knew the majority of them, though, and they knew her. They were rooting for her. She handed the microphone off to the Oshiros and glided through the crowds towards him, towering over everyone in her heels and shining like a beacon in her gown. Now he was the one underdressed, in his jeans and blazer.

She reached him in the back, and she had to lean down to whisper in his ear. "I'm sorry I didn't believe I was good enough to keep you. I won't make that mistake again." She pulled back, just enough to look pensively into his eyes. "Did I get it right?"

One hand settled on her hip, fingers threading into the twisted silk cords. "Exactly right, doll. Exactly." The other cupped her flushed face and brushed against a tear. He felt incandescent with happiness, every nerve ending shouting in a way that threatened to shatter his careful composure. His right hand and left hand argued about whether the silk or her skin were softer. He wanted to kiss her but couldn't decide if he should start with her pink mouth or the tear on her face or the hollow of her throat.

"I'm so glad," she said, beaming. "Because I put this dress on your card and it was *so* expensive." He drew down her face and kissed her like the world was ending.

When they came up for air he said, "What if we got out of here?"

Her eyes darted to Jason for some reason. "Um...it's my first night in this job..."

Jason rolled his eyes. "Get the fuck out of here, French."

She beamed and took Dennis's hand. "In that case...yes *please*, Sir."

April & Dennis

April could feel every nerve in her body singing. As she had sat in front of the mirror doing her makeup for tonight, she'd felt something very like the dreamy unrealness and floaty drift of subspace filling her up; in her surrender to the moment, in her helplessness to know how he would react, in her fear and longing and pride to be on that stage, she had transcended herself and her body for a moment. She already felt as raw and vulnerable as she ever had, and she knew the night had just begun.

Her fingers laced with his and raised his hand to her lips. She kissed each of his fingertips and flicked her tongue over his thumb in a way that caused the knuckles of his other hand to tighten on the steering wheel. She could see his self-control charring in his eyes, and the fire lit her up.

He cleared his throat as they got on the highway. Most of

the traffic was going the other way, thank God, into the city for the night. "Have you come yet, doll?"

"No, Sir," she said softly. "I was hoping..."

"Me too," he said. "So much."

"I missed you," she said. Her voice was vibrating with emotion and she wasn't trying to hide it. He let his free hand fall to where her neck met the rising slopes of her shoulders. His fingers clasped the back of her neck and just squeezed, as he had the night they first met. The pressure of his fingers wrung out the tension of her moment onstage, of the slow terrible walk through that crowd. The clasp of his hand brought her back under control with a click that felt like it should've been audible and a moan that just barely was. Her eyelids fluttered shut.

Dennis could see that they were dusted with gold. Every inch of her presentation was perfect; she'd made a wonderful shimmering doll just for him, and his lust for the image she'd created and his love for the woman who knew him so well twisted and tangled and planted deep roots in his chest.

"I missed you," he said huskily. Her skin was soft and hot under his hand, the seam between them burned and sizzled, and he wanted to make this heat grow, to press together skin to skin and let the flames engulf them.

They came to a stop in the driveway of his house, and he was already pulling her towards him, lips searching for hers, painted pink pink pink to guide him in.

They kissed in the car for long stolen moments: her twisted sideways in the seat and half-climbing up onto it and over the center console, him pinned in by the steering wheel but too enthralled to suggest a change of venue. They devoured each other, and he let his control slip entirely for a moment, knowing that inside he would have to pick up the role of dom again for both of them, eager for that, but eager first to plunder her mouth with his and wrap his hands in her silky hair and ruck up the gorgeous dress she'd let him pay for. To lose his mind in the car after a date like he was sixteen again. Until—

April saw him seemingly seize control of himself and the situation all at once, like a shutter closed behind his eyes, and his strength made her shiver. "Come on, doll," he growled, and pulled himself away from her needy pawing.

For a moment she couldn't disentangle herself from the car. She was too tall to sit like this, limbs too disarranged to successfully back out the passenger side door, but then he was there, and he solved it by the simple expediency of gripping her hips and lifting her out. The bite of his fingers and the flex of his arms (and the spikes of her heels) made her wobble and fall against him, and she could feel his heart pounding.

He took her hand and drew her towards the house. She was fascinated to see it finally finished, but he didn't leave her much time to look around, leading her up the dark stairs, past his bedroom to a door further down the hall. He opened it and tugged her inside, flipping on the lights.

"Ohhhh, Sir…"

It was a playroom, or dungeon, or whatever you wanted to call it. The lighting was warm and soft. Custom-built and fully outfitted. Built-in storage overhead to keep the floor open, benches of different widths, suspension points and D-rings anchored in the ceiling and along a load-bearing wall. Quirts of rope, handcuffs, spreaders and other bondage delights hung from hooks. It looked like the well-organized workshop of a meticulous professional who worked in a very strange craft. Which in a way was what it was. The floor was slightly springy underfoot—some kind of rubbery mat stuff.

"It's wonderful," she said, stumbling forward on the squashy floor and sinking onto a padded bench.

"I like how it came out," he admitted. "It's been torturing *me*, these last few weeks," he added in a grumble.

"Oh Sir, I'm—"

"No."

Dennis said it with as much force as he could bring to bear on one word. Which right now, was a lot. "No more apologies tonight." He stepped forward and drew her to her feet, snagging a length of rope off the wall and threading it through the rings of her cuffs. "I just need you to wait a moment." Using the rope, he pulled her arms up into the air and looped the rope over a suspended hook, drawing it taut and tying it off.

"Good?" he said.

"Well, it's not *comfortable*," she said, in a teasing tone.

He snorted and walked towards another door set in the wall.

April could see a bathroom through it—the en suite for his bedroom. Then he shut it behind him and left her to wait. She sighed and let her weight hang from her arms for a moment, feeling the deep knot between her shoulders and the kinks of anxiety in her back protest and then give in. Soaked in her helplessness. If she stood up straight, she could lift the rope off the hook, but…that wasn't the point.

He was gone long enough to let her start to become bored, then squirmy; long enough to wonder if doms got together and traded notes about the optimal amount of time to leave a sub in suspense.

Suspense. That was a good one! You could also say he left her hanging…

Round and round her mind went, from boredom to silly amusements to frustration to surrender to boredom again, and again and—then the door was opening,

Her arousal had never flagged, even in her waiting, but

now a delirious spike of need hit her, ripping from her groin to her chest and making it hard to catch her breath. He had gone into the other room to change.

He was just fixing onyx cufflinks in the cuffs of a crisp white shirt, half-unbuttoned over a bare chest she wanted very much to kiss. Black slacks, and the oxblood Oxfords she loved. "Now," he said, with a voice like a razor. For a moment in the car she'd seen him almost unmanned, but now the Sir was back with a capital *S*, and he was ready for her. "Let's begin."

He circled behind her, and she didn't try to follow, although she hated to take her eyes off him. She felt his fingers trailing over her back, touching her skin through the gaps in the weave of silk ropes. "Hm... I could cut this off," he said thoughtfully.

No! a part of her screamed, but she remembered her position and swallowed it. "You paid for it, Sir," she said coolly, knowing that would inflame him.

"Hm." She felt his fingers curl around the loose weaving of the skirt, and then drag it up above her hips. His hands trailed over the tight fabric of her underwear; she'd have loved to wear a thong or go commando under a dress like that, but the realities of her situation meant a compression garment was needed. As he peeled them down her legs she groaned in relief as her trapped clit was freed and throbbed in the cool air. He took them all the way down to her ankles and knelt behind her to unwrap the bindings of her heels. As he took them away, she had to balance on her toes to keep her height, and suddenly the suspension wasn't so funny anymore.

Dennis smiled when he heard her gasp—not that she could see it—and skimmed his hand up her legs. God, she was smooth. When his hand reached around to her groin, he began to stroke her, and the muscles of her legs flexed, and she whimpered as her weight settled again on the hook and on her arms.

He didn't squeeze or pump; just lifted her clit slightly with his fingers and ran one finger back and forth along the underside, where sticky wetness had drooled and spread. She made the most delightful noises.

"Are you ready for sex tonight?" he asked.

"I'm ready for anything, Sir," she said, in a voice that rasped. She flinched at it, and flinched again when he lifted his other hand to her ass and parted her cheeks to begin to lick and tease while he stroked.

"I—I—oh *Christ*, Sir—I—please!" she cried out, in no time at all.

"Hm," he said, smiling to himself again. "*Now* I believe you've been waiting all this time." Before he rose, he slid a plug into her, provoking another heartfelt moan.

He rose and circled back to the front of her and dragged over a bench.

April watched through hooded eyes as he settled in front of her, looking smooth and unflappable and unbearably *smug*; the flames in his eyes were banked and under control again, and he lifted the pink silicone vibrator he'd taken down from the shelf. He ran it over her length again and again, first off and then switching it on, stopping when she cried out and resuming once she got herself under control. He put his other hand between her legs, cupping her, and probing the folds of skin below her clit. Feeling for the shallow canal that lay there beneath the skin and gently fingering it as he teased her erection. Twice he pressed the vibrator against the base of the butt plug as he took her into his mouth; she bit her lips savagely and tried frantically not to come, desperate not to make him stop but unable to withstand it. Both times she only lasted a few seconds.

Time telescoped and warped for her as she dangled at his mercy. This time she didn't get bored when he stood up and stepped away for a moment; she just floated. He circled in front of her, holding a black flogger. "I haven't used one of these before," he admitted. It was a vulnerable thing to say, but her eyes searched his face and posture and saw no fear or insecurity. Only the iron-hard certainty of a powerful dom. "So it's very important you tell me if it goes too far. Do you understand, doll?"

Her head bobbed loosely on her neck. She felt like she was a liquid, something delicious and sparkling like champagne. "Yes, Sir."

"Yes Sir what?" he said.

Oh. Um. She focused. "Yes, Sir, I'll tell you if it's too much. Red yellow green."

"Good girl."

Dennis *was* nervous, but he knew she had done more impact play than him. It would likely be fine, and she would safeword if she needed to. Still, he felt better once he was out of her eye line and could relax his face.

He trailed the flogger over her shoulders and down her back, letting the tails slither between the ropes of her gown and tickle her sensitized skin. She gasped and giggled and almost fell off her tiptoes again, and that's when he decided to swat her ass the first time.

She let out a heartfelt cry that was clearly pleasure, not pain, and he continued to smack the leather over her ass and thighs, sometimes harder, sometimes just letting it flap against her. He thought for a long moment before he snapped it up between her legs. She moaned long and low and dropped as her toes curled, her weight falling on her arms again. He quickly moved forward, wrapping an arm around her waist and holding up her weight until she found her feet again.

"Th-thank you, Sir," she whispered.

"Should I put some slack in the rope?"

"Maybe just a bench to kneel on?" she asked.

"Of course, darling." He kissed the side of her face and pulled the bench over, and also adjusted the rope slightly.

"Okay," she said, in a brave, swimmy voice. "Let's do it."

April hadn't known what to expect; he was a novice when it came to this kind of play, and he might have gone too hard right out of the gate or pulled his strikes too much out of fear. But he was a natural. Of course he was.

Once she was off her toes, she could really just let go of everything and let the sensation consume her. She had never in her life gotten so close to orgasming from impact play, but six months of denial combined with the intense intimacy of the evening made her feel like every draft or breath of air would push her over.

As the intensity consumed her, she began to lose sight of her body, the time, the place, as she had with Sandra, unplugging bit by bit. She felt the ghost of the fear of punishment, of Marie and her hateful games, but this time the steady strokes of the flogger and his gentleness gradually dispelled it.

Dennis stopped once again to check on her, and realized she was far gone in subspace, her head hanging loose on her neck and her weight once again transferring to the rope. He let out a shuddering breath and reached up to unhook the rope, careful not to let her fall off the bench. She hung on to his shoulders and took a few stumbling steps before her eyes fluttered open.

"Where are we going?" she asked, with mild curiosity.

"Time to get out of this dress finally, doll," he said tenderly.

I love you, he thought, as he'd thought with each stroke of the flogger. He knew he hadn't said it back yet, but he wasn't sure this was the time or place. Surely it would mean more separated from sex and kink? But it was all he could think as she languidly allowed him to undress her, as she sank onto the bench, as he unbuttoned his fly and steered her towards his hardness.

I love you. I love you. I love you.

April had reached the point of surrender where she accepted each turn of events placidly. *We're getting undressed? Okay. We're sucking cock now? Okay.*

More than okay. "You have a great dick," she said dreamily. "It does good things."

When they first got together, she'd been intimidated by the fact that he was uncircumcised; she'd had a lot more experience by now, and she loved the extra sensitivity of his glans. She bobbed and licked and stroked in a timeless haze, stopping a few times to just press against the flesh of his thigh and take in the smell and heat of him before resuming. He moaned beautifully, and it gave her a wonderful illusion of power.

"Maybe I won't let *you* come," she said playfully, and as she had half-hoped this spurred him to tighten his fingers in her hair and fuck her mouth; she let go and let the moment engulf her, and then he was coming, in her mouth and running down her chin, she was so greedy for him and it was good, good, good—

"I love you," he gasped, and then it was something beyond that.

Dennis sank onto the bench beside her, his legs weak and his need for her overwhelming. He wrapped himself around her and kissed her deeply, tasting himself. "I love you," he said again, and then *she* kissed *him*, lunging for his face and biting his lips hungrily.

"I love you," she said back, and they went on like that for some time, both thoroughly out of their minds.

Gradually, though, his sense returned, and he began to

scheme again. He pressed her back until she was supine on the bench, then rose to grab handcuffs and ankle restraints to bind her to it face up.

She lay back and waited for him; she watched intently as he plugged in a Magic Wand and knelt beside the bench.

"How long has it been since you came?" he asked.

"A million years," she estimated.

"Do you want to come?"

She eyed him. "Is this a trick question again?"

He shook his head, switched on the vibrator and pressed it up into her groin, beneath her clit. She keened, and he moved it away. "No tricks. Just treats. Do you want to come?"

"*Yes!*"

April almost screamed. "*Please. Sir. So bad!*"

"Hmmmm," he said, and she almost sobbed.

"I knew it was a trick, I knew it, I hate you."

"No, you love me." So smug.

"Please let me come."

"You know what I was thinking?"

She did sob.

"What if we waited until New Year's?"

That...that was only another six weeks. Maybe...maybe she could live with that...

"How about New Year's, onstage at Frankie's, so everyone can see what a good girl you are?"

She gasped and tried to sit up, yanked against the handcuffs and fell back. "*Dennis Martin!*" She sounded outraged.

"Well, all right," he said. "You can come tonight. Maybe onstage next year."

"Wait, next *year*?" And then he pressed the powerful vibrator back up against her core, and she was falling over the edge even as images burned in her mind of herself, dressed up and restrained, tied to a St. Andrew's Cross on the stage at Frankie's coming again and again and again…

He continued pressing and teasing and drawing out orgasms until they were dry spasms and she was begging him to stop. "Okay, doll. Okay." He knelt again to remove the restraints on her arms and legs. He toweled her off, then carried her through the interior door that connected to the en suite bathroom of the master bedroom from the other side. Where there was a hot tub.

Dennis grinned at the way she moaned when the hot water hit her. She sounded almost the same as she had orgasming. The fourth one. "This is amazing. I'm never having kinky sex without a Jacuzzi nearby again."

"Is that so?" he asked, easing in himself once her hair was secured in a bathcap.

"I dunno. I'm mush. I've only got mush thoughts." She tangled up with him. "Help, I'm mush."

"That's okay. Just be mush, then. I'm gonna clean you up, though."

"I came *so much*, Dennis. I came so much."

He laughed. "Mm-hm. Well that's what happens when you wait six months." He maneuvered her around in the water to rub her shoulders; he'd put them through it tonight.

"Did you really say something about next year?"

"Just talk," he said patiently. She twisted her neck to narrow her eyes at him.

"I don't *believe* you." He just kept rubbing. "Dennis, I can't go a whole year."

"Of course not," he agreed mildly, and leaned forward to kiss her ear.

"Not a whole year. Dennis. Promise me it won't be a whole year."

"Technically, if it's New Year's, it'll be more than a year."

"*Dennis.*" Her voice was almost a sob. "I can't."

"Then we won't," he said, moving his arms down now to just hold her. "You're always in control."

"That doesn't really help," she said sulkily.

"Why not?" he asked. He had been doing a bit of a taunting all-knowing dom schtick, he would admit, but he genuinely didn't know what she meant.

"Because I'm a slut for denial," she said mournfully, and he burst into laughter. She did not, although a smile cracked her plaintive pose. "I'll sell myself out in a second." After a moment, she surrendered to laughter, too, and the tension—the delicious, precarious tension of the scene—bled away into echoes in the clean white tiled room.

Eventually they made their way out of the water and into bed. He thought that surely they were both exhausted, but as she curled against his chest they began to kiss and twine around each other and then he was inside of her and they found they were each capable of one more after all.

April woke up in Dennis's bed, at Dennis's house, in Dennis's arms, and everything was right. She felt sore in all the good ways, and so relaxed she thought she might float away without the heavy comforter.

She tilted her head to kiss him, their faces nuzzling together, and felt a troublesome patch on her skin brush against his stubble. For a moment, it sent a nasty sizzle down her nerves, and she had time to wonder if she could steal away and shave without waking him. Then a sleepy, heavy hand curled around her hip and pulled her close, and she surrendered to the moment. It could wait.

They stayed in bed a long time that morning, until other biological necessities forced them out. She was studying her face in the mirror—making sure she'd gotten all the shaving cream and admiring how the electrolysis was steadily thinning out the blue shadows under her skin—when Dennis returned from the other door into the en suite from the playroom. He had a flat square box in his hands and a smile on his face.

"What's that?" she asked, perking up. So many fun things could fit into a box like that.

"I got it while we were apart…my way of holding on to hope, I guess," he rumbled.

She opened it. "Oh, Dennis…"

It was a collar; a very traditional collar, of heavy black leather, with a stainless steel O-ring at the throat. It matched the cuffs he'd given her.

"I thought you'd need a different one for everyday," he said. "Although, if you're going to work at Frankie's—well. You can decide that."

She bit her lip and turned. "Will you put it on me?"

He smiled. "Yes please."

She looked in the mirror, lifting a hand to touch it. "I love it." She was nude, and sometimes these days she could even look at herself in the mirror like this and feel good, but right now she looked… Wow. She looked at the curve of her cheeks, and the flare of her hips, and her small breasts, and her long hair, and the petite pink bump of her soft clit, and the leather encircling her neck, and she felt…

"You're beautiful," he said, folding her into him.

"Not underdressed?" she asked with a giggle.

"Not at all. I'd take you anywhere like this."

She shivered delightedly. "Now…what you were saying about the stage at Frankie's…and about *next year…*"

Epilogue

They spent Thanksgiving in Illinois, of course. "She's just a little ray of sunshine," his mother said, speaking of a woman at least a foot taller than her. "I like her."

For Christmas, April's parents invited her home. Her grandmother was visiting the Maryland cousins. She told them she would come home if she could come in a dress, and her boyfriend would be with her.

So instead, they spent the holiday in Austin. Dennis's long-delayed housewarming became a Christmas party, and the Carltons mixed with Pride & Progesterone—tentatively at first, until someone brought out Apples to Apples.

For New Year's Eve, there was a show at Frankie's, and April *was* onstage, but not performing, and sometimes she was so busy running around being in charge, she forgot to look for him in the crowd. But his collar was always around her neck, and his love and his power wrapped her up from head to toe.

So that was all right.

In the year that followed, Ed O'Reilly retired after yet another heart attack, and that was a fresh adventure as Dennis found himself unexpectedly backing Leo Graham for the position, over much worse choices from the consulting side of the business. It kept things interesting, at least.

And as April had feared, she did *not* get to orgasm again until the following New Year's, but they weren't onstage at Frankie's for that, either, because they were on their honeymoon.

★ ★ ★ ★ ★

To learn more about Penny Aimes and her upcoming books and story teasers, please visit her website at pennyaimes.com

Acknowledgments

Any novel should probably have credits as long as a Hollywood blockbuster to acknowledge all the people who left their thumbprints on the work. Here are a few people I couldn't bear to leave out:

Rebecca Fraimow, midwife of this book and a talented author in her own right;

May Peterson, a ground-breaking trans romance author;

Lynn Brown, at Salt and Sage, who helped with sensitivity reading;

John Jacobson and Ronan Sadler of Carina Press, who went above and beyond;

And my wife, who wanted to know how it ended.

Navy Chief Derrick Fox enlists his best friend's little brother to pull off a big, showy, and totally fake homecoming. When their gangplank smooch goes enormously viral, they're caught between a dock and a hard place. Neither of them ever expected a temporary fake relationship to look—or feel—so real. And Arthur certainly never considered he'd be fighting for a very much not-fake forever with a military man.

Keep reading for an excerpt from
Sailor Proof *by Annabeth Albert!*

Chapter One

Derrick

It was going to happen. Today was finally the day I was going to deck an officer and thus end any hope I had of ever making chief of the boat, and probably earn myself a court-martial to boot. But Fernsby had it coming, and he knew it, the way he met my eyes as he gave a cocky laugh. He might be a junior-grade lieutenant who had to answer to the other officers, but he wasn't stupid. It didn't matter how much he had it coming, a chief fighting with an officer of any rank over a personal matter was going to be harshly punished.

But it might be worth it.

Fernsby had been goading me the entire long deployment, every chance he got, which, considering the close quarters on a submarine, was pretty damn often. And now here he was, joking with another officer about winning the first-kiss raffle for our homecoming, knowing full well that I was standing right there. And that he'd be kissing my ex.

Personal matter indeed.

And totally worth punching that smug smile away.

"I hope we go viral. Social media loves two hot dudes kissing." Fernsby smirked as he waggled his eyebrows at the big-eyed ensign who'd been hero-worshipping him all damn tour. And of course he was smirking. First kiss was a storied tradition for most navy deployments, and sailors loved vying for the honor of being first to disembark and greet their loved ones. Usually I was happy for whoever won, and over the years I'd seen more than one proposal as a result of that first kiss.

God, I hoped Fernsby wasn't planning *that*. Bad enough that he couldn't stop ribbing me that Steve chose him over me and that I'd been the last to know Steve was cheating. Watching them be all happy was going to suck.

"I'm gonna get so lucky." Fernsby's knowing gaze met mine over the ensign's head.

An angry noise escaped my throat. "And I hope—"

"Fox. A word. *Now*." My friend Calder appeared seemingly out of nowhere in the narrow corridor and hauled me backward, effectively cutting off my tirade along with a good deal of my circulation.

"Yeah, Fox. Go on with you." Fernsby made a dismissive gesture as I growled, but Calder kept moving, giving me little choice but to follow. He dragged me past various compartments through the mess, where two of our fellow chiefs were playing cards. He didn't stop until we were in the chief's section of the bunking with its rows of triple beds, steering me into the far corner by our bunks and about as close to privacy as we were going to get.

"What the fuck?" Calder wasted no time unleashing on me.

"It's nothing." I looked down at my narrow bunk. I had

the bottom bunk, another chief had the middle, and the top bunk was Calder's. And I was more than a little tempted to disappear into mine and pull the blue privacy curtain. "Fernsby was running his mouth again."

"You sure as hell looked like you were gearing up to slug him. I saw your clenched fist. I'm surprised smoke wasn't coming out of your ears."

Calder wasn't wrong, so I shrugged. "I need to stop letting him get to me. I know."

"Yeah, you do." He shoved my shoulder the way only a longtime best friend could get away with. We'd been lucky, meeting up in submarine school, both getting assigned to Bremerton, and then ending up on the same boat together as chiefs. Calder had a vested interest in me not fucking up, and my skin heated from how close I'd come to doing just that.

"I'm pissed because it looks like he won first kiss and now I have to watch that," I admitted in a low whisper.

"What you need is a kiss of your own," said the guy who probably had different dates scheduled for each of our first three days home.

"Ha. Would be nice, but not happening." It went without saying that I wouldn't have anyone in the throngs of family and friends waiting on me. Simply wasn't how my life was structured, and most of the time I was fine with it. Calder was the one who would have a big contingent of friends and family. And I was well acquainted with his undying belief that the solution to one terrible relationship was to find another more casual arrangement. "I'm not exactly a rebound sort of guy."

"Everyone knows that about you." Calder rolled his eyes. He was both taller and broader than me, which was saying something because I wasn't exactly tiny. However, his playful demeanor always made him seem younger. "But you should be. And I'm not even talking about getting laid. I'm saying you need to make Fernsby and Steve-the-lying-ex-from-hell jealous by having some hottie there to greet you."

"God. I wish." I let my head thump back against the panel where the bunks met the wall. Unlike Calder, I wasn't counting down the minutes until I could get lucky, but I had entertained more than one fantasy about how to pay Steve back. A rebound held limited appeal from an emotional standpoint. But jealousy? Yeah, I wouldn't mind trotting out someone hotter than Steve, who always was a vain fucker. "But we're only a couple of weeks out from homecoming, and I'm not exactly in a position to meet someone while we're deployed."

Unlike some other deployments, the submarine force had very limited communication access. No cell phones, no swiping right, no mindless surfing of hookup sites. Hell, simply getting messages to friends and family could be challenging, let alone trying to conduct a revenge romance on the down-low.

"Call in a favor?" Calder quirked his mouth. He undoubtedly had multiple persons who would love nothing more than to pretend to be madly in lust with him.

"From who?" My back tensed and my nerves were still jangling from listening to Fernsby brag. "It's not like my contact list is awash in friends with benefits or even friends period."

"You need to work on that whole brooding loner persona." Calder clapped me on the shoulder, nicer now. "It's not doing you any favors."

"Why be the life of the party when I have you?" I laughed, years of shared memories flowing between us. Any social life I did have I owed almost entirely to Calder. He'd even introduced me to Steve.

"I do like to bring the party."

"You do." Closing my eyes, I took another deep breath, trying to steady myself. I truly did not want to fight Fernsby even if my fist tended to forget that. "You're right though.

Someone there, even pretend, would make me feel less like a fucking loser."

"Exactly," Calder agreed a little too readily, making my gut clench. Maybe I was that pathetic.

"But I'm not doing something stupid like an ad." I cracked an eye open in time to catch him laughing at me.

"Of course not. You save your stupidity for fighting with officers."

I groaned because he was right. "I'm not the personal ads type. But who do you know? Surely there's a guy into guys who owes you a favor whom you could loan me?"

I wasn't too proud to borrow from Calder's vast social network.

"Hmm." Tilting his head, Calder narrowed his eyes, the same intense thinking he did when poring over the latest supply manifest. As a logistics specialist, Calder had a solution to almost every problem that could crop up, apparently my love life included. He muttered to himself for a few moments before straightening. "Arthur would do it."

"Ha. Very funny. Try again." I kept my voice down, but my laugh was a lot freer this time. *Arthur.* The nerve. I had to go ahead and sit on a bunk before I lost it laughing.

"He would," Calder insisted, serious expression never wavering. "He owes me."

I shook my head. *Arthur.* I'd known Calder's family for a decade now, including his spindly youngest brother, who was some sort of musical genius. And also terminally hopeless. "You want me to use your too-nerdy-for-band-camp little brother to make Fernsby jealous?"

"He's almost twenty-five now. Not so little. He's been out since high school, so no issues about a public kiss. And Haggerty said Arthur's hot now. Kid went and got all buff in Boston."

"Haggerty said that? And you let him live?" Our mutual

friend did like them young and pretty. I had vague memories of Arthur having a riot of unruly hair, far redder than his
brothers', and big green eyes, but he'd been barely legal last
time I'd seen him a couple of years back. And as I'd already
been seeing Steve, and Arthur was Calder's little brother, I
hadn't looked too terribly hard.

"It was an observation, not a request to go break his heart."
Calder kicked my foot. "Come on. It's perfect. Arthur has
always liked you, but he doesn't *like* you."

"Hey!" I should have been relieved that Arthur wasn't har-
boring some giant crush, not indignant.

"Yeah, yeah, you're a catch." Calder fiddled with the strap
on his bunk. Everything got strapped down on a sub, even
us. "But he's always said he'd never get involved long-term
with someone military."

"I don't blame him." This was why I was never doing
another relationship myself. Romance and the navy simply
didn't mix, especially not submarine personnel. We were bad
relationship bets, and I could admit that.

"See? This is why he'd be good for this. He can fake it
long enough to get Steve and Fernsby off your back, but it's
not like he'd actually date you."

"Of course not."

"Plus all that experience as a dorm RA has him good at
shit like signs and banners and cutesy gestures. And he's been
back in Seattle a couple of months now. He'd do it."

"I can't believe I'm actually considering this. How are you
going to get a message to him, anyway?" The last thing I
needed was anyone else getting wind of this ill-advised plan.
There was no such thing as privacy on a sub.

"Trust me. I've got my ways." Calder's voice went from confident to hushed as voices sounded near the front row of bunks.

"Dude. Did you hear about Fernsby?" asked one of the

youngest chiefs, a nuke with a chipped front tooth and no filter. I couldn't see him or his buddy, but his surfer-boy drawl was unmistakable.

"Yep. Fox is gonna be so pissed." The other person had to be Beauregard, who worked with me in Weapons. The Southern accent gave him away. "It's a wonder they haven't murdered each other this whole deployment. If a crew member stole my girl—or guy—I'm not sure I could stand the humiliation."

"Shush." A third voice sounded further back, and then there was a lot of fumbling around before Beauregard slapped his bunk.

"Okay, okay, here's my new deck," he announced as the three of them exited the quarters.

"See?" I gestured up at Calder. "It would be justifiable homicide."

"It would. But wouldn't revenge be better?"

"I dunno. Fernsby's head would look pretty great mounted on my wall back on base." I groaned as I thought about returning to my little room in the barracks. I'd let Steve keep the apartment, because I was such a nice guy and all. Damn it, I was tired of being nice. Tired of being taken advantage of and pitied and gossiped about. Fuck it all. "Okay. Whatever. See what you can arrange."

"Leave it all to me." Calder straightened to his full height, which came just shy of the low ceiling. "You won't regret this."

"Oh, I'm pretty sure I will." Dread churned in my too-empty gut, but it was a distraction from all the weeks of hurt and anger I'd been stamping down. At least we had a plan.

Don't miss Sailor Proof *by Annabeth Albert,*
out from Carina Adores!

Copyright © 2021 by Annabeth Albert

Discover another great contemporary romance from Carina Adores

Danny Ip walks into every boardroom with a plan. His plan for struggling tech company WesTec is to acquire it, shut it down and squeeze the last remaining revenue out of it for his Jade Harbour Capital portfolio. But he didn't expect his best friend's younger brother—the hottest one-night stand he ever had—to be there.

Tobin Lok has always thought the world of Danny. He's funny, warm, attractive—and totally out of Tobin's league. Now, pitted against Danny at work, Tobin might finally get a chance to prove he's more than just Wei's little brother…

Hard Sell by Hudson Lin is available now!

CarinaAdores.com

CARHLHS0821TR